The Vampire
and the Devil's Son

The Vampire
and the Devil's Son

(a.k.a. *The Baron's Dead Wife*)

by

Pierre-Alexis Ponson du Terrail

translated, annotated and introduced by
Brian Stableford

A Black Coat Press Book

Acknowledgements: We are indebted to David McDonnell for proofreading the typescript.

English adaptation, introduction and afterword Copyright © 2007 by Brian Stableford.
Cover illustration Copyright © 2007 by Nathalie Lial.

Visit our website at www.blackcoatpress.com

Introduction

Pierre-Alexis, Vicomte de Ponson du Terrail, was born in 1829 into a minor aristocratic family that had fallen on hard times since the Revolution of 1789. He was the nephew of General Toscan du Terrail, and claimed descent from the illustrious Captain Pierre Bayard du Terrail (1473-1524). His family apparently intended him to make a career in the Navy, but his lack of the mathematical skills necessary for navigation made that impossible. His early literary ambitions were displayed in a manuscript composed and circulated in 1845, *Un amour à seize ans*, signed George Bruck.

Ponson was in Paris when the Revolution of 1848 broke out, and volunteered for the *garde mobile* that attempted to defend Paris against the Revolutionaries–a task that swiftly proved impossible. When the members of the *garde* were offered dispersal into the regular army, under the command of the new government, he declined. Publication was difficult in the immediate aftermath of the Revolution, but he started to publish short pieces in some profusion in 1850. His movement into the field of popular fiction was not immediate, but he began publishing his first newspaper serial in 1852 with *Les coulisses du monde* [*Society's Wings*, "wings" being understood in the theatrical sense].

French popular fiction had enjoyed a tremendous boom in the 1840s thanks to the success of the *romans feuilletons* serialized in newspapers, which had become an important aspect of fierce circulation wars fought by publishers competing for the attention and loyalty of a population moving towards universal literacy. The two brightest stars in that firmament

5

were Alexandre Dumas and Eugène Sue, and their closest follower was Paul Féval. All three men had made a great deal of money from the production of *romans feuilletons*, but their works clustered around markedly different points of a political spectrum.

Although Dumas often afforded monarchs and carefully-selected aristocrats relatively lenient treatment in his accounts of French history, and he was certainly no apologist for the excesses of the Terror, he was a fervent Republican, who saw the underlying pattern of French history as a progressive one. Sue was much further to the political left–an evolutionary socialist if not a revolutionary one–who fervently believed and asserted that all the past miseries of the French people had been caused by the twin curses of Royalty and Catholicism. Féval, on the other hand, was an ardent royalist, although a bourgeois one–he was the son of a lawyer–and his real affiliation was to a nostalgic affection for the legendary chivalric code that he imagined to have been embodied in the knighthood of feudal Brittany, his birthplace and adopted homeland.

After the Revolution of 1848, the fortunes of these three writers diverged markedly. Sue accepted a post in the new government, while Dumas lent it his enthusiastic support–but both were undone by Louis-Napoléon's *coup d'état* in December 1851 and exiled from Paris. Both had just embarked upon works presenting vast panoramas of history, which they intended to be their respective masterpieces–Sue on *Les mystères du peuple* [*The Mysteries of the People*] and Dumas on *Isaac Laquedem*–but both works ran into trouble with the Emperor's censors. Sue eventually finished his, although its publication was inhibited, and died shortly afterwards in 1857. Dumas, who returned to Paris under an amnesty, aborted his when the censors interrupted its serialization, and returned to safer literary ground–but he was never the same writer afterwards; his heyday was over.

Féval, by contrast, merely waited out the lean times and picked up where he had left off; even though he was probably not entirely untroubled by the censors–in terms of anxiety if not actual interference–his political views made him far less likely to attract their attention. Although he could hardly regard the Second Empire as a desirable phase in French political life, he was far less inclined to rail against its retrogressiveness than Dumas or Sue, and his career thrived as theirs went into decline.

Ponson must have observed all this with a certain amount of interest–and must have observed, too, that his own political stance was not unlike Féval's, with the added advantages of a certain authenticity and a blithe cynicism. Although Féval was related to aristocratic Breton families via his mother, he was not an aristocrat himself, but Ponson was; not only did he embody aristocratic ideals more plausibly, but he was well enough acquainted with aristocratic life, habits and pretentions to see through their various shams. The partial eclipse of Sue and Dumas had opened up a market space, and the possibility of colonizing that space alongside Féval evidently appealed to Ponson. Because he was a true aristocrat, though, and no mere pretender, he could not be content merely to imitate Féval; his objective had to be to outdo him, in every possible respect.

That was, in essence, what Ponson appears to have set out to achieve. Féval was a prolific and flamboyant writer, who had found his *métier* in producing adventure stories and mysteries at high speed, making up for an inevitable lack of planning by ruthlessly exploiting an assortment of melodramatic tropes, often combining them with a wry humor that had proved not to detract at all from their sensational effect. Ponson did all of that, but exaggerated every single feature. Nor did he have the slightest trouble with the censors–a fact that did not help his reputation among opponents of the *régime*.

Féval, at his peak, turned out approximately two million words a year, sometimes having three serials running simultaneously, although he only managed to maintain that level of production by dictating much of his work to a series of secretaries. Ponson, at his peak, topped Féval's two million words per annum by a further half-million, once had five serials running simultaneously and seems to have written every word himself, with no other technological assistance than a steel nib. Although numerous other writers have since topped the two-million-words-a-year level of production for years at a stretch, none has done so without an amanuensis or an efficient typewriter, so Ponson would probably be entitled to be reckoned an all-time champion were it not for his august predecessor, Voltaire, who did as much, to a higher standard, using goosequills.

When he was interviewed in *Le Journal* (June 19, 1861), Ponson informed his interlocutor that he rose between 4 and 5 a.m. every morning and did a five or six-hour stint of furious writing before taking a leisurely breakfast and delivering his copy–usually for publication the following day–in the course of a constitutional stroll. After that, he would spend his afternoons fencing–he claimed to be an expert swordsman–or doing what would nowadays be called "working out." Allowing for a certain amount of hyperbole (to which he was always prone), this presumably does represent his ideal, if not his average, working day. In the same interview, he gave an account of his standard sales pitch: *"Prévenez-moi trois feuilletons à l'avance, si ça ennuie votre public, en un feuilleton je finirai."* [Commission three episodes in advance; if that bores your readers, I'll finish it in one]. This too needs not be taken absolutely literally, but it summarizes his approach to his *métier*. The reverse also applied, of course; if a serial did prove popular, he was willing to spin it our indefinitely–the *Rocambole* saga, a.k.a. *Les drames de Paris,* ran for 14 years from 1857 until Ponson's death in 1871 and was still left unfinished.

The contents of Ponson's work exceeded Féval's in much the same fashion as his productivity. He never re-read his work, so he was rather prone to continuity errors, and was perfectly capable of losing his way in the middle of a sentence, let alone a plot. The oft-leveled accusation that he often reintroduced characters which he had killed off earlier, however, actually refers to a matter of deliberate strategy. Even though he recognized the melodramatic necessity of sometimes involving them in fatal climaxes, he was never one to waste a charismatic hero or villain, and was always willing to tell his readers, after a decent lapse of time, that earlier reports of deaths had been exaggerated, and that the character they remembered so fondly–or had loved to hate–was alive, well and back in business.

Ponson understood perfectly well that such flaws did not distract significantly from his readers' enjoyment, and such contrivances enhanced it. He knew that the nature of serial fiction greatly favored story at the expense of plot–which is to say that, provided that the present chapter of a narrative had sufficient excitement in itself to make readers avid to know what would happen next, the complexities of its relationship to some overarching textual scheme need not be taken too seriously.

The principal keys to success as a *feuilletoniste* were the maintenance of melodramatic pitch and the management of narrative pace, and Ponson took both crafts to new extremes. Hs adventure stories acquired a flamboyance so vivid that the French language required a new adjective to describe it, and thus preserved the name of his most popular hero, Rocambole, in *rocambolesque*. His dialogue became extraordinarily streamlined–although his various innovative practices in that regard were taken up by so many subsequent writers that they now seem perfectly familiar and quite normal.

What Ponson might have accomplished had he not died young, we can only guess, but his literary career was undone, just as his military career had been, by the intervention of political events. When the Franco-Prussian War broke out, he took part in another futile defense of Paris, then fled to an estate on the banks of the Orléans Canal, which he had acquired by a judicious marriage in 1857. There, he gathered a force of volunteers to engage the Prussians in guerilla warfare, but he was easily defeated, and the house he had used as a base was looted and destroyed; he died soon afterwards, in January 1871, at the age of 41.

Although Ponson's career lasted less than two decades, he was amazingly prolific, and did everything he could to assist his own legend. *Le Journal* credited him, in awed tones, with having published 67 volumes in the two years 1858-59. We must remember, however, that an octavo volume of the period was not necessarily overstuffed with wordage. The present novel, *La baronne trépassée*, which appeared in three volumes, is little more than 65,000 words long, although the two other works he published in 1853–one in three volumes and one in four–and the five four-volume works he published in 1854-55 all had more words per volume.

Such reported figures as the fact that his series devoted to *La jeunesse de roi Henri* filled 60 volumes, while the saga of Rocambole eventually filled 40, though correct, thus need to be regarded with a certain circumspection. The average wordage of an octavo volume of the period was probably about 40,000 words, so the 67 volumes he published in 1858-59 would have amounted to less than three million words–but we must remember, too, that not all of his work made it into volume form, so the 67 volumes observed by *Le Journal* would only have been a proportion of his actual output.

The fact that *Les drames de Paris* ran in *La Patrie* for so long without that paper's readers ever tiring of it had much to do with its introduction of Rocambole, initially as a teenage *gamin*, although he grew up quickly enough to take on the principal burden of the serial. *Les drames de Paris* was, in essence, a soap-operatic series, and it was broken up into convenient sections for book publication, appearing as a sequence of multi-volume novels.

Rocambole's popularity was such that Ponson soon brought him back in *Le Petit Journal* in 1865, where *La résurrection de Rocambole* was said to have almost doubled that periodical's circulation to something over 280,000. The editor of *La Patrie* immediately commissioned *Le dernier mot de Rocambole*, which ran from 1866-68, boldly printing an extra 100,000 copies of the issue in which it made its debut. Several further sequels followed. Nor did the story end there–Rocambole's adventures were continued by Constant Guéroult in *Le retour de Rocambole* and *Les nouveaux exploits de Rocambole* in *La Petite Presse* in 1875-76, and various 20th-century writers added further sequels.[1]

It was in Rocambole's heyday that Ponson hit his peak; while Rocambole was the mainstay of *La Patrie*, Ponson was still producing serials on a daily basis for his other regular markets. For long stretches in this period, he was also the only serial-writer employed by *Le Petit Journal* and *La Petite Presse*; they were three of the outlets in which he once had five serials running simultaneously, the others being *L'Opinion Nationale* and *Le Moniteur du Soir*. To write a new episode of five different serials before breakfast every morning, six days a week, making all of them up as he went, was no mean feat, although his bouts of physical exercise presumably gave him abundant space for planning.

Not everyone, of course, approved of what Ponson did, and the fact that he outdid Féval in all the key features of popular serial fiction meant that he bore the brunt of criticism leveled at the intrinsic defects of that kind of work.

In particular, he attracted the vitriolic ire of the Comte Auguste Villiers de l'Isle Adam, whose satirical novella "*Claire Lenoir*"[2] (1867) features an anti-hero named Tribulat Bonhomet, supposedly an archetype of bourgeois crassness, who waxes lyrical on the virtues of the unnamed but easily recognizable Ponson, his favorite writer. Villiers' objection to Ponson was, however, as much personal as literary.

As an impoverished aristocrat, whose entitlement to bear a name made famous centuries before was more than a trifle dubious–he expended a great deal of time and effort in genealogical research trying to prove it–Villiers had very strong ideas about the prerogatives and responsibilities of aristocracy. He considered it beneath his dignity even to contemplate the possibility of writing for money rather than for art's sake–a position he took so seriously that he brought himself literally

---

[1] (See Notes p. 251.)

to the brink of starvation before accepting a compromise. Ponson, however, took exactly opposite position; he thought that the only excuse for a true aristocrat to do something as essentially bourgeois as literary work was financial need, and he appears to have taken as much pride in his total lack of artistic ambition as he did in his phenomenal productivity and his enormous sales. He gladly declared himself the most successful writer of his age, but flatly refused to hang out with other literary men. If he ever read "*Claire Lenoir*," we can be reasonably certain that he would have been quite unconcerned by Villiers' assault, regarding it as the spite of a mere poseur, and would not have felt the need to cry all the way to the bank.

Villiers was not alone in his condemnation, but some of his contemporaries were moved to utter a few words in defense. Théophile Gautier, for instance, declared that there was much to be said for *Le chambrion*, one of Ponson's several novels redeploying Gothic imagery. Ponson had several admirers among his fellow *feuilletonistes*, especially Léon Gozlan, who adored *Rocambole*. The highest compliment of all, however, was uttered by Prosper Mérimée, in a letter to Stendhal written in 1865: "*Il n'y a plus qu'un homme de génie à présent, c'est M. Ponson du Terrail. Avez-vous lu quelques-uns de ses feuilletons? Personne ne manie comme lui le crime et l'assassinat. J'en fait mes délices.*" [There is but one man of genius at present, and that is Ponson du Terrail. Have you read any of his serials? No one handles crime and murder like him. I am delighted by them.]

La baronne trépassée (1852) probably ought to be reckoned as Ponson's third novel, although its production overlapped that of its two "predecessors"–*Les coulisses du monde* and *La duchesse de Valseranges*–and it beat them both into volume form, thus becoming his first actual book. Although, like the other two titles named, *La baronne trépassée* is a historical novel, it contrasts sharply with them by introducing and foregrounding some striking Gothic elements.

In choosing to resurrect such materials, Ponson was following a recent fashion. While newspapers and magazines had still been struggling against economic adversity in 1851, Alexandre Dumas had scored a massive hit with his play *Le vampire*,[3] which was a comprehensive revision of a similarly-titled play that had caused a parallel sensation at the Porte-Saint-Martin theater 30 years before. That earlier play had been cobbled together by Achille de Jouffroy, the theater's manager, Jean Toussaint Merle, and the father-figure of French Romanticism, Charles Nodier,[4] in order to cash in on the international *succès de scandale* occasioned by John Polidori's novella *The Vampyre*–a veiled attack on Lord Byron that was widely rumored to have been penned by the great man himself.

The fashionability of Dumas' revamped version of *Le vampire*–whose run at the Porte-Saint-Martin extended throughout 1852–promoted a significant revival of interest in Gothic themes, which inevitably spilled over into the *roman feuilleton*. Paul Féval's most obvious response was to produce *Le livre des mystères*, serialized in *Le Pays* in May-July 1852.[5] Féval's *La vampire* [6] was probably first published in the same year, although there is some dispute about that, some bibliographies dating its first publication a decade later.

Ponson's novel is a response to the wave of fashionability rather than a direct riposte to any of Féval's works in this vein, but *Le livre des mystères* was undoubtedly one of the texts Ponson read before undertaking it, and from which he took some slight inspiration. If he had had the opportunity to read *La vampire* too, he must have taken note of the striking quality of the remarkable hallucinatory scenes in which the eponymous character carries out her exotic depredations, and had them in mind when he wrote his own scenes of a parallel nature.

Because *La baronne trépassée* is a mystery, whose plot–cursory though it is–hangs on the ambiguity of its seemingly-supernatural manifestations, it would be highly inappropriate to give away too much of the story in advance, so I shall postpone detailed analysis of its subgeneric nature and historical significance to an afterword, but it is probably worth making some observations regarding the literary-historical context of its two principal Gothic motifs–the female vampire and the Black Huntsman–and their various foreshadowings of literary things to come.

A fairly detailed account of the history of French vampire fiction in the early 19th century is provided in the afterword to *The Vampire Countess*, and there is no need to repeat all of it here. Of all her predecessors, Ponson's vampire most closely resembles Théophile Gautier's "*La morte amoureuse*" (1836; usually translated as "*Clarimonde*"), both in the conspicuous eroticism of her visitations and in the specific mode of her predation. (Something of a sideline was created by the plays spun off from Polidori's *The Vampyre*, which had de-emphasized the neck-biting aspect that is nowadays a core element of the motif, so Ponson's vampire, in contrast to Féval's, now seems much more central to the tradition whose stereotype was eventually consolidated by J. Sheridan le Fanu's *Carmilla* and Bram Stoker's *Dracula*.)

Although Ponson's hero, the Baron de Nossac, correctly–but anachronistically–credits the popularization of Eastern European vampire folklore in France to Dom Augustine Calmet's treatise on the subject, first published in 1746, Ponson is perhaps more likely to have run across such material in a collection of Gothic folklore, *Infernaliana* (1822), which was subsequently attributed to Charles Nodier. *Infernaliana* recycles several of Calmet's "case studies," and it may be significant that its chapter on the "*Vampires de Hongrie*" is immediately followed by the "*Histoire d'un mari assassiné qui revient après sa mort demander vengeance*" [Story of a murdered husband who returned after his death to demand vengeance], that being what the Baron's dead wife appears to be doing.

The anecdotes reproduced in *Infernaliana* do not include the legend of the *Grand Veneur* [Great Huntsman] of the forest of Fontainebleau, but Ponson was undoubtedly familiar with it, and may well have read an account of one of several royal encounters recorded by Pierre d'Etoile in his *Journal de Henri IV*, in which the phantom huntsman is said to be entirely dressed in black, save for a red feather in his cap (symbolic of his infernal genesis).

By the time Ponson was writing, however, diabolical huntsmen had proliferated considerably in Gothic fiction, the most famous examples being German—the legend of the Wild Hunt, recapitulated in a famous ballad by Gottfried Bürger, *Der wilde Jäger* (1778), had presumably encouraged the development of similar figures—so it was entirely natural that Ponson should relocate his own example to Bohemia.

The most famous literary Black Huntsman, of whom Ponson was almost certainly aware, is the one featured in the famous opera *Der Freischutz* (1826), with music by Carl Maria von Weber and a libretto by Friedrich Kind, based on a short story by Johann Apel. An English equivalent is featured in a short tale embedded in Alicia Le Fanu's Gothic novel *Henry the Fourth: a Romance*, published in the same year, but Ponson is far less likely to have been familiar with that.

Kind's Black Huntsman is, in essence, the Devil in disguise, as is the Green Huntsman in Jeremias Gotthelf's *Die Schwartze Spinne* (1842; tr. as *The Black Spider*), but Ponson added a considerably more elaborate apparatus to his own character in making him the Devil's exotically-sired son. In this respect, Ponson went further than such celebrated German *schauer-romans* as Lawrence Flammenberg's *Der Geisterbanner* (1794; tr. as *The Necromancer*) and E. T. A. Hoffmann's *Die Elixiere des Teufels* (1815; tr. as *The Devil's Elixirs*), albeit with his tongue somewhat in his cheek.

French *romans noirs* of the 1790s and early 1800s, as produced by such writers as François Ducray-Duminil and Elizabeth Guénard, had never achieved the same level of popularity as the German *schauer-roman* or the English Gothic novel, even though translations of such fiction were very popular in France. French writers often preferred to embed their own Gothic motifs in fiction affiliated to the more playful tradition initiated by Antoine Galland's translation of

Les mille-et-une nuits [*The Thousand-and-One Nights*]. French fantasies often displayed Gothic tales within some kind of sportive frame narrative, and represented their more earnest aspects as fundamentally foreign–often specifically German– and manifestly barbaric. Ponson's legendary pastiche of the Black Huntsman follows this pattern exactly; his character's subsidiary account of his remarkable conception has a quintessentially Gallandesque quality to it.

It is possible that Ponson was familiar with the published fragments of what is nowadays the most famous of all Gallandesque Gothic constructions, the Jan Potocki novel known in English as *The Saragossa Manuscript*, which was originally written in French; the two major extracts from it in that language had appeared in 1814-15, and had attracted some subsequent attention by virtue of a debate regarding their authorship. The starkly conflicting explanations offered to the Baron of his experiences in the Castle of Holdengrasburg bear some resemblance to those offered to Alphonse van Worden by his tormentors in the first phase of his adventure.

Ponson forsook the use of Gothic motifs for some years after writing *La baronne trépassée*, but he returned to them in a later phase of his career, most notably in *Le trou de Satan* [*Satan's Hole*] (1863), *Le castel du diable* [*The Devil's Castle*] (1865), *Le chambrion* (1865), *La mare aux fantoms* [*The Pool of Phantoms*] (1865) and two further vampire novels, *L'auberge de la rue des Enfants-Rouges* [*The Inn in the Rue des Enfants-Rouges*] (1866) and *La femme immortelle* [*The Immortal Woman*] (1868). This later work does not, however, recover the same Gallandesque spirit; the hectic confusion of the network of conflicting accounts given to the Baron as explanations of the events of Part One remained highly exceptional, even within the pattern of his own work. *La baronne trépassée* thus remains a uniquely fascinating neo-Gothic endeavor.

Although they both continued identifiable literary trends, the vampiric Gretchen and the diabolical Black Huntsman are both historically significant in anticipating routes that horror fiction was to explore avidly in the latter half of the 19th century. It is, however, arguable that the most significant precedents set by *La baronne trépassée* are in Part Two, which embraces melodrama of a very different kind.

Ponson was, of course, active at a time when modern fictional genres had yet to be distinguished, and *romans feuilletons* were required to be all things to all readers, leaving no narrative hook untwisted. It may seem odd to a modern reader that Ponson blithely juxtaposes graphic horror motifs, whose usual appeal is to male readers, with accounts of feverish emotion that are nowadays confined to genre romances aimed at female readers, but it was a common strategy in *romans feuilletons*. The chapters of Ponson's narrative set in Brittany, therefore, represent a significant experiment in the depiction of heightened emotion whose results were to be so extensively recapitulated as to become significant clichés.

In this respect, Part Three of the novel is a straightforward extrapolation of Part Two, although it betrays the exhaustion of Ponson's narrative energy in its cursoriness as well as its abrupt conclusion. Curt and cursory as it is, though, Part Three confirms the essential literary truth that Ponson discovered, and demonstrated more extravagantly than any other writer of his day that nothing succeeds like excess.

Although Gretchen may seem to be a strikingly exceptional character in her amatory attitudes, certain key features of her character were to recur in a whole series of Ponsonian *femmes fatales* who combine or alternate fervent attraction with vengeful hatred, routinely seeking to torture the men they most ardently desire. Indeed, she is not unlike her rival, the Duchesse d'A*** in this regard. Rocambole's female counterpart and nemesis, Baccarat, is the most obvious and extreme of their successors, while Sarah in *Les Gandins* (1868-69) is perhaps the most refined.

Femmes fatales are, of course, a common feature of French literature, amply reflected in *feuilleton* fiction by the descendants of Alexandre Dumas' Milady, but Ponson's characters in this vein–especially Gretchen–are the most explicit in formulating and tailoring their policies of cruelty in direct response to the arrogance and brutality of contemporary male posturing. To the extent that Ponson was a forerunner of generic romantic fiction, he was more uncompromisingly feminist than any other writer of that sort.

Ponson's work poses problems for the translator because of the multiplicity of his mistakes, and such habits as extending sentences far beyond their natural length by the reckless accumulation of subclauses. Had he been writing in a different milieu, a copy-editor would undoubtedly have cleaned up his trivial errors and ameliorated the effect of some of his more profound eccentricities, and I have taken the liberty of doing a certain amount of petty labor in this vein, while also attempting to retain the unique flavor of Ponson's style. I have annotated a few instances where the decision to correct or refrain from correction was marginal, and have also used the textual notes to point out the most significant errors arising from Ponson's casual attitude.

The text I have used for translation is the Marabout reprint published in Verviers (in Belgium) in 1975. The titles in the Marabout line are usually very reliable in their reproduction of the originals, so I assume that it is an accurate rendition of the primary text, and that the continuity errors in the text are Ponson's rather than resulting from the accidental omission of text.

Brian Stableford

Prologue

I

"Duchesse!"

"Baron..."

"Do you have news of Monsieur le Régent?" [7]

"None since yesterday."

"That worries me seriously, my poor Duchess, and I strongly fear..."

"Fear not, Baron—your appointment must already be confirmed."

"The Lord hears you, Duchesse!"

"So you need this governorship desperately?"

"Why, judge for yourself, Madame. I summoned my steward yesterday evening, and I demanded a clear and succinct statement of my business affairs..."

"At a guess, you are ruined..."

"Worse than that, Duchesse. I have debts of a million and no more credit."

"You don't pay your debts, my poor Baron."

"I've already thought of that, Duchesse—but how does one run up more?"

"Child! You're going to be Governor of the Province of Normandy for his Majesty King Louis XV."

"All well and good—but if not...?"

And the Baron, who was still in bed, extended his slender and aristocratic hand towards the bedside cabinet, took up his golden casket, and coquettishly smudged the ruff of his shirt with the yellow powder known as Spanish snuff.

The Duchesse, seated in a large and well-upholstered armchair, tapped the floor impatiently with the toe of her high-heeled shoe, and replied: "You're rather impertinent, you know, Baron."

"Pray tell me how, Duchesse?"

"How–a fine question! Do you doubt my influence?"

"Oh, Duchesse!"

"Without a doubt–for you suppose that you might not be appointed..."

"I may hope, then..."

"Without the least anxiety."

"And sleep peacefully..."

"When I have departed, Baron."

"Oh! Not before, Duchesse."

"My God!" the Duchesse said, ingenuously. "You gentlemen are so discourteous since the death of the great King..."

"Give me your fairy's hands, Duchesse, and come sit down here... Come closer..."

"What a child you are!"

"I'm going to tell you a secret..."

"Bah! Some intrigue hatched in Porcherons [8] and unraveled..."

"Nowhere, Duchesse. It's been suggested that I marry."

The Duchesse, who had sat down on the edge of the bed, got up abruptly and went back to her armchair with a frown and a peevish attitude that elevated the Baron's self-esteem considerably.

"Ah!" she said. "And... to whom?"

"Oh, don't be jealous, Duchesse. It really isn't worth the trouble. She's the daughter of a tax-farmer..."

The Duchesse's pretty face cleared immediately. "This might be serious if you weren't a Nossac, my dear Baron," she said.

"My God!" said Baron de Nossac carelessly–he being the man we find lying abed–"I'm well aware that it will be a misalliance..."

"An enormity!"

"But what can you do? Misalliances have been all the rage for a century."

"You think so?" said Madame d'A***, whose forehead became furrowed again as her face suddenly paled.

"Without a doubt, Duchesse. Did not Queen Anne of Austria marry Mazarin?" [9]

"Secretly, Baron."

"Of course–but what does that matter? Did not *La Grande Mademoiselle* marry Lauzun and Louis XIV Maintenon? Has not Monseigneur le Régent similar peccadilloes within his family?" [10]

"So," said the Duchesse, getting up angrily, "you would dare..."

"I don't say that, Duchesse, since you've obtained a governorship for me. But then, if I don't have that... what the Devil can I do? My future father-in-law has enough money..."

"To make you overlook her humble rank, no?" said the indignant Duchesse. "Truly, gentlemen will do anything!"

"When they do not hold governorships, Duchesse..."

"And who has proposed this marriage to you?" she said, adopting a disdainful and mocking tone.

"Simiane, Duchesse.[11] He offers me a wife who is pretty, clever, well-mannered, and afflicted by I don't know how many millions."

"Accept her, Monsieur," said the Duchesse, pursing her lips. "I would never stand in the way of your happiness..."

"Now, Duchesse, don't sulk. I've refused."

"Definitely?" asked the Duchesse, with a joyful gleam in her large blue eyes.

"Almost. Simiane's coming back again today."

"But you'll refuse again?"

"Just so," Monsieur de Nossac replied. "If I get my governorship..."

"That's fair," said the Duchesse. "But you'll have your governorship."

"I ask for nothing else, Duchesse."

"I shall hasten to the Duc."

"Go, Duchesse."

"And your letters patent will be dispatched in an hour."

"I'm counting on it, Duchesse."

Without compromising his imperturbability in the slightest, the Baron de Nossac pointed a finger at the clock. "I'll give you one hour more, Duchesse," he said. "It's noon; Simiane will be here at one o'clock; he'll remain here until two."

"Well," said Madame d'A***, "if your letters of appointment have not arrived, you'll be free to give your word..."

"I have not given it to her, Duchesse, but I give it to you."

"One moment!" exclaimed Madame d'A***, rising to her feet. "I want you to make me another promise."

"Which is?"

"That if you get married..."

"Oh, Duchesse, you don't expect that."

"No, of course not–but can one foresee every eventuality?" A smile full of mockery glided over the Duchesse's cherry-red lips.

"Bad girl!"

"If you get married," she continued, "you promise to grant me another 24 hours after today."

"With all my heart, my beloved."

"Twenty-four hours of my own choice, you understand?"

"What do you mean?"

"I mean that, when I appear before you, by day or by night, and say to you Baron, my 24 hours are due, at that very moment, if we are in the street, you will climb into my carriage, and if we are in your house, you will take up your hat and your sword and follow me."

"And if I'm somewhere else?"

"Likewise, Baron."

"On my faith!" Monsieur de Nossac exclaimed. "I see nothing inconvenient in that. Duchesse, I give you my word as a gentleman to be your slave for 24 hours, to follow you wherever you desire for that space of time, and to obey you blindly."

"To begin from the day when I learn of your marriage?"

"So be it," said the Baron. Then he added: "That's not a very useful promise, Duchesse."

"Who knows?" she said, extending her hand to him. "Adieu..."

"*Au revoir*, Duchesse!"

The Duchesse took a few steps towards a little door masked by the wall-hangings, opened it and disappeared.

That door gave out on to a hidden stairway, which descended into the gardens—gardens that were located quite close to the place where the Rue de Helder and the Rue de Provence now stand. The townhouse where Monsieur le Baron de Nossac received the Duchesse d'A***, the mistress of the old Duc de Saint-Simon, who enjoyed his great favor, was, you see, his *petite maison*. [12]

II

Monsieur le Baron Hector de Nossac was a young man of 26, of fine appearance, excellent nobility, high spirits and proven courage. At court, he enjoyed the reputation of a very lucky man; never had a reputation been better deserved. The Baron was handsome, magnificent, fickle, quarrelsome and fond of gambling. He had a slight weakness for Spanish snuff and Aï wine. [13] The Duchesse du Maine had inducted him into the Order of the Honey-bee; he had steeped himself in the Cellamare conspiracy, and Dubois had had him imprisoned in the Bastille. [14] On the worthy Cardinal's death, Simiane had reconciled him with the Regent, and the Regent had given him a regiment. A wink from Madame de Phalaris had got him into trouble with the Duc d'Orléans again, and the Duc had withdrawn his commission.[15]

An uncle, of the sort one no longer sees, had died the day after his disgrace, leaving him an annual income of 200,000 *livres*. The Baron had spent the aforesaid income, and more, within six months. Then he thought of returning to court, and, deeming it absolutely necessary for that purpose to have a suitable mistress, had conceived designs upon the Duchesse d'A***. The latter, at the outset of the story that we are about to relate, was on the point of obtaining for him the governorship of the province of Normandy. Now, the day when we have just seen the Baron de Nossac chatting from his bed with the Duchesse d'A*** was, to be precise, December 2, 1723.

As the Duchesse was climbing into her carriage, which was waiting for her at a side-gate in the gardens, another carriage came in by the main entrance. A gentleman, who was tall but very thin, got down and asked to be taken to the Baron immediately. This gentleman was Monsieur de Simiane.

"Ah. There you are, my dear chap!" the Baron said, negligently.

"Yes," Simiane replied, excitedly.

"My God, what a state you're in! What's happened, Marquis? Where have you come from? Has some jealous husband had you beaten by his servants?"

"My dear chap," Simiane said, without replying to Nossac's rather impertinent question. "It's merely time to get you married."

"What a pity, my dear chap! I shan't be getting married–I've got my governorship."

"You think so, Baron?"

"I'm perfectly certain of it."

"Personally, I'm certain of the opposite. The Regent didn't have time to sign your letters."

Monsieur de Nossac shrugged his shoulders. "What does that mean, Marquis? In what sense did he not have time?"

"He didn't–because the Regent died last night."

The Baron released a cry.

"He died of apoplexy."

"You're dreaming, Marquis–it's impossible. The Duchesse d'A*** has just left. She knew nothing about it."

"There are many others who don't know, and won't know until tomorrow. Moreover, I'll wager that the Duchesse d'A*** will be arrested."

"Why's that, Marquis?"

"Because she's the sworn enemy of Madame de Prie."[16]

"So what?"

"So what?" Simiane exclaimed. "Where have you been, my dear chap? Don't you know that the Marquise de Prie is the Duc de Bourbon's mistress?"

"Yes, of course."

"Well, I have something to tell you: the Duc de Bourbon is Prime Minister."

The Baron went pale.

"Monseigneur de Fréjus," Simiane continued, "has generously stood aside. That gentle prelate is never in a hurry. Be tranquil, though–he will lose nothing by waiting." [17]

"So my governorship...?"

"The wisest thing would be to don your mourning-dress."

"And this marriage...?"

"It's necessary to conclude it immediately, or to forget it."

"Why is that?"

"Because Monsieur Borelli, the excise-farmer–who believes he is making a good bargain by giving you his daughter today, having had wind of your governorship–will retract the offer tomorrow, when he finds out that you're in disgrace,"

"But my dear Marquis, one cannot marry between one day and the next."

"One can marry between evening and morning. Consent, and you shall be married this evening."

"Truly?"

"I'll see to it. I'll persuade Borelli that it will reflect well on him to give you his daughter in a spirit of complete disinterest, before your appointment as the Governor of Normandy."

"Bravo!"

"Then I can put the wheels in motion?"

The Baron consulted the clock. "Wait ten minutes," he said. "If my commission hasn't arrived by two o'clock, you have my word."

"Very well."

"The Regent's death will not be made known today, then?"

"No, there are measures to be taken. You'll be married this evening, at midnight, and you can take your wife away to whatever château you might wish."

"Not at all–I'll remain in Paris."

"The marriage will take place in her father's house on the Île Saint-Louis, without pomp..."

"Not at all–I want a splendid feast; I want to do things in broad daylight."

"In complete darkness, at any rate." [18]

"So be it. You'll be in charge of the invitations. Those who don't come will indicate how I'm to treat them in future."

"Oh, don't worry; misalliances are so fashionable that everyone will come. Besides, your wife-to-be is rather beautiful..."

"Really? Anyway, that's a matter of indifference. For what I want to do..."

"She has a fine air about her, and a beauty unmatchable anywhere. She'll provide us with a footstool after the storm."

Two o'clock chimed; the door opened.

"My God!" cried the Baron. "Here's my commission."

The Baron was mistaken. It was merely Duc d'A***'s manservant, who was coming to warn him, confidentially, that the Duchesse had been arrested in her carriage an hour before, as it arrived back at her townhouse.

"Poor Duchesse," said the Baron, philosophically.

"What do you say, my dear?" asked Simiane.

"I say, Marquis," the Baron replied, phlegmatically, "that you can get everything ready: I'll marry Mademoiselle Borelli tonight."

III

Mademoiselle Hélène Borelli, the daughter of the excise-farmer of that name, was 23 years old. She had a Grecian head, large black eyes bordered by long lashes–velvet eyes, as the saying has it–a fine figure, a little on the tall side, well-sculpted hands and dazzlingly white skin, so lusterless that when she stood still one could easily mistake her for a marble Madonna.

At two o'clock in the afternoon, Monsieur le Baron de Nossac had not yet seen his bride; at four, he was introduced to her; at six, he dined with her in his future father-in-law's house; and at eleven, he climbed into a carriage to go to Saint-Germain-l'Auxerrois, where the Abbé de Morfrans, his cousin, was to celebrated the wedding mass.

"Well," Simiane asked the Baron, as he led his bride to his carriage, "how do you like her?"

"In truth, my dear chap," the Baron said, complacently, "she's beautiful enough. I believe I'll love her for an entire month, straight away."

"Monsieur le Baron," Hélène said to him, in a soft voice, "I'd dearly like to talk to you privately for ten minutes. Would you please ask your friend the Marquis de Simiane to travel in my father's carriage?"

"Marquis," said Monsieur de Nossac to Simiane, in a whisper, "it's the first, and doubtless the last, chance that I shall have to speak one-to-one with Mademoiselle before she becomes my wife..."

"I understand, Baron–don't worry about it..."

And Simiane got in with the tax-collector, who spread himself out in his gilt-embroidered coat on the brocade cushions of his carriage.

The whole society of city and court had been invited to the wedding supper at Borelli's house, but the Marquis de Simiane had had the exquisite tact to invite very few people to the wedding mass, so there were only a dozen carriages behind that of the future spouses.

"Monsieur le Baron," Hélène said to her husband, as they set off, just as eleven o'clock chimed, "we shall not be married until midnight."

"That hour will be a century, Mademoiselle," the Baron replied, courteously.

"Will you allow me a quarter-hour of serious conversation?"

"I am entirely at your disposal."

"And reply to me with complete frankness?"

"On my honor as a gentleman!"

"Well then, Monsieur le Baron, I will be frank too. My father wanted our marriage for reasons of ambition and pride. I, on the other hand..." The young woman hesitated.

"You?" the Baron prompted.

"If I were not so close to being your wife, I would not dare admit it–it is for love."

"Ah, Mademoiselle!" said the Baron, joyfully. "You know me, then?"

"I saw you once, two months ago. Now, Monsieur, I know perfectly well that you cannot say as much to me, and that this marriage is not, for you..."

"This marriage," the Baron put in, "even yesterday, could only have been a speculation on my part. Today, everything is changed; I love you."

"Are you telling the truth?" Despite the semi-darkness in which they were plunged, the young woman fixed an ardent gaze upon Nossac.

"Can you doubt it? You are so beautiful!"

"It's just that I don't want to deceive you," Hélène said, "and it's essential that you know me well..."

"Oh!"

"You tell me that you love me, and I believe it–but if you deceive me..."

"Oh, fie!"

"I shall never forgive you as long as I live." A spark of light flared up in Hélène's black eyes, which caused the Baron to shiver. "My God, yes!" the young woman continued. "I am not an aristocrat, my father is not even a military man, and there is no churchman in my family. We are poor bourgeois folk enriched, and I imagine that a gentleman who would deign to raise us up to his level would have no scruples about deceiving a woman of my sort."

"I swear to you that the thought never entered my head."

"I believe you again, Monsieur le Baron–but listen: we shall be married in an hour, and there is still time to break the engagement."

"What! What a thing to say!"

"Will you swear to me that you will forsake the some-what debauched existence that you have led until now?"

"I swear it to you."

"You will never give me the right to be anything other than an honest wife?"

"Oh, never!"

"If, one day, I should take a lover, will you have the courage to kill me?"

"Yes," the Baron said, resolutely.

"And will you give me the same right?"

The Baron hesitated, but he darted a glance at the young woman, and found her so beautiful that he replied immediately thereafter, in a firm voice: "Yes, I give you that."

"And you swear to me that you love me?"

"I swear it to you."

"Enough, Monsieur le Baron," Hélène said. "I shall be your wife in the eyes of men in a few minutes' time; I am already your wife in the eyes of God." And she offered him her ivory forehead, which he kissed.

The carriage stopped at that moment beneath the porch of the old church.

The Baron got down from the carriage first, then offered his hand to his wife. She leant on his arm with a noble leisureliness, and went up the temple steps with him. She paused on the last one.

"There is still time, Monsieur le Baron," she said, looking him in the face. "Would you like me to release you from your promise?"

"What madness!"

"You will keep your oaths?"

"Yes."

"Be careful! They are burdensome for a man like you."

"They might be, with regard to another woman, but not with regard to you. I've told you, Hélène, you're beautiful... and I love you!"

"Very well," she said, while her velvet eyes shone with a chaste flame. "Let's go, then–I will be your wife!"

The priest was at the altar; the spectators had already taken their places in the choir-stalls. Simiane and Villarceaux were the Baron's witnesses, the Chevalier de Mirbel and the Comte d'O*** the young bride's.[19]

At half-past midnight, the nuptial blessing had been given to the spouses, and Hélène Borelli climbed back into the carriage as the Baronne de Nossac.

"Whew!" murmured Simiane. "That's done! Old Borelli will no longer refuse me the 200,000 *livres* I asked to borrow from him, on my lands in Sault, which are already heavily mortgaged."

"Whew!" murmured the Baron, at the same time. "They can now announce and lament the death of Monseigneur le Régent. I'm rich enough to do without the proceeds of my governorship of Normandy."

"Whew!" murmured old Borelli, simultaneously. "They won't say that I'm no sort of a man any longer, I imagine.

30

Nossac is my son-in-law, and we shall soon have the governorship of Normandy." He added, with a hearty laugh: "One more gentleman mixing with the riff-raff!"

As for Hélène, she whispered to herself: "He's handsome; he loves me; I'm happy!"

IV

The supper and the ball that followed the wedding ceremony were splendid. The Regent's death had not yet been divulged, and society had come to watch the Baron de Nossac go slumming. But the universal curiosity was cheated; no one, except for the witnesses and the audience at the nuptial mass, saw the new bride. She had refused to attend the feast and had returned home.

The young Baronne de Nossac was sitting next to her fire, her head lolling backwards, in the serious and melancholy attitude that expectation adopts when it is tempered by a vague anxiety. The young Baronne had tears in her eyes. Would he love her for long? The poor child did not doubt the sincerity of his promises, but to promise and to keep a promise...

It was to think about such matters that Hélène de Nossac had wanted to be alone for a few hours more; it was for this reason that, while the music of the ball resounded on the floors below, she had taken refuge in the bedroom she had occupied as a child, in order to weep and dream at her leisure...

As two o'clock sounded, the Baron came in.

At the sight of him, Hélène was overcome by emotion, and hid her head in her hands. The Baron went to her, took her in his arms and kissed her on the forehead.

Almost immediately, though, someone knocked softly at the door.

"Oh, what is it?" said the Baron.

It was a lackey who had been searching all over the house for him, and had pursued him as far as the nuptial

31

chamber. "Monsieur le Baron," he said to him, "there's a carriage at the door of the house. Inside, there's a gentleman who wants to speak to you immediately."

"What's his name?"

"I don't know, but it's on urgent business."

"My God!" said the Baronne, fearfully.

"Calm down, my dear child," said Monsieur de Nossac. "I'll come straight back."

"Oh, come back quickly... Armand."

"Instantly, my dear angel."

The Baron went downstairs, saying to himself: "It's one of my creditors, pressed to sign something, who wants to be sure I can pay my debt. Scoundrel!"

He arrived at the front door of the house, and saw the carriage parked on the roadside.

"Baron," said a faint and high-pitched voice, when he reached the carriage-door, "I learned of your marriage 20 minutes ago."

The Baron shivered, and darted a glance into the depths of the carriage, where he perceived the Duchesse d'A***, brazenly dressed in a musketeer's doublet.

"Baron," the Duchesse went on, "you promised me this very morning to give me 24 hours, of my choice..."

"Yes, Madame," murmured the Baron, pale and trembling.

"Well, my dear, I opt for today."

"But Madame... That's not possible..."

"Why is that?"

"Because... because..." the Baron stammered, "...my wife is waiting for me."

"Well, you'll find her again tomorrow."

"But it's my wedding night..."

"You shall spend it with me. Now, Baron, climb up here, next to me."

"Madame!" cried the Baron. "For mercy's sake!"

"You have very little yourself, coming here to talk to me of your wife. Let's be off, my fine friend–I have your word."

"But must I not, at least, go fetch my sword?"

"No need–there's one here."

"My hat?"

"Again, there's no need. We're going to your house."

"To my house!"

"Of course. Remember your oath: you promised to follow me wherever I desire."

"But people will know."

"And you will not be dishonored by that, my dear. I am still beautiful enough for someone to devote himself to me without shame."

The Baron, bound by his word, climbed into the carriage, cursing and swearing. It drew away immediately.

"What a wedding night!" he murmured.

"What ought to console you," the Duchesse replied, with a mocking laugh, "is that your wife will not have a better one... Unless Simiane..."

"Madame!" the Baron exclaimed, angrily, "I have given you my word to belong to you, body and soul, for 24 hours; I keep my word, but that does not give you the right to insult me. My wife's honor is my own!"

"Baron!" cried the Duchesse. "It's noon–would you like to summon your servants and have my dinner served?"

The Baron, pale and livid, was sitting in a corner of the room, his head in his hands and his forehead charged with a cloud of concentrated wrath. He got up slowly, like an automaton whose springs were at full stretch, he took hold of a tassel of silk hanging down beside a Venetian glass set above the fireplace, and tugged it violently.

"Hold on," the Duchesse continued. "Here's the key to your apartment, which I prudently extracted, for fear that the whim might take you to slip away."

"Madame!" said the Baron, angrily. "Have I ever broken my word?"

The Duchesse did not deign to reply to this exclamation, but she added with her habitual mockery: "Then you'll ask for your carriage."

"Why would I do that, Madame?"

"Why, to go out, it seems to me. I have a frightful migraine." She added, with scant compassion: "Let's see, what time is it?"

"Noon, Madame."

"What time was it last night, when I picked you up?"

"Half-past two, Madame."

"You're my slave for 24 hours, Baron. Count up... nine and a half and 14 and a half make 24, so you still owe me 14 and a half hours."

"And you won't do me the favor of letting me rest?"

"Not for a second, my dear."

"But that's a barbarity without a name, Madame!"

"Fie, Monsieur. Is it a torture, then, to keep me company?"

"No, of course not," said Monsieur de Nossac, jeeringly. "But I have a wife... A wife who is waiting for me..."

"And who must be prey to a cruel anguish, must she not? Be tranquil, Baron–we shall take pains to reassure her. Hold on–I perceive that there is paper and ink on the night-stand. Go to the night-stand, Baron."

"What do you want me to do, Madame?"

"Keep going... Good. Now sit down. You realize that it won't be me who writes to Madame de Nossac."

A thin and mocking laugh spilled from the Duchesse's rosy lips. Monsieur de Nossac took up a pen and wrote the following lines:

My dear angel,

The Regent died last night, Monsieur de Bourbon is Prime Minister, and I write to you from the Bastille...

The Duchesse extended her slender fingers towards the letter, seized it and read it. "My God!" she cried, bursting out laughing. "A pretty lie! Are you a liar, then, my poor dear?"

"What do you want me to say, then," the Baron stammered, "to excuse..."

"The truth, Baron."

"Impossible!"

"You're a simpleton. Do you imagine that I carried you away last night in order that you could be billing and cooing at your wife's feet this evening, while she is perfectly convinced that you have come from the Bastille?"

"But what do you want to do?"

"Nothing much—dictate your letter."

"What! I'll never consent to that!"

"You're forgetting one important thing, my dear Baron."

"What?"

"That you're my slave until tomorrow morning."

"Well?"

"Well, you must show me absolute and passive obedience. Write, Baron—I have your word."

The Baron reddened with anger, but he took up the pen and another sheet of paper, murmuring: "I'm waiting, Madame..."

"Write," said the Duchesse.

My beautiful friend,

Before our marriage, I had promised a Duchesse, whom I shall not name, 24 hours of slavery. I always keep my word, and I kept it last night. I am writing to you from my home, where I am about to dine with my beautiful gaoler. My butler has popped the champagne-cork and lightly warmed the claret. The menu is excellent. We shall go out in a carriage later today, and tomorrow, at daybreak, I shall return to you, my beautiful friend, perhaps a little paler, a little wearied by my last youthful folly, but resigned in advance to the early acquisition of that florid complexion and marvelous plumpness that is and always will be the prerogative of married men.

I kiss your hands.

"And you're going to send that letter!" cried the Baron, stunned and pale with anger.

"Of course."

"But can't you imagine the fatal consequences it will have?"

"I'm trying, Baron,"

"It's my conjugal happiness, broken forever!"

"Agreed. For me, it's the satisfaction of a whim. When one is beautiful, and something of a Duchesse, my dear, one has the right to indulge expensive whims."

The Baron stared fixedly at his former mistress. He met her cold and haughty gaze, in which an implacable hatred burned. He understood that this woman, who had loved him the day before, and whose love he had offended, would be pitiless. He resigned himself to submit to his torture until the end.

Almost immediately, someone knocked at the door. Nossac went to open it.

"Monsieur le Baron is served," said a lackey.

"Baron," the Duchesse said to him, "go cast a quick eye over the supper menu that your butler has prepared, and please send in my chambermaid, who should have arrived by now. I have to get dressed."

Ten minutes later, Madame la Duchesse d'A*** and Monsieur le Baron de Nossac were at the dining-table. The Duchesse devoured a partridge's wing, crunched a few delicate morsels, moistened her lips with the best Aï wine, shelled a pomegranate candied with caramel with the end of her rosy fingernail and ate an atom of plum pudding–a dish recently imported to the tablecloths of the city and the court from the far side of the Channel. Then, when she was replete, she got up and said to the Baron: "Have your horses prepared."

The Baron gave the order.

"Now," she continued, "please go to your bedroom and change into the complete costume that your valet has prepared according to my orders. For my part, I shall go modify my own dress with the help of my maids."

The Baron knew now that he really was a slave, and that he could utter no criticism of the strange desires of his imperious mistress. He delivered himself into the hands of his valet, who dressed him in the uniform of a mere guardsman; then he rejoined the Duchesse, whom he found dressed as a sutler.[20]

The soldier and the sutler made a fine couple.

"Where are you taking me, Madame?" asked the Baron, in a tone that implied: *From what torture am I condemned to die?*

"To Porcherons, my fine friend."

"In a carriage?"

"Only to get out of Paris After that, we'll go on foot across country, arm in arm, like a true guardsman and an authentic sutler."

"And what shall we do in Porcherons?" Nossac asked, his irritated voice catching in his throat.

"What everyone does there, Baron. We shall amuse ourselves. We shall dine in the arbor of an inn; we shall drink frightful wine the color of indigo, and we shall eat a nameless cuisine, which will make you miss, ever so slightly, the future table of Monsieur the tax-farmer Borelli, your father-in-law."

The Baron bit his lip. "Let's go, Duchesse," he said, offering her his arm. "Come on—I'm in a hurry to leave."

"Are you worried that Madame de Nossac might come looking for you?"

The Baron had not thought of that, but the idea made him shudder.

"Be reassured, my dear," the implacable Duchesse said to him. "If she comes, she will come in vain; I will not give you up."

They climbed into the carriage and left Paris at the gallop. Then, having arrived quite close to the place where the circling wall now stands, which separates Paris from Batignolles, they sent the carriage and its lackeys back and went on foot, arm in arm with one another, across the fields, like a true guardsman and an authentic sutler, just as the Duchesse had said.

At Porcherons, the Baron de Nossac found abundant company, and his disguise lent a little extra luster to his escapade. It was undeniable that Monsieur Borelli was a man who had been well and truly turned over, and that Madame de Nossac would have nothing from her husband but his name... and his creditors.

V

It was broad daylight when the Baron, finally at liberty and rid of the Duchesse, left his house on foot and headed for the Île Saint-Louis, where Monsieur Borelli's townhouse was located.

Despite the early hour, the servants were all at work and the windows wide open. *Oh! What does this mean?* the Baron thought. *Has my wife taken a second husband?*

The servants bowed respectfully as he passed by, but none of them addressed a word to him. Disdaining to question them, Monsieur de Nossac went straight up to his wife's apartment.

Both sections of the double door were open, and the rooms were completely deserted. *My wife is with her father,* he thought, and went to the tax-farmer's quarters. Like his wife's, they were deserted; the bed was undisturbed.

"What the Devil!" the Baron exclaimed. "There's a fine mystery here."

He went back downstairs and asked the first servant he encountered: "Where is Monsieur Borelli?"

"Monsieur Borelli left last night for his estate in Normandy."

"Ah!" said the Baron, stunned.

"He left a letter for Monsieur le Baron with his steward."

"Summon the steward for me."

The steward appeared, a letter in his hand.

The Baron opened the letter precipitately and read the following:

Monsieur le Baron,

You only married my daughter with the objective of paying your debts. Your objective is fulfilled; your debts are paid. I enclose the receipts from your creditors with my letter, to which I do not desire any reply. I leave you my house in Paris and have retired to my estate at Caux, where I do not expect ever to receive you as a visitor.

A man who is extremely sorry to have you for a son-in-law.

Borelli.

"But where is Madame de Nossac?" cried the Baron.

"Gone, Monsieur le Baron."

"With her father?"

"No, Monsieur le Baron."

"Then where is she?"

"On the road to Brittany, where she has a château."

"When did her carriage set off?"

"Yesterday evening, Monsieur le Baron."

"That's good!" said the Baron, angrily. "Go find me two post-horses immediately. I want to leave right away."

The Baron was obeyed with admirable promptness. Twenty minutes later, he climbed into the post-chaise and shouted: "I might break 20 horses, but I'll catch up with my wife!"

VI

The Baron kept the first part of his promise.

Thirty leagues from Paris, however, as his horses were being changed, a very well-dressed gentleman arrived behind the Baron, doubtless after having achieved similar feats of celerity, and said to him gravely: "My name, Monsieur, is the Chevalier de Courceneuille, and I am, since yesterday, the lover of the Duchesse d'A***..."

"Oh!" said the Baron, taking a step back.

"It appears, Monsieur, that you have gravely insulted the Duchesse, for she has sent me to provoke you..."

"I accept the challenge, Monsieur," the Baron replied, immediately drawing his sword.

The Baron had fenced on many occasions with the Regent, who was an expert, but that did not prevent his receiving a forceful sword-thrust, which laid him abed for a week in the wretched inn that served as a relay-station.

That ensured that he was unable to catch up with his wife.

VII

Eight days later, however, Monsieur le Baron de Nossac was able to continue on his route, and within 48 hours, he arrived in Léonais, the province where his wife's château was located.[21]

At the final relay-station, he was told that the roads he must follow henceforth were impassable by carriages. The Baron demanded a horse, and went on his way, despite the lateness of the hour. He rode all night. At daybreak, he attained the summit of a hill from which the grey towers of the château for which he was headed were visible.

It was a fine winter morning, devoid of the dull mists that normally extend over the bare fields and yellowed pasturage, creeping before the cold and rainy north wind. The Baron felt a slight outburst of joy in his heart and urged his weary horse forward.

Suddenly, in the midst of the pleasant calm of the fields, the sound of a bell reached him, slow and measured. It was sounding a funeral knell. The Baron shuddered and dug his spurs furiously into his horse's flanks. The horse resumed its gallop and sped like an arrow to the gate of the château.

The Baron went into the courtyard; it was silent and deserted. He dismounted, went up the steps to the main door, then climbed the interior staircase with its golden balustrade and stone steps. Both sets of stairs were empty of servants.

Guided by a mysterious and sinister presentiment, he passed through several rooms, similarly empty, where the sound of his spurred boots echoed lugubriously. Finally, he heard a confused murmur in the distance, at the far end of the series of apartments through which he was passing–a vague and monotonous murmur resembling the psalmodic chanting of monks in the depths of a cloister at the nocturnal hour of matins. Guided by this noise he continued onwards, his heart tremulous with emotion and sweat pearling on his brow.

He arrived in this manner at a closed door. Behind that door, the murmur that he had heard became distinct; it was indeed a litany. The Baron felt his hair bristle. Suppressing his terror, he knocked.

The litany ceased instantly; both sections of the door opened, creaking on their hinges with a funereal sonority. The Baron recoiled before the spectacle thus displayed to his eyes, and released a cry.

Extended inanimately on a bed of state was Madame la Baronne de Nossac. A surpliced priest was kneeling at the head of the bed, reciting the prayer for the dead. Weeping servants were kneeling all around it. A mortuary candle was burning on the night-stand. Propped up on that candle was a large envelope, bearing the following inscription:

To Monsieur le Baron de Nossac

The Baronne de Nossac had passed over the previous evening. It was her funeral knell that the Baron had heard.

He marched straight to the bed, as stiff as a statue, and placed his hand on the dead woman's heart. The heart was no longer beating. He approached his tremulous lips to hers... but her lips were cold. He took the icy hand of the deceased in his own, lifted it up and let it fall. It fell inertly.

The Baronne de Nossac was definitely dead.

He went to the night-stand then, broke the seal on the envelope and opened it avidly. The envelope contained nothing but the deceased's will, a testament conceived in these terms:

I appoint Monsieur le Baron de Nossac as my sole heir, on condition that he remarries within an interval of two years and lives in my house on the Île Saint-Louis, in Paris, whenever he stays in the capital.

Baronne Hélène de Nossac née Borelli

P.S. If Monsieur de Nossac is widowed again before the expiration of the two years, he must remarry, in order that my inheritance shall not return to my family.

Not a word of love or anger was appended to this testament. Was that silence menacing or disdainful?

VIII

The Baron arranged his wife's funeral ceremony. Then, he put a pistol to his head, intending to kill himself–but he recalled that he had not built her a mausoleum, and thought that it would be more fitting to attend to the construction of that edifice than to blow his brains out.

The mausoleum was constructed at great expense and placed in the grounds of the château, with the following inscription:

HERE LIES
BARONNE HÉLÈNE DE NOSSAC
NÉE BORELLI
DIED A VIRGIN
AT THE AGE
OF
TWENTY-FIVE YEARS
D.P. [22]

When this was done, the inconsolable Baron took up his pistols again and went to the tomb in order to sacrifice his life there to the manes of his unfortunate wife.[23] However, a gentleman from Paris arrived there at the same time, at full gallop, and said to him:

"It's perfectly proper for a gentleman to mourn his wife, but, as for sacrificing his life to her–that is not allowed. A gentleman's life belongs to the King."

This gentleman was the Marquis de Simiane, who had brought the Baron a commander's commission, and orders to report immediately to the army in Germany.

The Baron resigned himself to live, swearing meanwhile that he would never be consoled.

As things transpired, however, he was.

Part One

I

It was one year to the day since Madame la Baronne de Nossac had been carefully interred by her husband in the grounds of her château at Léonais. We rejoin the Baron several hundred leagues from his wife's tomb, aboard the flagship of the French fleet assembled at Danzig under the command of the Comte de La Motte.[24]

King Stanislaus of Poland, an ally of His Majesty Louis XV, was blockaded by the Russians in his last stronghold, Danzig. Lacy, the supreme commander of the Tsar's armies, had proclaimed Prince August King of Poland and Grand Duke of Lithuania at Varsovie. Danzig, thus blockaded, could not hold out for long, and the capture of Danzig would send Stanislaus' head rolling on the scaffold.[25]

Three men were in council aboard the flagship: the Comte de La Motte, the Admiral-in-Chief; Baron de Nossac, an army commander in charge of a force of marine infantry, and Comte Bréhan de Plelo, a Breton gentleman, the French Ambassador in Copenhagen.[26]

"Messieurs," said the Admiral, "we have five ships of the line and three corvettes, and a force of between 7,000 and 8,000 men. The Russians camped outside the walls of Danzig number 30,000. They are well-entrenched; the fortress of Weshulmund has surrendered to them and their batteries dominate both banks of the Vistula. Disembarkation is futile; there is nothing to be done. We cannot help Danzig."

"Monsieur," replied the Comte de Plelo, with icy dignity, "there is a King in Danzig whose life is under threat–a King whose head might fall beneath the axe, like that of Charles I of England. Consider that..."

"I know that, Monsieur, but what can I do about it?"

"Consider also," Baron de Nossac said in his turn, "that all Europe has its eyes upon us. If Danzig is taken tomorrow, and a military tribunal of Russian officers convenes, tries and condemns King Stanislaus on that same day, and his head rolls on the scaffold the day after, while those eyes are turned towards us, all Europe will raise a cry of reprobation against us, which will say: There was, a league from Danzig, a squadron of the army of King Louis XV, a friend of King Stanislaus. That squadron, that army, remained contented spectators and watched the head of a King fall, without any of their gun-ports throwing a single cannonball, or any of their muskets a bullet!"

"Messieurs," said the Comte de La Motte, haughtily, "you speak nobly and well, but our master the King has invested the supreme command in me. In that capacity, I must render him a strict account of his soldiers. To attempt to carry provisions to Danzig would lead them to certain death, without any hope of success. I am opposed to the disembarkation."

"Monsieur," said the Comte de Plelo, "there is an old proverb–a chivalric proverb, as it happens–which is popular in France, especially in Brittany. I am a Breton–would you permit me to quote it? *Do what must be done, come what may!* Well, I, Comte de Bréhan de Plelo, summon you to the salvation of a King allied with France! Before I became a statesman, I was a swordsman, and I take upon my own head, in advance, the entire responsibility for the hazardous expedition that I am proposing to you. Are you satisfied?"

"In that case, Monsieur," the Admiral replied, "we can disembark. I am ready to die at your side."

"After me, Comte," Monsieur de Plelo said, proudly. "The first gentleman who will die for King Stanislaus will be me."

"And I," said Baron de Nossac, "swear to you, Messieurs, that if I must pass over the corpses of an entire Russian army alone, I shall reach His Polish Majesty; I shall place myself at his right hand, and if I do not save him, if I do not snatch him from the headsman's grip, at least I shall ensure that not a hair falls from his head until mine is no longer on its shoulders."

The Comte de Plelo held out his hand. "Baron," he said to him, "you are the finest gentleman I know, and you prove to me once more that gallantry and bravery, spirit and nobility, will always be combined in you."

"I shall take the measures necessary for the disembarkation," said Monsieur de la Motte.

"I shall command it," said the Comte de Plelo.

"And I," Nossac added, "shall revert to the status of a mere gentleman. I shall resign my General's powers to one of my Colonels."

"Why is that, Baron?"

"Because I want to get to the King, and I do not intend to lead my army to him."

"What chivalrous folly!" murmured the Admiral.

"Follies of that sort," replied Monsieur de Plelo, "outweigh wisdom and diplomacy."

II

The attack and the disembarkation took place on the same day. Monsieur de Plelo and Monsieur de Nossac, with 200 men, got past 10,000 Russians and arrived at the very gates of Danzig. There, however, Monsieur de Plelo fell, riddled with bullets, while his companions were captured or killed. One man alone, bloody and covered in mud, with his sword in his fist, his clothing in tatters and scored by bullet-wounds–minor, for the most part–contrived to come through the enemy lines, to fall exhausted and dying at the palisades of the besieged city. This was the Baron de Nossac. The Comte de Plelo and he had each kept his word; one of them was dead, the other had reached King Stanislaus.

III

It is not within our remit to relate in a detailed manner the miraculous escape of King Stanislaus–which, at the time, astonished all Europe by the boldness with which it was conceived and executed. We shall limit ourselves to a brief summary.

The Danzigers had mounted such a vigorous opposition to the Russian army only because the presence of their King enthused and stimulated them. They were quite prepared to be buried beneath the ruins of their city, on condition that the King perished there with them. Now, the King knew that while he remained in Danzig, Danzig would not surrender, and that if he did not want the city to be bombarded and starved any longer, he had to leave.

Never had any flight appeared so impossible. The Russians were blockading Danzig; Danzig, in its turn, had its self-esteem at stake, and would not allow its King to depart. The King had therefore to protect himself from his friends as well as his enemies. Three men, however–three alone, without accomplices or auxiliaries, with nothing to aid them but their audacity and their swords–resolved to save the King and succeeded in reaching him. These three men were the French Ambassador to Danzig, the Marquis de Monti, General Steinflich and Baron de Nossac.[27]

The Marquis procured a peasant's costume for the King, and a pair of old boots from a officer of the garrison–boots for which he dared not ask, and had stolen by the officer's batman. General Steinflich prepared a boat which, on a dark night suited to such an event, was moored beneath the rampart extending along the Vistula. The King, followed by the General and the Baron, both disguised as he was, arrived at the rampart and presented themselves at a postern gate opening on to a winding stairway, whose foot plunged into the river.

At that postern a Swedish officer was on guard.

"Who are you?" he asked the King.

The King hesitated for a minute, then elected to depend on the loyalty of the officer and said to him: "I am the King of Poland."

"I cannot let Your Majesty pass," replied the officer, "without the permission of the Major in charge."

That was impossible. The Major was opposed to the King's flight.

"Monsieur," the Baron de Nossac then said to the officer, "are you a gentleman?"

"Yes, Monsieur."

"Are you quite convinced that if Danzig is captured, the King will be beheaded?"

"Yes," replied the officer, "but we shall die with him."

"Monsieur," the Baron went on, "when I was very young, I knew a Scottish gentleman who was almost 100 years old, who always wore a black velvet mask over his face and a mourning-band upon his arm. Do you know why?"

"No," said the officer.

"Because he had been the first Scottish officer to abandon the cause of King Charles I. In the many years that had elapsed since then, he had not contrived to forget his treason or stifle his remorse."

"What is there in common between him and me?" asked the officer.

"This–that he was the primary cause of his sovereign's death, and that if, in three days' time, the head of King Stanislaus is divorced from his body, you will be able to say to yourself: I am the one who killed my King, by my obstinacy and my passive obedience to a discipline that ought no longer to hold sway when the life of a crowned head is in peril."

The officer reflected for a minute; then, placing his hand on his heart, yielded passage, saying: "The King may pass!"

The King went down, followed by his two companions, found the boat, manned by a *znapan*–a sort of Bohemian mercenary soldier quite common in Germany at that time–took his place there, and cut the mooring-rope himself with his dagger.

As for the Swedish officer, on the following morning, when the boat was far away, he went to find the Major in charge, told him what had happened, and said to him: "Now, sir, as it is unnecessary for two officers simultaneously to fail in their duty, you may assemble a court-martial and have me shot this very day."

"You were right," replied the Major, offering his hand. "You are a true gentleman."

"No," said the officer, "I am a traitor, but I have saved the King. I shall die content."

If one searched for such men nowadays, where could they be found?

IV

The King reached the marshes into which the Vistula sinks before uniting itself with the sea. He remained in hiding in a peasant's hut throughout a long day, and did not resume his route until night fell again. Finally, after ten similar nights–ten nights of continual peril–passing through the entrenched Russian and Imperial forces, sleeping badly, scarcely eating anything, and always escorted by Steinflich and the Baron, he succeeded in reaching the bank of the Nogat. There, Steinflich left the King, but the Baron wanted to continue accompanying him. The King crossed the Nogat with him; then, on the other bank, reached a village named Bialagora, where he bought a horse and cart.

In that rig, two days later, King Stanislaus of Poland made his entrance into Marienwerder.[28] He was out of danger and far from the Russian axe. Then the Baron took his leave of him.

"Adieu, Sire," he said to him.

"You're leaving me?"

"I'm returning to my post, Sire."

"Alas!" said the King, with a sad smile. "I no longer have a kingdom and I am the poorest of Poles. I can, in consequence, offer you neither honors nor a fortune to retain you by my side, and I release you."

"Sire," the Baron said, proudly, "God is my witness that if I were a Pole, I would gladly follow you to the ends of the Earth, even though both of us should lack shelter and bread—but I belong to the King of France, and I can only serve you by escorting you."

The King offered his hand; Nossac bent his knee and kissed it. Then he bowed and made ready to depart.

The Baron made his way to a hostelry, at which a *znapan* had just arrived, covered with dust, apparently having come a long way, asking to speak to him. The Baron was still dressed in his peasant's costume, but the *znapan* went straight to him and said to him: "General, I've come to you on behalf of General Steinflich."

"Why is that?" asked the Baron, shivering.

"To warn you that an ambush has been mounted on the other bank of the Nogat."

"What ambush?"

"For you, General. The Russians have promised that you shall pay dearly for the removal of King Stanislaus."

"So I must remain here?"

"Yes, General, unless..."

"Unless?" Nossac prompted.

"Unless you trust me enough to venture forth in my company, across country and through the forest. I know roads where neither the Russians nor the Imperial forces ever go, and I promise you that you will be at the Prussian frontier within a fortnight, where you can take ship."

"Damn!" said the Baron. "I like that much better."

He took off his disguise, procured suitable clothing and a horse, then said to the *znapan*: "We'll depart before dawn tomorrow, if you wish."

The *znapan* bowed, suppressing a diabolical smile that rose to his lips, while he murmured to himself: "The Castle of the Black Huntsmen is still a long way off, but we shall get there!"

V

The Baron slept badly in a miserable bed, which was the best the inn at which he had fetched up had to offer. The nightmare, that painful dream which normally follows great fatigue, assailed him for several hours and unfolded within his impressionable mind the strangest tales and the blackest legends then current within the mysterious land of Germany—which, even in our day, is not completely free of the superstitious and supernatural traditions of the Middle Ages.

All of a sudden, a slow, monotonous and bizarre voice awoke him with a start. The voice was singing a Slavonic song,[29] whose first two verses went as follows:

The old castellan with furrowed brow,
Is still sitting up as midnight passes,
In his huge antique armchair.
The last fire-brand is going out,
Time hastens on and the tint of dawn
Is already upon the horizon.
What does the dark and ominous face
Of the old castellan hold secret?

In the dark forest, the old castellan,

As the day faded into twilight
Must have seen the eternal huntsman pass by,
All clad in black on his black horse:
The Black Huntsman who never rests
With his whip in his hand from dawn to dusk,
Following the hunt with his horn to his mouth...
There'll be deaths in the manor by morning!

This song, springing up suddenly in the nocturnal silence and awakening harmonious echoes in the surroundings, astonished the Baron sufficiently to make him leap from his bed and run to the window overlooking the courtyard of the inn. By the moonlight that fringed the great black clouds with silver, lending objects a strange and tormented appearance, he perceived a man busy harnessing two horses. It was the *znapan*.

Reassured, the Baron returned to his bed, took his watch from the bedhead, and consulted it. It was barely one o'clock in the morning. Well, he thought, the odd fellow is in a great hurry to depart. He returned to the window and called out. The *znapan* turned his head.

"Good day, General," he said. "Since you're awake, get dressed right away."

"We're leaving in the morning..."

"It's a long way."

"Let's be on our way, then," said the Baron.

He dressed hastily, went down to the courtyard without making a noise, put his prudently-loaded pistols in their holsters, carefully buckled his sword-belt and climbed into the saddle. The *znapan* leapt on to the bare back of his own horse with the fantastic lightness of Hungarian and Bohemian cavaliers, and went on ahead.

They left the village in this fashion and took a stony and undulating by-road, flanked by tall hedges. At first, they plunged into the middle of a fog-enshrouded plain, then made a sinuous ascent of the steep slopes flanking a mountain clad in black fir-trees, which suddenly opened like a gigantic mouth, bisected by a profound gorge leading south-eastwards.

As soon as the Baron had heard the *znapan*, the latter had cut short his song. With other preoccupations preying on his mind, the Baron had not paid any heed to the sudden silence. Rocked by the rhythm of his mount's movement, he soon allowed himself to fall into the kind of melancholy reverie that so easily takes possession of a nocturnal traveler in pleasantly mute surroundings, troubled only by a light breath of wind or some nocturnal bird or cricket.

The Moon, passing behind the clouds in quick succession, projected clear-cut stripes of bizarre and gigantic shadow. Sometimes, it disappeared completely; the obscurity was profound then, and the Baron had all the difficulty in the world seeing his guide's horse three strides ahead of him.

The clouds drew closer together by degrees. At the moment when the two horsemen reached the entrance to the gorge, the clouds were no longer divided. forming a single black and menacing expanse. The Moon disappeared entirely, and the darkness became so profound that the Baron felt his horse shivering instinctively beneath him.

At once, the *znapan*'s voice rose up anew, continuing his song:

> *That evil Huntsman has Satan for a sire;*
> *He is all-powerful upon the Earth;*
> *He has a silver castle in the woods.*
> *His feverish hounds have rendered a ten-point stag*
> *Breathless in scarcely an hour.*

"Hey there, rogue!" cried the Baron, affected in spite of himself. "What's that you're singing to me?"

"The ballad of the Black Huntsman."

"Who is the Black Huntsman?"

"As you've just heard, General, he's the Devil's son."

"Shall we encounter him on our way?" Monsieur de Nossac asked, laughing.

"God preserve us from that, General."

"Why is that?"

"Because those who see the Black Huntsman die within 24 hours."

"Really?"

"Unless they have a daughter to marry off..."

"Ah-ha!"

"For it's said that the Black Huntsman is in want of a wife–but that no one, peeress or peasant, will have him."

"I have no daughter to marry off, but I'm in need of a wife myself. If the Black Huntsman has one on offer... by God, I believe I'd marry her!"

The Baron had scarcely completed this sentence in a light tone when a strident voice rose up in the depths of the gorge, 500 yards in front of the horsemen. This voice, quite differently accented and more terrible than that of the *znapan*, intoned a third verse of the ballad of the Black Huntsman–a verse doubtless unknown to the *znapan*:

> *Does the castellan with brow so severe,*
> *In the hour when all his lands are calm,*
> *Stay by the fireside while everyone sleeps,*
> *While a dead man comes to the infernal round*
> *That Satan hosts at the crossroads in the woods,*
> *Who also desires to sit down for an hour,*
> *Shivering and pale, by the fire in his hearth,*
> *To warm himself up before the green opal ray*
> *Glides tremulously from the clearing sky?*

"What voice is that?" demanded the shivering Baron, bringing his horse to an abrupt halt.

The *znapan* did not reply, perhaps because he was overwhelmed by terror or perhaps because he had not heard the question.

The voice continued:

> *The old castellan is sixty years old;*

The previous evening he saw the Black Huntsman,
Pass by on his ebony horse
In a clearing close to the manor.
So there'll be deaths today,
And the chaplain will say his dismal prayer tonight.
But that's not so, for the great Black Huntsman
Came howling about the manor a while ago
He said to the lord: "Tonight I want
To lie with your daughter all night long."

"But what voice is that?" cried the Baron de Nossac.

At that moment, a flash of lightning sprang forth from a crack in the vault of cloud. That lightning-flash lit up the gorge for two seconds, and by its sinister light the two travelers saw a black-clad horseman motionless in the middle of the road, mounted on a horse as black as himself, with a velvet mask upon his face and a hunting-horn slung over his shoulder.

"The Black Huntsman!" murmured the *znapan*, in a voice seemingly strangled with fright.

"By God's death!" cried the shivering Baron, desirous of taming the fear of danger with danger itself. "I want to see this terrible Huntsman at closer range!" And he urged his horse, which was trembling beneath him, forward.

VI

The Black Huntsman–for it was certainly him, to judge by appearances, so that is what we shall call him–remained motionless in the middle of the road, like some colossal guardian spirit set to defend the entrance to the black and mysterious valley against mere mortals.

He was, indeed, of truly gigantic stature, of a sort one no longer finds in Northern Germany. His horse, which was as black as he was, appeared to the Baron to be larger and stronger than other animals of its species. But if Monsieur de Nossac's first reflexive moment was fearful, he was brave enough to master his terror and emotion completely within the space of a few seconds. The time it took him to reach the Huntsman at the gallop, brief as it was, sufficed for him to recover all his composure. When he found himself no more than 20 paces away, he brought his mount to an abrupt halt and called out to the strange horseman: "Hey, master–give way, if you please."

The Huntsman did not reply, but he urged his horse forward in his turn and came to meet the Baron.

A second flash of lightning ploughed through the clouds, briefly illuminating the two horsemen as they came face to face, permitting them to look at one another.

"Well?" demanded Monsieur de Nossac, in a tone that was courteous but firm and frosty. "Will Your Infernal Lordship let me pass?"

"Ah!" said the Huntsman, with a mocking laugh. "Do you believe that you have recognized me, Milord?"

"By damn!" said the Baron. "I've heard the beginning of your story, and you've just told me the end, all in a prettily-rhymed ballad. You're the Black Huntsman."

"Just as you're the Baron de Nossac."

The Baron started with surprise and alarm on hearing his name pronounced. "Bah!" he said, immediately composing himself. "It's entirely natural that a son of the Devil should know the Grand Armorial of France by heart."

"And you have a fine enough place therein, Monsieur, if I remember rightly. It dates from the Crusades, I believe?"

"Indeed. Would it be inconvenient to Your Lordship if I continued on my way?"

"My dear Baron," the Huntsman replied, in a familiar tone. "You're at the edge of my domain; I own this valley and 20 leagues of forest to either side. I also have a rather fine castle ten leagues from here. You see that I'm a perfectly presentable lord, who would not cut a paltry figure at the court of any sovereign, be it my cousin in Russia or my cousin in Prussia."

"I congratulate you," said the Baron politely. "You have superb estates. Except that, if you would allow me to give you some advice..."

"Oh, don't apologize. I know by heart the work of one of your poets of the last century, Nicolas Boileau–a clever man, Baron, whom, I foresee, will be very badly mistreated 150 years hence by a school of Romantics who will have the defect of possessing more genius than sense.[30] I remember one rather remarkable verse: *Be grateful for the advice that is given to you*, and so on."

"Then I shall permit myself to suggest to you, Milord, that you light the roads of your domain a little better. It's as dark hereabouts as a Jansenist's soul." [31]

"You think so?" the Black Huntsman asked, earnestly.

"And I suppose that it would be easy enough to abstract a few of the brands from the stove at which His Majesty your father warms himself, since he grew tired of freezing in Heaven."

"My father is always cold," the Huntsman said, dryly. "But then again, his guests are so numerous that he could not frustrate them in that manner." He paused to laugh mockingly, then resumed: "However, Baron, if, when you are one of them, you would care to make me a gift of your portion of the fire to serve me as street-lights and lanterns, I shall accept the gift with great pleasure!"

"My regret has no bounds that it cannot be immediate," the Baron replied, in the same bantering tone, "for I dread that my guide might break his neck before much longer, he is so fearful already..."

"Your guide, Baron, is by the fireside at this very moment."

"What do you mean?"

"Look."

A third lightning-flash seemed to obey the Black Huntsman's mental command, and made the tortured rocks and dark thickets of the gorge resplendent within the radius of a quarter of a league. The Huntsman extended his hand; the Baron turned around. He explored and examined the road, searching... and saw nothing. The *znapan* had vanished.

The Baron exclaimed in surprise. "What has happened, then?"

"He's beside the fire you wanted to impoverish just now, in order to light my domains. He's an imp, whom my father lends me from time to time."

"Well," murmured the Baron, "I'm in a fine mess now."

"I shall serve as your guide, my dear fellow."

"Will you let me pass, then?"

"That depends. Yes, if it's to come to my home; no, if you wish to continue on your way."

"My dear infernal sir," the Baron said, phlegmatically, "either you're a tasteful trickster, whereupon I shall ask your permission to assure myself whether my sword is the same length as your hunting-knife...'

"Ah!"

"...Or you really are the son, the nephew or some other relative of the Devil, in which case..."

"In which case, Baron...?"

"Here's a weapon which might perhaps deliver me from you." And the Baron placed his hand on his forehead, ready to make the sign of the cross.

The Huntsman burst out laughing. "My dear Baron," he said, "I have Satan for a father, but my mother was a maiden of noble birth and a good Catholic. I was baptized 917 years ago, during the reign of Charlemagne, in the Cathedral of Aix-la-Chapelle, so you may sheathe your sign of the cross."

The Baron's hand fell back. "On what condition will your lordship condescend to let me pass?" he asked.

"I've just told you that I'm 917 years old–a fine and youthful old age, as you see, but I'm prodigiously bored. You're the wittiest gentleman in the French court, and I've sworn to have you under my roof for a few days. Can you refuse an old man that?"

"Have you drinkable wine?" Nossac asked, with superb calmness.

"I've a 1500 Chambertin, a 1630 Aï, a 1463 Johannis-berg, and..."[32]

"Enough, Milord! I'm yours."

"Very well," said the Black Huntsman, "let's be on our way then! And while Satan, my father, refuses me a firebrand, we'll have torches!"

The Black Huntsman put his horn to his mouth, and brought forth a powerful and raucous melody, which rather resembled one of those storm-winds that bend the crowns of an entire forest beneath their forceful flight. Immediately, the surrounding thickets lit up, and a dozen horsemen, as red as their master was black, surged forth, with blazing resin torches in their hands.

Decidedly, the Baron thought, I really am dealing with the Devil.

VII

The torch-bearers were uniformly dressed in red cas-socks and culottes; their faces, masked like their master's, were concealed beneath red velvet.

Behind one of these masks the Baron thought he could see embers sparkling that were adequate replacements for eyes. *Ah!* he thought, *the Black Huntsman lied–there's an atom of the paternal stove there.* The stare seemed truly infer-nal, moreover, and the French gentleman required all his brav-ery to resist being frightened by the sight of this black colos-sus surrounded by these red phantoms, all lit by the flickering and sinister light of the resin torches. The Baron's heart did not beat any more rapidly, though, and his forehead remained smooth and calm.

"My dear future host," he said to the Black Huntsman, "I see that you have an impressive household, and I wish that I were already in the manor to appreciate the rest."

"We cannot get there before this evening."

"Bah! When one has the Devil for a father, one ought to be able to cover 18 leagues in two hours."

"Doubtless–but my name is sufficient indication that I hunt every day, and I intend to hunt today."

"Ah!"

"I take your skill as a hunter on trust, Baron..."

"You're a thousand times too kind."

"My sons are scouting the woods. I'll call them."

"You have sons, then?"

"Four, Baron."

"I thought you were celibate, Milord."

"You haven't heard the final verse of my ballad, then?"

And the Black Huntsman's resounding voice intoned the last lines of the strange song that had apprised the Baron of his existence and presence:

But that's not so, for the great Black Huntsman
Came howling about the manor a while ago
He said to the lord: "Tonight I want
To lie with your daughter all night long."

"Of course," said the Baron, laughing. "But that doesn't tell us anything."

"Wait," said the diabolical hunter. "Listen." And he resumed, with a note of ardent joy in his voice:

The old castellan has died of sorrow,
Found rigid, with his hand on his heart,
While the monks in the cloister sang matins;
But his daughter and the Black Huntsman
Have already fled far from the manor;
They're in love, it's said–and when silver bells

Resound in the distance of the evening,
Singing is heard in the deep of the woods,
A voice that is powerful, a voice that is loud,
Makes the mountains tremble and the plain shake,
A voice which says: From the chatelaine's
Three confinements, four black hunters are born.

"So your lordship has four sons?" said the Baron, quite phlegmatically.[33]

"And a daughter, my dear gentleman."

"God!" cried Monsieur de Nossac, gaily. "I'm reassured. I have such little fondness for drinking without female company that I would have hesitated to swill your marvelous vintages while faced by your bearded and masculine visages."

"You shall have a woman at your right hand, Baron."

"Your lordship's daughter?"

"Yes, Baron."

"All right! Is she as black as you?"

"Not at all; she's white."

"So much the better!"

"She has an immense dowry."

"So she's to be married, then?"

"Undoubtedly; I've committed her to you."

"To me?"

"To you, my dear gentleman."

"Of course!" cried the Baron. "Better her than another— and my friends at Versailles will be amused to see me as the prospective son-in-law of the Devil's son."

"It was for that reason, Baron, that I sent you the subaltern imp who led you here."

"So it was a trap?"

"Not at all. To prove it, if you refuse to become my son-in-law, there's still time for you to retrace your steps. I'll take you back to Marienwerder and I shall hunt alone."

The Baron hesitated for a minute. "What if your daughter is ugly?" he said.

"If you find her so, you may refuse."

"By my faith!" Nossac said, cheerfully. "1500 Chambertin, 1463 Johannisberg and a pretty girl is well worth the trouble of an adventure. I'll follow it to its end! Whether they lead to the Devil or to God, to Paradise or the Inferno, vintage wine and beautiful women deserve no less."

The Black Huntsman put his horn to his lips and blew a fanfare so loud and powerful that the thickets and crags trembled, and the echoes, near or distant, multiplied in a howling chorus.

As the last echo died away, the same fanfare began again, simultaneously and with similar vigor, from four different directions in the surrounding woods. Almost immediately, four horsemen, as black as the Huntsman and similarly masked, with similar horns to their lips, appeared in the south and north, the sunrise and the sunset. Their eyes of flame shone from behind their masks.

"These are my sons," said the Huntsman.

Two of them were as big as their father, as well-built and as tall as he, but beneath the mask of one of them a beard protruded that was already grey, while the other had one that was uniformly black and sleek, testifying to his youth. The first might have been 20 years older than the second.

The two others, less tall and less strongly-built, were exactly the same height, and they both had blond beards. They were twins.

They approached their father one after the other, bowing to the Baron and speaking to the Black Huntsman in an unknown language that resembled neither German, nor Slavonic, nor Russian–a language entirely different from those employed by mere mortals of either hemisphere.

"North Wind," said the Huntsman to the eldest, "what spoor have you found?"[34]

"A buffalo, father."

"And you, South Wind?" he said, addressing the second.

"A bear, father."

"And you, Winter Wind?" the Huntsman went on, addressing one of the twins.

"A wild boar," replied Winter Wind.

"And you, Night Breeze?"

"An elk."

Oh! thought the Baron, *here are four hunters who have singular names.*

"You think so?" said the Huntsman, replying to the Baron's thought. "It's perfectly simple, though. I called the first North Wind because he scouts the forest to the north, the second South Wind because he comes from the south, the third Winter Wind because the winter wind hereabouts blows from the west, and the fourth Night Breeze because the nocturnal exhalation that stirs the thickets arrives from the Orient and carries the scent of the eastern forest."

"That's quite ingenious," murmured Monsieur de Nossac.

"Each of them," the Huntsman continued, "has another name, but that is a saint's name that my wife gave them, which they only bore when the priest baptized them."

"Ah!"

"Now I cannot find another," the Huntsman said. "All the men who see me have a habit of dying of fright."

"Am I so very brave, then?" said the Baron

"So brave," replied the Black Huntsman, "that I believe I have finally found a son-in-law. I've been searching for ten years."

"Indeed?" said the Baron, disquieted. "How old is your daughter, then?"

"Twenty-five years of age."

"No more?"

"That's quite enough."

"And she's mortal, is she?" the Baron continued.

"Alas!"

"Ah–so much the better," he murmured, relieved.

"Why so much the better?"

"Because a wife sometimes becomes rather tedious after eight or ten years, and might become unbearable were she eternal."

"Be tranquil," said the Black Huntsman, sadly. "I alone am immortal; my children are subject to the common law. For proof, look at North Wind's grey beard. He's 50. South Wind is only 30, and his beard is black. Night Breeze and Winter Wind are scarcely 18, and theirs are blond."

"Very well–I'm reassured."

"Now, Baron," the Black Huntsman continued, "it's time to hunt. Choose–what do you fancy today: a bear, a buffalo, an elk or a boar?

The Baron reflected. "A bear or an elk–both are pleasant prospects."

"In that case, it shall be both."

"In one day?"

"Why," said the Huntsman, pointing towards the east, which was lightly tinted by a mixture of white and opal, "it's scarcely four o'clock, and it isn't raining. The conditions are right."

The Baron raised his eyes to the sky in his turn. The leaden vault of dark clouds that had earlier been opaque and heavy had broken in a thousand places, allowing the appearance of patches of ash-blue sky, and the lightning-flashes that had ploughed through them incessantly were dying away one by one, like lamps running out of fuel. His son's torches had doubtless prompted Satan to make economies in his lighting.

"Right, then!" cried Monsieur de Nossac. "Until now, my dear host, in spite of everything marvelous that had occurred around me, I was unable to believe in this role of the Devil's son that you play so well, but I am now constrained to admit that you must certainly be a supernatural being. When someone commands the storm and disperses the clouds in the sky within a few seconds..."

"He must be the Devil, or at least his son, must he not?"

"Exactly."

"Since you require the supernatural to convince you, Baron, I shall provide it for you. We have plenty of horses and hunters here, but we lack hounds. Well, you shall see them."

The Black Huntsman brought his terrible horn to his lips, and began his fanfare again.

As soon as the first notes sounded, an unparalleled storm rose up in the neighboring thickets: an infernal concert of baying, a gigantic chorus of deep and high-pitched voices. The stunned Baron put both his hands to his ears, and cried: "Do you have 10,000 dogs, then?"

"Not 10,000, but 500 or 600. See for yourself."

As he had shielded his ears, the Baron had instinctively closed his eyes; when he opened them, he perceived that the valley, half-lit by the torches and half by the first rays of dawn, was entirely covered in dogs, all linked together, divided into four packs and respectfully held by grooms entirely dressed in white, as the huntsmen were in black and the torch-bearers in red.

The first pack consisted of a 120 Finnish mastiffs, striped in black and fawn, as big as donkeys, with square heads, teeth as long as thumbs, and eyes that were bloodshot and inflamed. This was the bear-hunting pack. The second, for buffalo, had a equal number of Cape hunting-dogs, equally fiery and just as large, but slimmer and less shaggy than the mastiffs. The third, for wild boar, had been recruited from the magnificent Céris dogs of Saintonge, one of the most handsome breeds of large Western dogs.[35] The fourth, finally, which was for elk, was even more handsome. It was composed of 80 harriers, all black, of that fine Breton breed–almost extinct today–as tall as Corsican horses, with heads as long as a king's foot and claws hooked like a cat's, which the Barons of the Middle Ages employed to hunt peasants who had taken refuge in the woods, refusing to submit to the *glebe* and the *corvée*.[36]

The Black Huntsman threw his horn over his shoulder again, and the dogs abruptly fell silent.

The Baron studied them admiringly. "My splendid host," he said to the Black Huntsman, "won't you include a few of these superb animals in your daughter's dowry?"

"All of them, if you wish, Baron."

"By God!" exclaimed Monsieur de Nossac, "I'd be content with a dowry like that. The King of France would give me five or six of his provinces for them."

"To the hunt, Baron! To the hunt! Here's daylight coming, and I cannot see the Sun."

"Why is that?"

"Because we're on bad terms, that's all."

"But if you hunt every day?"

"My forests are too dark for its light to penetrate them. To the hunt!"

He took up his horn again and made as if to sound the departure, but he paused. "Baron," he said, "your horse is worn out. Dismount–here's another."

The Baron looked up and saw a magnificent stallion, as white as snow, richly caparisoned, held by the bridle by one of the torch-bearers. He did not wait for the injunction to be repeated, and leapt from one saddle to the other without touching the ground. Immediately, it seemed to him that an unknown and unparalleled force screwed him to the saddle of his new mount, and that the stirrups gripped him like a vice, clamping his feet in place.

Was that illusion or reality?

The fanfare resounded–that colossal fanfare which resembled an earthquake. The dogs were released, to hurtle into the forest, and the horsemen bounded after them. The Baron was seized by vertigo. He shivered yet again as he felt himself transported by a horse whose hooves seemed not to touch the ground, so rapid and hectic was its course. He saw the Black Huntsman galloping at his side, conversing with his four sons in their unknown language.

The Black Huntsman had told the truth; his forests were dark, and the red light of the torches, which ran through the trees in every sense of the term, like a frenzied dance of phantoms and will-o'-the-wisps, was scarcely sufficient to bring an imperfect illumination to the profound darkness. The dogs set an infernal pace, and seemed now to have but one formidable voice as they gave forth together. From time to time, the Baron saw them appearing and disappearing in the distance–followed close behind by the red-clad horsemen, their torches held in their fists like pikes or blunderbusses–hot on the heels of a gigantic bear, which sometimes turned round, mingling its terrible and heavy roars with their howling harmony. At the same time, the five hunters, with their horns in their mouths, sounded a signal no less resonant than their famous fanfare.

Then the noise of the hunters' horns, united with the baying of the pack, became so loud that a delirium soon took hold of Monsieur de Nossac. He thought he was having a long and painful dream.

He witnessed the death of the bear, then heard the call and set off after the elk without being fully conscious of what he was doing, what he heard of what he saw...

Finally, after ten hours of that infernal race, he suddenly saw the torches go out, disappear and vanish along with the red-clad horsemen who carried them. When the dark vault of foliage under which he had been running since morning was succeeded by the starry vault of the sky, brightly lit by the rays of the Moon, he thought he was emerging from a burdensome nightmare, and that he had slept for a century. He had passed from one night to the next without having seen the daylight that separated them.

In the distance, on a precipitous crag overhanging a torrent, was a gigantic and somber mass, dappled here and there with points of luminosity. "There's my castle," said the Black Huntsman, extending his hand. "The lamps are lit, and we're expected."

VIII

The Baron followed the direction of the Black Huntsman's hand with his eyes, examined the castle rapidly, and then turned round.

The dogs, grooms and torch-bearers had all disappeared.

The Huntsman's four sons were galloping to either side, while the Devil's son took the lead.

What had become of that strange crowd, that nameless admixture of men, horses and dogs?

The sudden solitude and instantaneous silence, succeeding the tumultuous hurly-burly that had surrounded them shortly before in a matter of seconds, had a sobering effect on the Baron, and he recovered all his composure.

Well, he thought, I'm definitely dealing with the Devil; there's no longer any doubt of that. What has happened to me is more than supernatural.

Despite their ten hours of steeplechasing, the horses did not seem to be out of breath. They were still galloping with fantastic speed. They crossed the interval of a league that separated the castle from the edge of the forest in 18 minutes or thereabouts, and soon paused at the edge of the torrent, which eroded and polished the crag on which it was proudly established. The torrent was copious and deep; it made a lugubrious noise as it ran.

The Baron could not see any bridge at first, but when he looked more attentively he noticed the trunk of a fir-tree extended across it, joining the two banks by means of its narrow surface.

"Are we to pass over that?" he asked, with a certain anxiety–for the water was roaring dully two fathoms below, in a fashion to chill the boldest of men with fear.

"Of course!" replied the Black Huntsman, vigorously urging his horse forward. It placed an assured foot on the narrow platform and set off across it at a trot. The four sons set off after their father. The Baron did not hesitate any longer. He spurred his mount, which also crossed at a rapid trot, without flinching over the abyss.

When all five of them had reached the other bank, the Black Huntsman turned around. Without quitting his saddle, he lowered himself to the ground like one of those circus riders who pick up a staff in the arena, at the gallop and without pause. Bracing himself with one hand on the pommel of his saddle, he seized the end of the fir-trunk, lifted it up despite its enormous weight, swung it momentarily into empty space, then threw it down into the abyss, where it described a frightful somersault and plunged into the water with a loud splash.

"Here we are, at home," said the Black Huntsman, tranquilly.

The Baron shivered, marveling at that Herculean strength, then looked ahead. He was on a kind of terrace about eight feet wide, at the foot of a rocky peak supporting the imposing mass of the castle.

Unless these infernal horses have wings, Monsieur de Nossac thought, the ascent will be difficult.

The Black Huntsman resumed the head of the procession, and ten paces to the left brought him to the entrance of a sort of narrow, almost perpendicular stairway, which no pedestrian would have climbed without signing himself reverently several times over. Even so, the Devil's son's horse resolutely placed its feet on the first step, and commenced climbing at a rapid pace, striking myriad sparks from the polished rock, without ever flinching, as if steel crampons had suddenly sprouted from its iron shoes.

Good! thought the Baron, who was becoming accustomed to this succession of prodigies. *It appears that my host draws his horses from his father's stables. Only the inferno could produce their equals.*

This time, instead of bringing up the rear of the cortège, he moved ahead of the four sons and followed the Huntsman to the first step of the narrow stairway. The horse went up without any hesitation.

He's used to it, Monsieur de Nossac said to himself.

The stairway had 297 steps. The horses climbed them in ten minutes. The Baron and his hosts found themselves on a second platform, from which the walls of the castle rose up. It was a Gothic manor, with deep ditches cut out of the living rock, slender and pointed turrets, slim spires, sinewy and narrow arches, dull black loopholes, a gigantic belfry, a mossy roof, thick walls, formidable machicolations, rusty weathervanes groaning and screeching under the brutal caresses of the nocturnal wind, a coat-of-arms engraved on the main door, and subterranean passages a league in extent, hollowed out in the rock and corresponding mysteriously with the surrounding forests and plains.

The Baron, who was an amateur archaeologist, examined the castle attentively and found its style quite pure, with the exception of a few slight anachronisms that blended in quite well with the whole ensemble. Numerous lights were burning behind the colored panes of the arched windows. Opaque and semi-translucent shadows passed rapidly back and forth behind these same window-panes, but there was no noise–not a word nor a breath–to advertise the interior life and movement. The castle was as silent as the tomb.

The Black Huntsman halted in front of the drawbridge, which was raised, put his horn to his lips, and sounded the three blasts employed in the Middle Ages by knights errant asking for hospitality at an advanced hour of the night. The drawbridge was lowered, creakily, and the huntsmen passed over it. All five of them arrived in the courtyard of the manor, which was deserted. The Huntsman dismounted; his sons did likewise, and so did the Baron.

"Come, Baron," the Huntsman said, taking him by the arm. "I'm dying of hunger."

It seemed to the Baron that the Huntsman's hand was burning, and that it gripped him like a vice. He allowed himself to be drawn, and they climbed the steps of the *perron* side by side. The other four hunters came up behind them.

"What about the horses?" the Baron suddenly asked, turning round.

The horses had disappeared, without any stable-hand leading them away.

Damn! thought Monsieur de Nossac. *My adventure is assuming such proportions that if I were ever to tell the tale at Versailles, Richelieu himself would not be able to believe it.*

The door of the manor opened slowly, just as the draw-bridge had been lowered, without anyone appearing. The Black Huntsman crossed the threshold, still holding the Baron by the arm. They came into a vast hallway lit by four torches fixed to the wall. There was a large staircase in the middle, with steps of black marble sewn with white tears, like the design on the coat-of-arms.

The Black Huntsman and his guest climbed the staircase, turned right on the first landing, and went into a room no less vast than the vestibule, similarly lit. Its black walls were speckled with silver tears. They went through this room, then another and another, all decked out in the same colors, and arrived in this manner at the manor's dining-room. In stark contrast to the others, this room was decked out in white, with black tears.

"I approve of the lachrymal variety," the Baron murmured.

In the middle of this room stood a sumptuously-furnished table, on which the most exquisite dishes were steaming, mirrored by wines so clear and so brilliantly colored that it was easy to see that the lord of the manor had not lied about their vintage.

No servants were present; the room was deserted–except that, in a corner, on a rostrum covered in black velvet, there was a coffin. At the sight of it, the Baron took a step back, and shuddered.

"That's my wife's coffin," the Black Huntsman said, coldly.

"She's dead, then?"

"For ten years."

"And... she's there?"

"Yes, of course. Look."

The Huntsman drew the Baron forward; he followed without resistance. The Devil's son led him to the coffin and lifted the mortuary drape.

A woman was lying cold and motionless within. She was young, to judge by the ebon color of her hair, whose curls streamed upon the snowy shroud; she was beautiful, if one studied the lower part of the face–for a mask like those worn by the hunters covered the upper part.

One might have thought that she was asleep, so well had her arms conserved the gentle suppleness of their joints, and so clearly visible were the blue veins beneath her translucent skin, which still appeared to enclose blood in full circulation.

"But she can't be dead! It's impossible!" the Baron exclaimed.

"She died ten years ago."

"Ten years. And she's conserved in this state?"

"It was my father who embalmed her."

"But what age was she?"

"Sixty-nine."

"One would have thought her scarcely 30!"

"My father returned her to this state in embalming her. He was in a good humor that day."

"And you leave her here? You haven't buried her?"

"No," said the Huntsman, "for it requires the hand of a Christian to bear her into the ground."

"You're one, it seems to me."

"Half only. It requires a pure Christian–I thought of you."

Nossac shivered, and looked at himself in a Venetian glass that was facing him. He was very pale and his lips were quivering.

"To the table, Baron," said the Black Huntsman. "I'm hungry."

Nossac went to the place indicated by his host. The four sons placed themselves one beside another. Then the Baron observed that one empty place remained next to his and another next to the Huntsman. The door opened at that moment, and a woman came in.

It was a young woman of 24 or 25, blonde and dazzlingly beautiful. She had large blue eyes full of a vague and suave languor, a delicate pearly-pink mouth, small, slender diaphanous hands with tapering fingers, fairy-like feet that scarcely brushed the ground, and a supple, svelte figure replete with amorous undulations.

At the sight of her, the Baron released an exclamation of admiration. He forgot the terrors of his journey, the Black Huntsman, his silent and dejected sons, and the coffin set facing the table as if to diminish their appetite and forbid them any joy. He no longer saw or heard anything but the young woman, who made a circuit of the table, placing her rosy lips upon her father's ebon forehead while saying to him: "Good day, dear Black Huntsman, my father," and then going to each of her four brothers, kissing each of them on the forehead and greeting them by name. Then, she bowed deeply to the Baron, and came back to sit down to her father's right.

"Here is your wife," said the Black Huntsman.

The Baron thought that he could see, in the midst of these infernal hosts, Heaven opening up before him—but his intoxication was chilled and suddenly repressed to the utmost depths of his heart by a voice that resounded at the far end of the room, fresh and sonorous, but full of mockery.

The startled Baron raised his eyes, and saw the mortuary drape that covered the coffin rise as the corpse sat up.

"Baron de Nossac," the dead woman said, "since you must bear me into the ground, you cannot refuse to serve as my cavalier this evening and escort me to the table. Come give me your hand."

The Baron felt his hair bristle, while a cold sweat broke out on his forehead. He summoned his presence of mind and self-assurance to his aid in vain, and he would surely have fallen backwards if his bewildered eyes had not encountered the hypnotic, celestial and supplicant eyes of the young woman, which seemed to be saying to him: "Obey!"

He felt his fear ebb away then. He got up and marched resolutely towards the dead woman, who got down stiffly and impassively from her coffin, and he bowed to her with a courtesy redolent of the heyday of Versailles.

"Thank you," said the dead woman, placing her icy hand in the Baron's–who prickled and shuddered anew at that contact.

IX

The dead woman leaned on the Baron's tremulous arm, and marched toward the empty place that was presumably reserved for her with the slow rigidity of an automaton. She sat down to the right of her cavalier, and said to him: "To the table, Monsieur le Baron; your appetite must have been put to the proof by a day's hunting."

"Indeed," stammered Monsieur de Nossac.

The Black Huntsman took out his hunting-knife, which still hung from his belt, carved the haunch of venison that was steaming on the table with consummate skill, then gave a slice to each of his guests. He began with the Baron, following to the conventions of German hospitality rather than those of France, which give precedence to the women. Monsieur de Nossac was undoubtedly distressed, but terror never overcame him so completely as to steal the last vestiges of his self-assurance. In consequence, he noticed this lack of gallantry, and corrected it as best he could by offering his plate to his neighbor, the dead woman.

"Thank you," she replied, in an icy voice. She placed the plate in front of her, but she did not touch it again.

Five minutes later, one of the dead woman's sons–the oldest one, who called himself North Wind–got up gravely and came to remove the plate, which was still full, and which he replaced with another, similarly charged. Baron de Nossac thought that he was dreaming. Had it not been for the radiant visage of the young woman, who smiled at him from time to time in an ingenuous and candid manner, he would certainly have doubted his own existence. The meal had a funereal color, in perfect harmony with the decoration of the room and his strange hosts.

The Black Huntsman ate with Teutonic gluttony; his sons imitated him quite well. The young woman, however, scarcely touched her glass or the food that was given to her, like a dainty and flirtatious bird which, having found itself in the same flock as voracious vultures and famished ospreys, desired to give them a lesson in delicacy and etiquette by pecking at the occasional tiny grain of millet. As for the late lady of the manor, she did not eat at all–but each of her sons took turns to renew her plate and change her glass.

The Baron, having been momentarily distraught with terror, recovered his composure and wit and ended up returning to his first hypothesis–which is to say that was it was all some terrible deceptive trickery, to which he must not fall prey at any price, if he were eventually to triumph. Aided by the soft gaze of the young woman, he was the first to speak.

"My dear host," he said to the Black Huntsman, "you're as silent as Madame la Châtelaine's tomb."

"You think so?" said the Huntsman, in a sullen tone which gave the Baron to understand that the pleasantry was out of place.

At the same time, four flashes of light sprang simultaneously from the masks of the Huntsman's sons, and the young woman's forehead darkened with a grave and sorrowful melancholy. The Baron understood that he had committed an error, and silence fell again–but the dead woman, who had been silent for ten minutes, took it into her head to break it, and she said to the Baron: "Are you not a widower, Monsieur de Nossac?"

The Baron shivered at this abrupt question, asked in a bantering tone, and darted a fearful glance at the dead woman. A dull and mocking laugh sounded beneath her mask, while her eyes, which were as cold and dull as the eyes of death itself, glittered like daggers within the holes of the mask.

Monsieur de Nossac met that icy gaze and his tremulousness turned to terror again. "How did you know...?" he stammered.

"The dead know everything."

"That's true," the Baron murmured. "And yet..."

"I even know your wife."

Monsieur de Nossac started, went pale and choked. He would undoubtedly have got up from the table if the dead woman's icy hand had not been placed on his to retain him.

"Stay here!" she said, slowly. "You're petulant, like all the gentlemen of the French court. You forget that we're within the borders of Hungary here."[37]

The sweat of anguish was pearling on the Baron's temples. He was listening to the dead woman's voice with the dejected and despairing attitude of a condemned man listening to his death-sentence. As the voice continued to sound, however, as dry and metallic as the bronze works of a clock, it seemed to him that he had heard it somewhere before.

"They say in Paris that you're the widower of a rather beautiful woman," the dead woman continued, "who has, it's also said, left you a great fortune."

The Baron trembled in every limb, and looked at the dead woman in stupefaction.

"Don't be astonished to find me so well informed, Monsieur le Baron. My spouse there must have told you that I was the daughter-in-law of Satan, and Satan knows everything, as well you must know..."

Monsieur de Nossac opened his mouth and tried to speak, but no word could escape from his clenched throat.

The deceased lady of the manor continued: "The Baronne de Nossac, your wife, made a singular will, it seems. She imposed on you, it's said, the obligation to remarry within an interval of two years, on pain of seeing your fortune return to her natural heirs if you do not."

This time the haggard Baron could no longer hold firm, and he cried out, with his face contracted in fear: "Are you the

Baronne herself, come to reproach me for my lax conduct, having left the tomb to mock me?"

The dead woman replied with a burst of laughter. "My dear Baron," she said. "I'm beginning to believe that remorse is troubling your mind sufficiently to make you see your dead wife in me..."

"You have her voice..."

"Do you think so?" The dead woman's mocking and icy laughter broke out again, taking on a sinister note in that funereal room.

Again the Baron wanted to get up and flee, but the dead woman's hand nailed him to his chair, motionless.

"You're mad, Baron," the lady of the manor said, "but I pardon you, in consideration of where you are. Be certain of one thing, though: if I were your wife, as you claim, I would already have taken off my mask to show my face. The recognition would be interesting, to say the least."

The dead woman had attempted to stem the objection that rose to the Baron's lips–but Monsieur de Nossac was, above all else, a man given to brusque interruptions and spontaneity. "Why not take it off, Madame," he said, "to reassure me?"

"Because I cannot do that; nor can my husband or my sons."

"Why?"

"If you have given due consideration to the sinister words of the legend of the Black Huntsman, you will have taken note of the fact that the sight of his face strikes all mortal men dead."

"I admit that for the Huntsman and his sons... but you..."

"My husband has communicated the same fatal privilege to me."

"But your daughter...?"

"My daughter alone is exempt from that fatal gift. It's a whim of her ancestor, who wished it thus. In exchange, if ever we should unmask before her, she would die on the spot."

"God's blood!" cried the Baron, finally succeeding in overcoming his fear completely, and seized by a sudden fit of chivalrous audacity. "I want to clear all this up. If Mademoiselle will consent to leave the room, I'll ask all six of you to lower your masks, and I promise to look you in the face, even if your faces are as frightful as Satan's own."

"Take care, Baron," the dead woman murmured, the mocking tone of her voice suddenly taking on a hint of menace.

"My name is Nossac," the Baron replied, proudly.

The Black Huntsman and his four sons exchanged a menacing glance, but said not a word.

"Very well," said the dead woman. "Offer your hand to my daughter, and escort her to the next room. You may come back alone–if you dare!"

Whether or not he would have dared two seconds earlier, Monsieur de Nossac felt that he had the courage now that he had to touch the hand of the dazzling young woman whose smile had enchanted him. He got up resolutely, therefore, went to her, and offered her his arm.

The young woman had suddenly gone pale, but the dead woman said to her, imperiously: "Go! Go!" She got up in her turn and put her white hand between the Baron's. The hand was trembling.

"Come, Mademoiselle," said Nossac, whose voice changed again under the pressure of an indescribable emotion. But he walked slowly, as if he wanted to prolong the short journey for as long as possible, sensible of the young woman's hand in his own. They left the dining-room in this fashion and went into the room next door. There Nossac halted, hesitantly.

"Come on," murmured the young woman, still drawing him forward. "Let's go a little further."

They passed through a second room, and entered a third. In that one there was a huge sofa upholstered in black velvet–spangled, like the wall-hangings, with white tears. The Baron led his companion to it, sat her down in it, then stepped back in order to bow to her. Suddenly, the young woman put her hands together as if to pray.

"Don't go back!"

A slight smile stirred on the Baron's lips.

"I shall go," he said.

"You'll die."

"Are you quite sure of that?"

"Yes, yes!"

"Very well, listen to me."

"What do you want?" she said, with a charming and flirtatiously suppliant glance.

"Has anyone told you that I was your intended husband?"

"Yes."

"Does that distress you?"

The young woman hesitated. "No," she said, eventually.

"Could you love me?"

She hesitated again. "I don't know," she said.

"Very well. Given how great and terrible the danger may be, if you don't want me to succumb to it, you need only say one word."

She looked at him in astonishment.

"One word that might serve me as a talisman, one word that might protect me like a shield," he continued, fervently.

She looked at him again, but her astonishment had given place to prayer.

"Don't go back!" she said.

"I would be a coward if I hesitated."

"But you're going to your death!"

"Perhaps, if you refuse me the word. No, for sure, if it escapes your lips..."

"All right!" she said, taking his hand. "Well..." She stopped and blushed.

"Well?" he prompted

"Well, Monsieur le Baron de Nossac..." she resumed–and stopped once again, hesitantly.

"Oh, speak!" demanded the Baron, joining his hands in a suppliant gesture.

"I love you!" she murmured, hiding her face with her interlaced fingers.

"Thank you!" cried the Baron.

He put his arms around her and planted an ardent kiss on her reddening forehead. Then, with his hand on the hilt of his sword, his head held high and proudly tilted back, he marched with a firm step towards the dining room, where the terrible company awaited him. On reaching the door, he pushed it unhesitatingly.

The Black Huntsman and his four sons had lowered their masks, as had the lady of the manor. The Baron had scarcely looked at them, however, when he released a cry, put his hand on his heart and leaned on the wall for support, pale and on the point of collapse.

Before his eyes—apparently, at least—were six skeletal faces: six death's-heads placed on living shoulders; six frightfully constricted and grimacing skulls. Some were beneath fair hair, others beneath black or grey hair, and one—that of the dead woman—on the white neck of a swan, perfect in its form, its contours and its movements, beneath the silkiest and most beautiful tresses that ever crowned a woman's forehead. But what was most frightful of all were the ardent eyes that shone out of that fleshless face, half-eaten away by coffin-worms: those eyes, which looked up simultaneously, with an expression of menace and mocking challenge, at the Baron who had dared to confront such a spectacle.

"You're pale and you're shivering, Baron," said the dead woman, with her skeletal lips.

The Baron was indeed pale and shivering—but a challenge, no matter what mouth utters it or in what place it is issued, is a very powerful stimulant. The Baron suddenly raised his head again and replied: "I am so little distressed, Madame, that I should like to finish supper with you!" And he advanced towards the table with a stoical confidence, to resume the place that he had occupied before.

X

The six skeletons looked at him with astonishment mingled with admiration. The Baron's courage was now close to madness.

"Baron," said the dead woman, releasing a dire laugh from her fleshless lips, "I offer you a sincere apology. You're a valiant knight."

"You're a thousand times too kind, Madame," Nossac relied, "and if the proverb advice is worth as much as praise has any merit in it, I shall permit myself to offer a small prayer on your behalf."

"Ah!" said the dead woman. "Go on."

"Take up the corner of your napkin, Madame."

"Very well–and then?"

"You have a worm on your cheek."

A flash of anger sprang from the eyes of the five black hunters–but the Baron, excited as much by fear as by intrepidity, was now the master of the situation, although he had been chilled and dumbstruck only moments before. He cried, with a burst of laughter as mocking as the dead woman's tone: "You want to play at being terrible and frightful, Messieurs, damned souls and revenants. I am trying, as you see, to set myself at your level."

"Will you have a drink?" asked the Huntsman, laughing. "Dare you drink and eat?"

"Yes, if you will allow me to do that, masters–certainly, by God!–dead as you all are..."

"You are mistaken, Baron," said the Huntsman. "My sons and I are very much alive."

"Then why these fleshless faces?"

"Because my father, Satan, made love to my mother after her death."

The Baron shuddered slightly, but he pulled himself together immediately. "That must be a curious story," he said, losing nothing of his bantering tone.

"And I'm ready to tell it to you, Baron."

"I'm quite ready to hear it–but first, my dear host, pour me some wine. At the rate you're going, you and your sons, it could well be that the decanters will be empty before long. That's what I was about to say just now."

"Drink, sir! And when the decanters are empty..."

"You have plenty more, I presume?"

"Of course."

"Let's empty them, then. I am curious finally to see your servants. Until now..."

"You have been speculating about them, you mean?"

"Precisely."

"I borrow my domestics from my father."

"Ah! God! Let's have the story."

The Huntsman brought his full glass up to his skeletal lips. When the Baron gave him permission by bowing to the dead woman, he expressed himself as follows:

"I have already told you that I was born in the reign of Charlemagne. My mother lived in that era. My mother was a demoiselle of the highest nobility and accomplished intelligence. In the century of ignorance in which she lived, when people took pride in not knowing how to write, my mother spoke and wrote several languages, including Hebrew and Syriac.

"Moreover, my mother was skeptical regarding several dogmas of the Christian faith; she was entirely doubtful of the existence of the Devil, and hence of Hell. Her chaplain preached to her morning and night, discoursing eloquently on the place of torment and eternal expiation over which my father presides, but in vain. Her mother, a pious woman, said to her: 'Daughter, you will be damned as a punishment for not believing in Hell,' but my mother smiled and shrugged her shoulders.

"Satan, my father, heard these impious words, and laughed in his turn, but my mother was so beautiful that he was momentarily seized by the desire to be a mere mortal in order to marry and make love to her. Now, one day, it occurred to him that it would be easy for him to achieve this end by taking human form. He lodged himself in the body of a handsome and moderately well-dressed knight, who was about to get himself killed in a war against the Saracens, and he presented himself at the demoiselle's house, after having sent her his squire, Seduction, a bearer of riches and rare presents. But the demoiselle was virtuous, despite being skeptical, and my father could make no headway. She remained a virgin in spite of everything. Fortunately, my father thought, the girl is damned, and will die sooner or later.

"My father's anticipation was fulfilled. One day, mounted on a white hack while on her way to watch a tournament held by King Charlemagne, my mother passed close to an old tower, which was falling into ruins and was tottering in the wind. At the top of this tower, a German poet was dreaming beside a stork's nest. Seeing my mother approaching, the poet, who was curious, interrupted the Latin dactyls that he was in the process of composing and leaned over. The stone on which he was leaning fell away, and he found himself launched into empty space. As chance would have it, he fell and broke his skull ten paces in front of my mother, who died of fright almost immediately.

"Once my mother was dead, her soul took the straight road that leads to Hell, whose existence she had always denied. She found my father Satan at its very gate, who offered his hand with exquisite gallantry and escorted her to the eternal hearth, before which she was destined to roast in a little fire during the consummation of the centuries. My mother, while living, had been something of an expert in the use of perfumes and mysterious waters invented and traded all over the world by vagabond Arabs. She grimaced in disgust, therefore, as she approached the paternal furnace, which he keeps so warm in every season. She bitterly repented her incredulity–but it was, alas, too late.

"My father took pity on her, though, and said to her: 'Gentle demoiselle, if you will consent to make love to me for eight consecutive days, I will render you to God–who has given you to me–and he will place you in his Paradise, where the breeze is fresh and the fire less ardent.'

" 'Make love to you?' said my mother, disdainfully. 'Let's get on with it!' And she sat down in a corner of my father's fire, with stoic resignation.

"For eight days, she had the courage to burn, but on the ninth, she could no longer stand it. 'So be it!' she said.

"My father, whom the burning atmosphere in which he ordinarily dwells has rendered very sensitive to cold, wrapped himself in his cloak and ascended to the Earth. Guided by the Moon's rays, he hastened to the cemetery where my mother was interred, scraped away the dirt with his cloven hooves, exposed the coffin, opened it and drew out my mother's corpse, in which he replaced her soul, which he had brought with him in a corner of his cloak. The soul readmitted to her body, my mother stood up and walked, enveloping her shoulders and face in the folds of her white shroud.

" 'Let's be on our way!' my father said to her.

" 'Where are we going?'

" 'Home, to your castle.'

"The dead woman walked slowly towards the town of Aix-la-Chapelle, where her father, who was a rich nobleman, had a sumptuous palace. She arrived at the door of this palace, followed by my father, who was shivering with cold. The door opened before her. She went in, climbed the stairs, arrived at her apartment, which had been deserted since her death, and bolted the door once my father was inside. My father rubbed his hooked fingernail against one of his horns, striking a shower of sparks that lit up a torch attached to the wall by an iron bracket. Then, by the light of that torch, he examined my mother–but he had scarcely looked at her when he released a cry of horror. During the eight days that her corpse had spent in the coffin, the worms had had time to eat away her face.

"My father had but one word, though; he had promised, and he kept his promise–and I was born nine months afterwards, I resembled my mother, however, and it is for that reason that I wear a mask, in order to be less hideous. My mother came out of her tomb to bring me into the world. My grandmother found me one morning on her daughter's bed and, without having any idea where I had come from, she had me baptized anyway.

"The priest who administered the holy water died of fright. Nevertheless, I was a Christian. Unfortunately, my father carried me off scarcely a month afterwards, and I only gained one thing by my baptism: to be proof against the sign of the cross. In every other respect, I am the Devil's son!"

The Baron had listened to this strange story quite calmly. When the Huntsman had finished, he exclaimed: "Your tales are as marvelous as your wines. Let's drink, mine host!"

"Drink," replied the Huntsman. "And now, my dear Baron, it's late. You must need to rest. Your apartment is ready." As he spoke, he struck a gong.

The young woman who had made such a strong impression on Nossac appeared immediately, came towards him smiling, and took him by the hand.

"Come," she said.

The sight of the young woman restored some presence of mind to the Baron, who was beginning to get drunk.

She led him through the rooms through which they had already passed, and had him climb the great staircase to an upper floor. There she opened a door, and introduced him into a bedroom with black wall-hangings similar to those down below, but furnished as comfortably as possible–a room such as travelers dream of in uncultured and barbaric lands where they are deprived of all luxury.

"Sleep," she said to him, showing him the bed.

Her smile was soft, innocent, almost angelic.

In the presence of that radiant child, the Baron shook off the drunken torpor that had invaded his limbs and constrained his reason. Kneeling before her, placing his lips on her diaphanous hands and looking at her in a suppliant manner, he said to her: "Oh, tell me that I am dreaming–a frightful dream–and that it is impossible that you, so beautiful, so pure and so innocent, are of the same family as all these instruments of Hell that I have just left. Tell me that all this is a nightmare, that I am sleeping standing up, that it is impossible."

"Shush!" she said, putting her slender pink fingers upon his mouth. "Shush!"

"Oh! No! Let me question you... ask you... It is impossible that you, so beautiful, could be..."

The young woman appeared hesitant, anxious, distressed. Then, suddenly making a supreme effort, she put her lips to the Baron's forehead, and murmured: "Perhaps I'm bringing death upon my head, but I love you! I will tell you everything!"

"Oh, speak!" cried Monsieur de Nossac. "I am here to defend you!"

"Very well!" she said, shivering. "You have been a lion thus far, be one until the end. Put your sword under your pillow, and stay awake. You are the victim of a terrible comedy!"

She fled, as if she dreaded having said too much, and closed the door behind her. Nossac wanted to run after her, but an invincible force–the inertia of drunkenness–nailed him to the spot, and his head began to spin again. He only had time to place his sword at his bedhead and to throw himself on the bed. He was immediately claimed by an unparalleled lethargy and sank into a leaden slumber.

Immediately, the door closed by the young woman opened noisily. A white form entered the room, and moved slowly towards the bed at the slow and measured pace of a phantom.

XI

In response to the noise, Monsieur de Nossac awoke with a start, opened his eyes, and tried to get up–but the reawakening was more moral than physical for he was unable, no matter how hard he tried, to move any of his limbs. He watched the impassive and mute form approach him without his tongue being able to utter a cry, and without being able to recoil into the gap on the far side of the bed.

The white form came up to him, and placed something cold upon his forehead. That something was a hand. Then it sat down at the head of the bed and immediately leaned over the Baron.

The Baron was in a terrible situation. He watched this strange being whose sex and species he could not quite make out. He saw it lean over him, and felt its breath, as cold as its hand. His forehead shuddered at the contact and his hair stood on end, but he could neither cry out, nor struggle, nor ask for mercy or reason.

The phantom, as it undoubtedly was, abruptly lay down side by side with Monsieur de Nossac, then applied its lips to his bare neck. Monsieur de Nossac suddenly felt a light prick, which was hardly painful at all, but frightened him regardless. He was dealing with one of those monsters known in Hungary and Bohemia as *vampires*, about which a monk, Dom Calmet, had published a book only two or three years earlier, in which he offered proof, as clear as daylight, that nothing is more natural than vampirism.

The Baron's anguish, throughout the time that the fatal suction lasted, is difficult to describe. Struck by paralysis in his every limb and in his very tongue, he had conserved the senses of touch, hearing and sight. He could see and hear the vampire, which was breathing in fits and starts. He could feel it extended upon him, sucking his blood with ruthless avidity. Strangely enough, despite the fear and pain he felt, he experienced a sort of indefinable voluptuousness, a bitter enjoyment of that atrocious contact.

And as the vampire drank his blood, the initial pain that he had experienced lessened, and passed into a state of pure sensation, while he, becoming increasingly numb, felt the heaviness of his head fall upon his heart. A seemingly-extraordinary weakness—which was merely the inevitable corollary of his loss of blood—extended through all his paralyzed limbs.

After 20 minutes or so, the vampire paused. "Your blood is rosy and fresh, Baron," it murmured.

The Baron would undoubtedly have started had he not been completely paralyzed. The voice was the one that had already excited and distressed him so powerfully—that of the dead lady of the manor with whom he had drunk and danced. An imperceptible tremor was the only indication the vampire received of the effect that its voice had had.

"Ah!" it murmured. "Do you recognize me, Baron?"

The Baron shivered again, and made a supreme but futile effort to speak and struggle.

"I believe," the dead woman continued, "that there is no need to explain to you by means of a lie how it comes about that, ten years after my death, I have such supple flesh, such rounded arms, and a neck so pink and white. You can see that I am a vampire. You have excellent blood, Baron; I swear to you that I shall be thrifty with it, and make it last a long time. I grant you a full month of life."

Monsieur de Nossac could neither budge nor cry out, but the moral anguish he experienced on hearing these words was such that a cold sweat ran from his hairline along his temples.

"And now," the vampire went on, "sleep and take your rest, to replenish the loss that you have incurred to my profit."

So saying, the late lady of the manor emptied the contents of a little phial upon the Baron's neck. The liquor that escaped from it was tepid and viscous; it seemed to the Baron that all of it entered into his veins, impoverished by the wound that the vampire had made with its teeth, and that it spread an indefinable sensation of well-being throughout his body.

The vampire got up then and said to him: "Adieu–until tomorrow." It went out at the same measured pace, and closed the door behind it.

Almost immediately, the Baron's eyes–which had been open all the while that the vampire had been beside him–closed beneath the weight of an invincible sleep. He was, however, freed from the heavy and punitive drunkenness to which he had surrendered at first, after the departure of the young woman. He slept peacefully, yielding to a need for rest motivated by an unaccustomed feebleness.

The Baron slept for several consecutive hours. When he awoke, the rising Sun had just illuminated the middle of the room he occupied. He got up precipitately and ran to one of the casement windows. He threw it open it violently, and plunge his avid head and ardent eyes outside.

He had before his eyes the most charming landscape that ever sprang from the palette of the Eternal. Beneath the walls of the castle a grassy plain extended for a league around, planted with trees. In the middle of the grassland was a stream; at its extremity was the edge of a forest of birch trees and firs, thick and bushy but shaking its green plumage in the most natural fashion in the breath of a morning breeze, with nothing in the least frightful and satanic in its appearance.

Between the plain and the forest a little village extended, with a procession of gardens, weeping willows and hawthorn hedges. Around this village a population of peasants, shepherds and laborers were occupied in various agricultural tasks.

Monsieur de Nossac was stupefied by this calm and bucolic scene. The precipitous crag, arid and desolate, looming over a wild and furious torrent, and the torrent itself, had disappeared as if by magic.

The Baron had expected to wake up in the middle of a wild and tormented place, no less infernal than the castle that sheltered him and that castle's masters. On the contrary, he found himself in the very heart of an illustration of a Florian pastiche,[38] with beribboned shepherdesses, laborers singing merry refrains, farms as spruced-up as cottages, and a castle which, in spite of the imposing attitude of its Medieval style, had, in broad daylight, the gentle and peaceful appearance of an old lord returned from the crusades, having become indulgent and generous towards his serfs and his vassals, for the sole reason that he had been a slave of the Moors himself for some ten years.

This was the first occasion for some considerable time on which the Baron had found himself alone, with his mind almost completely composed. He set himself, therefore, to think and reflect, attempting to analyze—or, rather, to explain—the various sensations and strange events into the midst of which he had been plunged.

Monsieur de Nossac belonged to the most skeptical and philosophical of all the centuries. A product of the orgies of the Regency, he had been a incredulous two days before as the most hard-headed materialist. After what he had seen and heard, however, skepticism had become impossible. He had sternly repeated to himself that there was a deliberate mystification at the bottom of all these mysteries, but he could not convince himself that the supernatural had not played the principal role in all that had passed before his eyes the previous day. Nevertheless, in rolling out his still-confused memories one by one, he remembered the words let slip by the young woman, who had seemed so beautiful amid those frightful skeletons—words that became the next best thing to a revelation: *You are the victim of a terrible comedy!*

But what of those fleshless faces, crawling with hideous and fetid worms? The cadaver descending from her tomb? The vampire sucking his blood?

Monsieur de Nossac ran to a mirror, which he recalled having seen, the previous evening, on the chimney-breast, and examined his neck. His neck was speckled with several drops of blood, and there was a slight cut in the middle of them—a scratch of scant importance, whose true cause was difficult to determine.

He had not been dreaming, then!

Decidedly, he thought, *such extraordinary things have happened around me that if I had not practiced chemistry with the late Regent, commanded the Régiment de Royal-Cravate and spent six years in the gutters of Versailles, I'd be a madman fit for a straitjacket.*[39]

Another thought, frightful and desperate, immediately assailed him as the pronounced the word *madman*.

"What if I were?" he said.

He returned to the window and looked out toward the blurred and vaporous horizon again, scanning the more clearly-delineated village and meadows, slowly taking account, with the logical reasoning of a mathematician, of the actual sensations he was experiencing. Finally convinced that his intellectual faculties were fully operative, he was obliged to say: "I am not mad."

He lost himself in contemplation again for several minutes, then added: "Now, if ever, I may say: the Devil alone knows the answer to this puzzle; I can't even begin to make head nor tail of it."

The Baron's laborious reflections were interrupted by a spontaneous burst of dainty laughter, sly and flirtatious–the laughter of a young woman, half-innocent and half-debauched–which sounded beneath the window. He redirected his gaze, which had wandered to the horizon, to the strip of grass that girdled the castle. He recognized one of the Huntsman's sons and the young woman who had served as his guide, walking in the grass with their arms around one another.

The hunter wore the same costume as the day before, as did the young woman–except that the hunter was unmasked. The Baron thought, yet again, that he must be dreaming with his eyes open, when he saw that, instead of his fleshless skeletal and worm-ridden visage, the young man without the mask had a near-beardless face that was pink, frank and open, brightened by two large blue eyes, and radiant with a fine and expansive smile that was not in the least infernal. As for the young woman, she seemed even more beautiful to the Baron than she had the previous day.

Monsieur de Nossac, whom neither of them had noticed, leaned out as far as possible in the hope of catching a few scraps of their conversation, which appeared to be lively and cheerful.

They were not speaking the bizarre language of the Black Huntsmen, but the good German of Berlin, Stuttgart or Heidelberg–a very pure and very correct German. The young huntsman, who must have been Winter Wind or Night Breeze, was now called Wilhem by his sister, and addressed her as Roschen in his turn.

The Baron's stupefactior increased further when, heaping astonishment on astonishment, the two sections of the door opened to give passage to the Black Huntsman and his other three sons, all four of them unmasked, with laughing eyes and faces as fresh as any human being's could be.

The skeletal faces had disappeared.

XII

The Baron's stupefaction was immense.

The huntsmen's faces were perfectly human, and rather comely besides.

The first–who was the father of the others, or had at least passed as such–was a man of about 58, but still hale and sprightly, to judge by the veritable feats of strength and youthful intrepidity that he had accomplished the day before. His hair was still black, speckled here and there with a few thin streaks of silver, while his beard was completely black and bushy. His eyes shone; his lips were red, turned up in the Austrian fashion; his nose was raptorial and his teeth were sharp and white.

The second–the eldest, who had been called North Wind the previous day and had been grey-bearded beneath his mask–was scarcely 30, with a jet black moustache and a pointed beard. Where, then, was the grey beard?

The third, South Wind, strongly resembled his brother, but was younger by two or three years; his slight beard was blond, not the black of the previous day.

The fourth and last, Night Breeze, was as ravishing an adolescent as ever sat upon the benches of the universities of Oxford, Heidelberg, Bonn or Salamanca in orange stockings with cherry-red or claret ribbons. He had blue eyes, ash-blond hair, a fine nascent moustache coquettishly curled up at the ends, scarcely distinguishable from his satiny and feminine pink cheeks. He had the mouth of a dreamer, having both the pleat of laughter and the pleat of tears at the same time: a mouth that could just as easily have dribbled a prayer of love–some melancholy stanza intoned by a page beneath a Spanish shutter in the decorative language of a loving poet pitilessly refused–or spouted, as occasion demanded, a sparkling and mocking hymn of intoxication: the cavalier and buoyant song of the German student, who attended his professors' lectures, in those days, with his rapier and rifle.

"Well, my dear Baron," said the hunters' father, "how did you sleep beneath my roof?"

"Marvelously," the Baron replied. "My night was as infernal as one could possibly desire, beneath the roof of one of the Devil's sons. I was fed upon by a vampire."

The Black Huntsman burst out laughing–a burst of laughter that was quite frank, entirely innocent, and companionable to the highest degree. "My dear Baron," he said, "you're the bravest man I ever met–you must be the most intrepid and the most accomplished gentleman in the service of the King of France."

"You think so?" Monsieur de Nossac asked, coldly.

"And I think it futile to submit you to further proofs. You are beyond the reach of any terror, my dear Baron. Before explaining the events that were accomplished before your eyes, permit me to assure you that neither I, nor my sons, have anything in common with the Devil, I am the Graf von Holdengrasburg, and these are my sons Hermann, Conrad and Samuel. Wilhem is with Roschen in the meadow; I shall introduce you to them shortly."

The Graf von Holdengrasburg leaned out of the window and called out, "Wilhem? Roschen?" Then he turned to the Baron, with a sincere and candid smile on his lips–but the Baron, in complete contrast, had become pale, his gaze sharpened like a steel point.

With his fist on his hip and his head thrown back, he studied the Graf von Holdengrasburg coldly, with a haughty expression. "Monsieur," he said, eventually, "you and your sons are gentlemen, so far as I can see. I hope that you and your sons comprehend the gravity and sadness involved in a trick played upon a gentleman. I am one such."

"I understand you. sir," the Graf replied, with cool dignity. "Neither I nor my sons will be found wanting, if you believe that you have been insulted. Will you grant me ten minutes?"

"To do what, Monsieur?"

"To justify our seemingly strange conduct."

"Exceedingly strange."

"And you will find that what you call a trick was, in fact, a necessity."

"Ah!"

"Will you hear me out?"

"I'm listening."

"I am not the Black Huntsman, that semi-fantastic person whose name is well-known in Bohemia, but tradition holds that I am directly descended from him."

"I approve of genealogy," murmured the Baron, sardonically.

"That descent is not a recommendation in these parts. My ancestors, poor and frozen with cold as they were in their cracked and crumbling castle, enjoyed an evil reputation hereabouts. They were honest men, but it's said that the sons of Satan play that loyal role hypocritically. They were humane towards their serfs and vassals, but the slanders went so far as to claim that, if they exempted unfortunates from the *corvée* and the whipping-post, it was mere insouciance, reserving the privilege of torturing their souls in Hell by way of compensation for sparing their bodies.

"Among the neighboring landholders, a few believed in our fabulous origin and feared us; others, bolder and less credulous, profited from it without any scruple. By a sort of tacit proscription or mute ostracism which injured us, they infringed by degrees upon our domains, stealing a plot of land here, a wood there. Our patrimony was diminished, and we did not dare to defend ourselves or complain, because judges and kings would have condemned us before hearing us. That lasted for several centuries; my father was the last victim of such rapines. He virtually died of hunger, having none but me at his death-bed.

"I was very young, no more than 15 or 16, and life presented a hard and inexorable prospect–but I triumphed over life. I took an old sword from my dead father's bedhead, which dated from the Crusades, girdled myself with a traveler's belt, and departed. I set off eastwards, begging for bread along the way, making my bed in ditches, but bearing myself proudly beneath my rags, and with a handsome enough face to attract the notice of women who watched me pass through the towns from their windows.

"I walked thus for a long time, sleeping in the open many a night, and eating the black bread of peasants and woodcutters more often still. Finally, I arrived in Bulgaria. They revere Mohammed there, and have never heard of the Black Huntsman or his family. I entered the service of a Bulgarian Prince; I became an officer in his army, then a General, and I was honored by his particular friendship. I married a Bulgarian Princess, by whom I had four sons and a daughter. But however oriental I had become, I loved my dear Germany above all else, and never resolved myself to forget her, or even to renounce the hope of returning there one day to die. Moreover, when my two eldest sons reached 15, I sent them to the University of Heidelberg to study. When the other two, who were twins, attained the same age, they went to join their brothers.

"I had grown old; the Bulgarian Prince, who had heaped wealth and honor upon me, had died, leaving the throne to his son, to whom nothing now bound me, and I had lost my wife a little while before. Then I remembered the vexations endured by my father and his family, under the pretext of a nebulous legend. I recalled the obstinacy of his enemies, his forbearance and that of his forefathers, and I thought of avenging him. I had four strong and valiant sons, immense wealth, a host of Bulgarian servants who did not know the German language and who could not betray us to the peasants of Bohemia. I wanted to be a true son of the Devil, and to resuscitate the Black Huntsman.

"My sons hastened from the University of Heidelberg; one night, I arrived here myself from the depths of Bulgaria, bringing an army of slaves and servants in my train. My castle was entirely ruined, not a single wall remained intact. The neighboring valleys are pitted with deep caverns, which served as our refuge by day, hiding us from all eyes. By night, we worked to rebuild my castle.

"One day, a woodcutter noticed that one fallen wall had been rebuilt sine the day before, and that a tower half-razed to the ground had grown by a cubit. He fled in fright and claimed that the Devil had taken it into his head to restore his son's castle. The news spread. Some believed it, others shrugged their shoulders. The following day, a number of curiosity-seekers arrived with the sunrise. The four towers had been re-roofed. Terror took hold of the land. Two days later, a wood-cutter saw me pass through a clearing clad as the Black Huntsman, with a mask on my face to hide my skeletal visage, blowing a wild and deafening fanfare on my horn. The terror became general.

"I organized a great hunt–a hunt like the one you saw yesterday and in which you participated, except that it lasted eight days. For eight days and eight nights my red-clad grooms and my white-clad beaters rode through the forests and valleys with torches in their hands, like a fiery hurricane, drawing lamentable and sinister plaints from the surrounding echoes, and exciting the formidable pack of hounds that you have seen at work. My castle was entirely reconstructed within a month. My neighbors, who had encroached upon my domains for centuries with their continual infringements, released their grip and recoiled in fright. One peasant, bolder than the rest, who dared to set himself in my path, fell stone dead on suddenly beholding my skeletal visage.

"For everyone–for the entirety of superstitious Bohemia, I became the Black Huntsman. By night, my castle was seen ablaze upon its rock like a gigantic lighthouse; by day, it was dismal, silent, deserted and menacing, dark in the rays of the Sun, like those phantoms which, having danced excessively at the Sabbath, are found in the morning with their limbs stiff, unable to return to the cemetery to stretch themselves out in their tombs.

"That has lasted for a year now. I have reconquered the ancient patrimony of my ancestors. I have developed a taste for hunting, and am perfectly certain now that no one for ten leagues around will poach a deer of any species."

The Black Huntsman–or, rather, the Graf von Holdengrasburg–paused, and looked at the Baron de Nossac.

The Baron was still cold and haughty. He had maintained his irritated gaze and his clouded brow. "That's all very well," he said, "but it provides no explanation whatsoever of the hoax of which I was the intended victim. I await enlightenment, Herr Graf."

"The explanation is simple, Baron. I have a number of spies on every road; I knew of your plan to deliver King Stanislaus before its execution. I followed you every step of the way. I saw you put your plan into operation with unprecedented audacity, and I wanted to find out for myself exactly how far your bravery extended."

"Are you quite satisfied?" asked the Baron, with heavy sarcasm in his tone.

"To the utmost degree. I am pleased to proclaim you the most intrepid gentleman in the world."

"You are a thousand times too kind. While you are in an explanatory mood, though, I hope you will do me the honor of telling me the purpose of that comedy of the coffin, and the dead woman who dances and talks."

One of the hunters, Hermann, let out a burst of laughter. "That's my mistress, a good and charming girl I brought from Heidelberg, who had a powerful desire to play the role."

"That's strange!" murmured the Baron. "I thought I recognized her voice."

"Oh! What do you mean?"

"Her voice resembles that of my late wife."

"Chance plays strange tricks, you know."

"True. But that same woman, dead or not, came here last night, took me in her arms, bit my neck and fed on me like a vampire."

The four hunters released a cry of amazement which, sincere or simulated, impressed the Baron deeply.

"That's impossible!" they cried.

"Why is it impossible?"

"Because she never left my room," Hermann said. "She left this morning for an excursion in the neighborhood, and will not return until this evening."

The Baron let out a cry in his turn and ran to the mirror that he had already consulted.

"Look," he said, pointing to the wound in his neck. "Touch it."

The hunters' surprise increased, but the Graf von Holdengrasburg examined it attentively and cried: "It's not a bite, it's a puncture." Then, running to the bed, he looked at the point of the sword that was projecting from the pillow under which the Baron had placed it, and broke into laughter. "Baron," he said, "you were drunk last night and you've had a nightmare. Your sword is the vampire accused by your imagination."

"By my faith!" Nossac replied. "So many extraordinary things have happened to me that I know longer know whether I'm asleep or dreaming."

"You're no longer dreaming, but you have had a dream."

"Oh! And yet, it seems to me that I can still feel her, next to me, sucking my blood and saying to me: *Your blood is rosy and fresh...*"

"Error and folly!"

"But tell me," Nossac said, excitedly, "by means of what strange phantasmagoria have you caused the bleak rock on which your chateau stood to vanish, along with the torrent it overhung and the wild terrain that surrounded it, in order to replace it all with that pretty pastoral scene that extends to the horizon?"

The hunters smiled.

"Come," said the Graf. "You shall see the key to the mystery with your own eyes." And he drew him into a neighboring apartment, took him through several rooms–from which the funereal decorations of the night before had vanished, giving place to sparkling and vividly-colored Oriental hangings representing the mysteries of the harem and the great hunt of India–then suddenly opened a casement window.

"Look," he said.

The Baron leaned out, and recognized the tormented landscape of the previous night. The explanation of the incomprehensible mystery was perfectly natural: the castle had two *façades*, serving to limit two very different horizons, one pleasant and calm, the other sinister and abrupt.

"I'm an idiot," he said. Then, looking at the Graf again: "Monsieur, I find your pleasantries excessively ingenious; but as I do not believe that I have merited them, nor provoked them, you will permit me to call you to account. A gentleman of my caliber and rank has little taste for practical jokes of this sort."

The four hunters burst out laughing. This laughter exasperated the Baron, who took a step back and drew his sword–but at that same moment, the door opened. The pure and dazzlingly beautiful young woman, Roschen, came in, supported on Wilhem's arm.

The sword slipped from the fascinated Baron's hand, its use prohibited.

XIII

Monsieur de Nossac felt his anger melt away under the gentle gaze of the young woman, as a storm-wind relents in its howling at the first kiss of the pale and indecisive sunlight that filters through the clouds. He looked at her mutely, almost ashamed of the reckless act he had been about to commit. Then he stared at Wilhem.

Wilhem resembled Samuel in such a surprising fashion that it would have been impossible to distinguish them clearly and precisely. They both had the same grave and melancholy smile, with a hint of irony. They both had Roschen's large blue eyes, and Roschen also bore a striking resemblance to them, except that she had features even finer, softer and more delicate than her brothers'. From Wilhem and Samuel, the Baron's gaze returned to the other three hunters. Their faces were frank, smiling, full of the courteous good humor that paralyzes the greatest irritation.

Monsieur de Nossac regretted and was ashamed of his foolish anger. He took a step towards the Graf von Holdengrasburg. "My dear host," he said, cordially, "since you have convinced yourself of my personal courage, you will not, I hope, see any cowardice in the excuses that I beg you to accept for my stupid susceptibility. Your jokes might perhaps have been hard, but I have had sufficient honorable triumph not to exact any reparation."

"Excellent!" cried the Graf, gaily. "You are the very model of the French gentleman, brave and clever."

"And if I regret one aspect of your metamorphosis, it is that the end for which the Black Huntsman brought me here has changed so completely." The Baron's voice had altered slightly.

"What do you mean?" asked the Graf.

"That the Devil's son challenged me by proposing that I should marry his daughter, while the Graf von Holdengrasburg no longer has any such motive to make me the same proposition, the terrible and frightful prospect of an alliance with the Devil now being set aside, of course." And Monsieur de Nossac darted a sorrowful glance at Roschen.

The Graf, however, extended his hand to the Baron expansively, and said: "You're more than brave and clever—you're endowed with an exquisite delicacy, Monsieur le Baron de Nossac. We are of sufficiently ancient nobility and wealth, rich and loyal; I ask again for the honor of your alliance—will you refuse me?"

Monsieur de Nossac did not reply, and looked at Roschen with a supplicant air. "Accept!" she seemed to say to him, by means of an imperceptible sign, while the incarnadine blush of modesty rose to her forehead.

"Herr Graf," Monsieur de Nossac said, solemnly, "I beg you to grant me the hand of Mademoiselle Roschen, your daughter."

"I grant it to you, Baron—and all the honor of the alliance belongs to my house." Having pronounced these words, the Graf took Roschen's hand, placed it in Nossac's, and added: "We change nothing of that which was agreed with the son of Satan; you are engaged; we shall celebrate the marriage in eight days."

Monsieur de Nossac's satisfaction, the tremor of happiness that climbed from his heart to his head, was so great at that moment that the phantasmagoria of the previous day and the bizarre events, the mysteries of which he still understood only imperfectly, were wiped from his mind. He believed completely that he really was in the home of a true Bohemian gentleman, a brave and honest man, who wanted nothing more than to disembarrass himself of his daughter and his millions in favor of someone presentable.

"Now," said the Graf, laughing, "if it meets your approval, we shall go down into the grounds, where breakfast will be served beneath a bower of honeysuckle and lilac. Give your hand to your bride, Baron."

Samuel and Wilhem opened the procession, supporting one another with an entirely feminine affected nonchalance, which betrayed the mysterious tenderness that exists between twins. The Graf took the arm of his son Hermann, and Conrad brought up the rear.

The Baron's surprise became more wondrous at every step. The castle, so dismal and lugubrious the previous evening, had a brisk and cheerful air, like one of those old men who are rejuvenated by a new marriage, blossoming as they make the rounds with their young wives on the arms. The green meadows that half-circled it and brushed it with a kiss of verdure, seemed to him to have sent the best part of its perfumes and its vivid light to the dwelling.

The Graf led his guest into the gardens where, as he had said, a table was laid beneath a bower.

The meal was Oriental in all its luxurious simplicity. There were baskets of fruit, vases of flowers, preserves from the harem and Albanian wines that Mohammedans can only drink in secret. All of it shone and sparkled, making a double appeal—to a painter's ennobled instincts by the richness and velvet quality of its colors, and to exquisite gourmet appetites by the penetrating perfumes it emitted.

At that moment, the hoofbeats of a horse resounded behind the arbor.

"Hello!" said Hermann. "That's Gretchen coming back—she wasn't due to return until this evening."

"Who is Gretchen?"

"Your dead woman of yesterday, Baron."

The horse halted directly in front of the arbor, and a woman with black hair and a forehead as white and pure as ivory leapt lightly to the ground. She was a ravishing young woman of 25 or 26, with red lips and profound black eyes, and a lithely nonchalant stride like the gait of a tigress.

With a smile upon her lips, she came into the bower of greenery and bowed to the Baron with respectful familiarity. At the sight of her, the Baron released a terrible cry of fright, such as the prodigies of the Black Huntsman had been unable to tear from him—not the dead woman rising from her coffin, nor any of the other vertiginous terrors to which he had been prey during the last 48 hours. It was a cry of pain and anguish, which made him pirouette on his stool, fall backwards and murmur in a faint and strangled voice: "My wife! It's my wife!"

XIV

The hunters looked at the Baron with an astonishment, which–whether it was true or feigned–produced a repercussion of surprise that was no less violent. In the midst of his fright, as totally terrified and overwhelmed as he could be by this apparition, he nevertheless had time to perceive that his hosts were dumbfounded, and had absolutely no understanding of the words that had just escaped him.

As for his wife–or, rather, the woman he had taken for his wife–she was just as surprised, utterly and innocently astonished, and she was looking at the Baron with an expression that seemed to say to him: "How the Devil could I ever have married you?" [40]

Monsieur de Nossac felt his hair stand on end. Either this was not his wife at all–in which case the resemblance was so perfect as to have driven him momentarily mad–or it was. In the latter case, given that he had seen her dead, and truly dead, had nailed shut her coffin and built her funereal vault, it would be necessary to overturn at a stroke all the received theories regarding the dead and believe that Madame Hélène de Nossac had emerged from the tomb, as young and beautiful as she had gone into it, in order to torment her unfaithful husband and demand that he account for his outrages.

It was certainly her, however, if the resemblance could be trusted: the same figure, the same bearing, the same calm and haughty smile, the same profound and confident gaze, the same slight dimple in the chin, the same voice, the same gestures...

Perhaps Gretchen had a few imperceptible lines furrowing her forehead, testifying to premature worries, which the Baronne had not yet acquired–but might they not have been engraved by the grave?

The eight people who were present remained silent for a long time, distraught and petrified. Framed as they were by the clumps of lilac and honeysuckle mounted on the invisible chassis of the verdant bower, they could easily have been taken for garden statuary. Finally, the Graf von Holdengrasburg broke the stunned silence that reigned within the arbor, saying to the Baron: "Is it impossible, Monsieur, that you might have been misled by a more-than-bizarre resemblance?"

"You...think...?" stammered Nossac, pale and breathless.

"I think so too," said Gretchen. "I saw Monsieur for the first time yesterday."

Instead of reassuring the Baron, these simple words redoubled his fright.

"Oh!" he said. "You have her voice too... It *is* you!"

"You're mad!" she said, emotionally. "I'm a poor girl from Heidelberg who has never been to France and who cannot speak French. How can you think that I might be your wife?"

The Baron continued to murmur: "You have her voice... You have her gestures, her gaze... The least mannerism..."

"Madness!" Hermann said. "I met Gretchen when she was scarcely 15 years old; she has never left me."

Monsieur de Nossac looked at Hermann. His expression was calm and honest; he did not seem to be lying. Then the Baron looked, in turn, at the Graf and his three other sons, and read the same assertion in their physiognomy. Then his eyes tried to meet Roschen's–but the blushing Roschen had lowered her eyes, and seemed distressed.

The Baron shivered, but he finished up telling himself that he had been deluded by a freak of chance, an unexpected resemblance. He attempted to smile. "Pardon my stupid fear, Madame," he said, "but my mind has been disturbed since yesterday, and your marvelous resemblance to the wife I have lost, combined with a dream that I had last night, which was so convincing in its appearance of reality that I needed the assurance of these gentlemen in order not to believe in it... Your resemblance, as I say, combined with the dream I had, is my only excuse."

"A dream?" said Gretchen, astonished.

106

"Yes," Nossac replied. "I had a dream. I believed that I saw my bedroom door open last night; you came in, with your mask on your face; you lay down next to me, and bit my throat like a vampire."

Gretchen first cried out in horror, then burst out laughing. "Look at me intently, Monsieur le Baron," she said, "and see whether I have the slightest appearance of being a vampire?"

The Baron looked at her again. She was gazing at him with the same suave and lascivious melancholy that he had seen in the eyes of Mademoiselle Borelli. Shivering anew, he thought about his wife, who had died of despair and jealousy, and his vile conduct towards her... and he forgot Roschen momentarily. For a brief interval, he remembered the tears he had shed over Hélène's inanimate corpse.

"Baron," said the Graf von Holdengrasburg, abruptly interrupting Monsieur de Nossac's painful thoughts, "be well and truly assured that our poor Gretchen had nothing in common with the late Madame la Baronne de Nossac. Dismiss the mournful memories that must have come into your mind, Let's take a walk in the grounds, if you care to, as one ought to before dining."

Monsieur de Nossac looked at Gretchen. Gretchen was carefree and calm.

"Madame," he said, unable to vanquish entirely the emotion that overwhelmed him, "will you allow me one question?"

"Speak, Monsieur," said Gretchen, in her soft and melancholy voice.

"How were you able to talk to me about my wife last night, in such precise terms?"

Gretchen smiled. "Ask Hermann," she said.

"Monsieur le Baron," Hermann said, "do you not have a friend called the Marquis de Simiane?"

"Yes, I have," said Nossac.

"A Colonel of Dragoons?"

"That's right."

"Who fought his last campaign in Germany?"

"Certainly."

"Well, as we have already told you, my brothers and I were students at the University of Heidelberg. Last year, Monsieur de Simiane, who had been wounded in the shoulder by a gunshot, came to Heidelberg for treatment. I was one of the assistant surgeons who dressed his wound. We became friends, and he asked me to continue visiting him after his convalescence. I brought Gretchen with me every evening, and every time he saw her, he could not help saying: 'You bear a vague resemblance to the late Baronne de Nossac.' "

"Vague? He thought the resemblance merely vague?"

"Yes, certainly."

My mind must be disturbed, the Baron thought.

"Now, one evening when he repeated that sentence," Herman continued, "we asked him who Madame de Nossac was. 'A wife who died a virgin,' he replied. And he told us the story of your marriage. You understand that we profited from it yesterday evening, and that Gretchen–who, good girl that she is, has a mischievous character and a liking for practical jokes–had no compunction about repeating, as completely as possible, everything that she knew." And Hermann put his Herculean hand around Gretchen's slim waist, and pulled her towards him to kiss her on the forehead.

Monsieur de Nossac felt a sudden shudder, and a vague pain in his heart and his head. That kiss had hurt him; he was jealous of it. Why? He immediately addressed that question to himself, of course, and charged himself, of course, with madness–for he immediately looked at Roschen, as if he were searching. in her gaze and in her love, for a protective aegis against poignant memories and the new image that had recalled them.

Roschen was suffering some distress. She had listened, with her eyes lowered, to the strange explanation that had been offered by Hermann and Gretchen to the Baron, and seemed more afflicted than astonished.

"Let's go, Baron!" said the Graf von Holdengrasburg. "Offer your hand to your fiancée..." He emphasized that word, and there was a brief flash of light–which the Baron did not see–in Gretchen's eyes. "Offer your hand to your fiancée," the Graf went on, "and let's go into the meadows, as far as the little village you see down there, which is inhabited by a Bulgarian colony."

The Baron went to Roschen and took her hand. Roschen's hand was trembling violently, and her heart was beating as if it were about to burst. The Baron took note of this emotion, but he attributed it to the scene that had just taken place and to the fright that it must have given the young woman.

Hermann and Gretchen went out of the arbor first and set off across the meadows, 20 or 30 paces ahead of the Baron and Roschen–who was walking silently, in some distress. Gretchen was leaning on her lover's shoulder with relaxed languor. Sometimes she talked to him distinctly, in a leisurely fashion, of matters of near-indifference. At other times, she leaned close to his ear to murmur soft words of love, which the Baron could not hear, by virtue of the distance, but whose content he guessed. Instead of thinking about Roschen–Roschen, whose arm was shivering on his, the pulsations of whose heart he would have been able to hear, so fervent were they–the Baron was following the least movements of Hermann and Gretchen with an avid eye, pricking his avid ears for the least insignificant word that a gust of wind might carry to them. He shook with anger at the little bursts of spontaneous, rebellious and mocking laughter with which Gretchen sprinkled her flirtatious and amiable chatter.

The poor gentleman was suffering, without knowing why. He asked himself, seriously, why he was so obsessed by a *grisette* from Heidelberg laughing on a student's arm–and while he was doing all this, Roschen too had to make an unprecedented effort to suppress the anguish which, to say the least, had overwhelmed her. She finally succeeded in that, and opened her mouth to speak to her escort.

At the sound of her voice, the Baron seemed to wake up from a painful sleep. In his turn, he forgot about Gretchen momentarily to return to Roschen. He looked at her; she was even more beautiful with the fleeting hint of vermilion coloring her cheeks and forehead. He squeezed her hand gently, then, and said to her: "I must appear extremely ridiculous to you, Mademoiselle."

"You?" she said, emotionally. "Why?"

"Because I give the lie to what you said yesterday–you are as brave as a lion–by falling prey to insane apprehensions at every instant."

"It isn't terror," she said, softly. "It's mere emotion."

One of Gretchen's bursts of mocking laughter reached the Baron's ears just as he was about to reply to his fiancée, and he fell silent abruptly. Roschen perceived this sudden interruption, and saw the Baron's brow become clouded. She shivered violently, and said: "I should dearly like to speak with you privately, Monsieur."

"Speak, Mademoiselle," Nossac replied, recalled to himself involuntarily by the distinctively harmonious tone of Roschen's voice.

"Oh, not now!" she said. "Not now."

"Why?"

"We can be seen."

"What of it?"

"What of it! If anyone knew what I intend to tell you..." Roschen stopped, trembling.

"If anyone knew...?" the Baron said, anxiously.

"I would be lost!" she said, in terror,

"Lost?"

"Wilhem would kill me."

Nossac looked at Roschen. Roschen trembled–but she looked at him lovingly, and seemed to be saying to him: "Oh! I would brave death for you... for I love you..."

"Well," he murmured, in a very low voice, "although I cannot guess or understand what you want to tell me, I shall wait patiently for the time and place at which you feel able..."

"This evening," she whispered, "in your room..."

"Very well," said Nossac, intrigued.

At that moment, they arrived at the edge of the forest that bordered the grassland, and the Baron saw Gretchen and Hermann disappear into a clump of fir-trees. He went pale with distress. A convulsive tremor took hold of the hand that was squeezing Roschen's hand, and Roschen guessed that he had just been overcome by a fit of jealousy.

"My God!" she whispered, so quietly that even Nossac could not hear her. "Does he love her still?" She stopped, chilled to the bone, with sweat on her brow. "And if so," she went on, "should I be jealous?"

XV

At ten o'clock that evening, after a supper at which, despite his best efforts, he had not been able to remain sober, Monsieur le Baron de Nossac retired to his bedroom and bolted the door.

Well, he thought, *what does all this mean, and in what sort of state is my poor heart? I loved my wife, and Gretchen resembles her in so striking a fashion that I am tempted to love her... I was jealous of her today. I suffered horribly during that walk through my host's meadows and woods, while she never quit the arm of that colossus of a student–and yet, it's not her that I love, that's impossible... I love Roschen...the beautiful Roschen, purest of the pure, who has vowed to love me...*

The Baron suddenly struck himself on the forehead.

What has she to tell me? What did she want to say to me? And why that terror, which overwhelmed her at the mere thought that we might be overheard...? Wilhem would kill her, she said. Why Wilhem, rather than one of the other brothers?

The Baron became pensive.

111

She'll come, undoubtedly, he said to himself. *She'll come... She told me so.*

At that moment, a sinister thought crossed the Baron's mind. He thought of Gretchen, who was doubtless on Hermann's arm, and he shook with anger. And then, as he had full possession of his reason, and as he had to chase away the phantom and get rid of that stupid jealousy, he summoned the image of Roschen to his aid, and murmured: "Roschen... Roschen... Come quickly."

But Roschen did not come.

The Baron found a small paper scroll on his bed, which he unfolded distractedly. The scroll contained a few lines in French, with no signature: *Wilhem is watching me. I can't come this evening. Tomorrow, we shall see.*

"Wilhem, always Wilhem!" murmured Monsieur de Nossac, angrily. "What fatal or evil influence does he have over his sister, then? His sister...? Is she his sister?"

As he felt his hair bristle at this terrible thought, in the same way that he had taken refuge in the memory of Roschen in order to flee from Gretchen, he now resumed thinking of Gretchen in order to avoid the doubts that were assailing him.

"Gretchen," he murmured. "Am I in love with you? My God! Am I in love with you?"

And he went to bed with that thought in his head.

As on the previous evening, he suddenly felt a strange numbness encircle his brain like a ring of iron, and he was scarcely able to place his sword at his bedhead, as was his habit.

Then, as his suspicions regarding Roschen had vanished, he tried to think about her, to see her again in his mind, in all her beauty and virginal splendor...

But the image of Roschen he tried to invoke would not come. Despite his effort, Roschen vanished from his memory. Roschen disappeared–and Gretchen, no longer the cheerful *grisette* of the meadows, but Gretchen the pallid dead woman, emerging from her coffin, masked and beautiful, as cold as a snake... Gretchen reassumed a despotic empire over his im-

pressed and fascinated mind. He cried out, silently: *Gretchen...*
Hélène... Whoever you are...I love you!

And immediately, whether he was dreaming or not–the
matter is difficult to determine precisely, because of the
strange malaise of his body and mind–immediately, as if she
were responding to his invitation, and even though the door
was bolted, Gretchen came into the room and walked slowly
towards the bed.

The Baron quivered, and tried to recoil–but he felt paralyzed in every limb. He tried to close his eyes, but could not
do it. Fear riveted his gaze to Gretchen's pale and ardent face.

The living Gretchen, the dead Hélène, approached the
bed, lay down silently beside the Baron, planted an icy kiss on
his forehead, then interlaced her marble fingers and said to
him: "Last night, I promised to come back. I have come
back... But be tranquil; your blood has done me good... I shall
use it thriftily!"

And, as on the previous evening, she sank her teeth into
his neck.

XVI

The sensation of that bite was experienced by the Baron
not so much a pain as an all-enveloping bitter voluptuousness.
As he felt his blood flowing, and the regular undulations of
vampire's breast and throat, he understood that it was drinking
deep draughts with a savage avidity...

Eventually, Gretchen, or the vampire, or Hélène de Nossac–for the Baron no longer knew which one he was dealing
with–that strange being, let us say, paused. Satiated, it
stretched itself out on the bed beside its victim, in a pose replete with voluptuous languor.

"Baron," it said, "I've taken too much of your blood today, and I'm displeased with myself... but I was so thirsty!
Then again, you see, I've been jealous since this morning, as

jealous as a tigress, because you love that little Roschen, and intend to marry her..."

Monsieur de Nossac made a supreme effort to speak.

"No..." he murmured.

"Are you telling the truth, my beloved?"

And the vampire placed its icy lips upon the Baron's tremulous mouth.

"My dear Baron," the vampire went on, "you were right to recognize me this morning; I really am your wife... your wife, whom you killed, and who loved you so much... your wife, who has covered 800 leagues on foot, enveloped in a white shroud, through the brambles, in the cold and the darkness, in order to warm herself up for an hour by drinking a little blood and stealing a kiss from you."

Monsieur de Nossac recovered some of his strength, and tried to push the vampire away.

"Do you know why the dead are always cold?" the vampire continued. "It's because they no longer have a drop of blood in their veins. If I had had the tenth part of what I have just taken from you, I would certainly not have been obliged to take my shroud in both hands and drape myself within it with such immense care, to protect me from the bitter caress of the wind. And the closer I came to the place where you were, you see, the more I felt the cold diminish. Yesterday, because I had drunk the previous evening, I was warm—towards evening, however, the chill took hold of me again; I felt the occasional shiver, and it seemed to me that the night was slow in coming...

"It has finally arrived. Now I have drunk, and have kissed you on the forehead and the mouth, I have warmed my heart and my body again... Oh, how I love you, my love! I would have been able to forget you, though, as you have forgotten me, ingrate! I would have been able, in the world to which my soul went, to marry an angel or a saint, both of us handsome and eternally young... I have not done that! I chose in preference to come back, to reanimate my corpse, which was sleeping peacefully in its coffin, sheltered from the bitter night air and the ardent rays of sunlight; I made it get up, that poor corpse, throw aside its tumulary stone, march every night without pause, from dusk to the following dawn–for I was obliged by day to enter into the first cemetery to be found on my route and to lay myself down there in an empty grave until darkness fell.

"I arrived thus in Heidelberg. There was a young girl named Gretchen in the city, who resembled me feature for feature. This young girl was the mistress of a student named Hermann von Holdengrasburg–the son of your host, Baron. Hermann had wanted to leave her for a long time, that poor girl, and he was waiting for an opportunity to present itself. His father, meanwhile, wrote to him and his brothers, telling them to return to Bohemia as quickly as possible. The opportunity presented itself. Hermann mounted his horse one morning and departed, leaving a few cold words of farewell addressed to Gretchen. Gretchen waited for Hermann all day; in the evening, she received his letter, fell ill, contracted a cerebral fever and died within 24 hours.

"I arrived in Heidelberg cemetery on the morning of the very day on which she was buried, and as I had not be able to find an empty grave, I was crouching in a cypress bush whose black foliage sheltered me from the Sun's rays. I saw Gretchen's bier pass close by Her coffin was open, according to the German custom, and I could see her face. I was struck by the extraordinary resemblance that Gretchen bore to me–so struck that I had the idea of rejoining you with the aid of a stratagem furnished by that resemblance.

"I spent the whole day in my cypress bush, waiting impatiently for nightfall. When darkness fell, I went to Gretchen's tomb. Having armed myself with a spade that the gravedigger had forgotten, I dug down into the freshly-turned earth. It was extremely difficult, because a long time had passed since I had had any blood–so long that I froze the ground on which I walked! I succeeded, however, in disinterring Gretchen, and when I had done that I undressed her completely and dressed myself in her clothes. I stole everything from her, including the golden cross that Hermann had given her, which as still hanging around her neck. Then, as I was still cold in spite of her clothing, I took her shroud, which I put on top of mine, and continued on my way. After eight nights of walking, I arrived here. I knew–for the dead know everything–that you would come here the following day. I found Hermann, sitting by the fireside chatting with his brothers and his father.

" 'What a pity I didn't bring that poor Gretchen!'

" 'Why is it a pity?' asked the Graf von Holdengrasburg.

" 'Because the Marquis de Simiane, whose wound I dressed, claimed that she strongly resembled the Baronne de Nossac, who died a year ago. Since we're awaiting the Baron, she could have rendered us a valuable service in taking the role of the dead woman in the comedy we're preparing.'

"I was still standing on the threshold, and they had not heard me come in.

" 'Gretchen accepts the role,' I said, all of a sudden.

"They turned round, stupefied. Hermann went pale and stuttered, while the Graf, whom I did not know, looked at me with astonishment.

" 'My dear Hermann,' I said to Gretchen's lover, 'you are an ingrate, and I ought to hate you–but I forgive you.'

"He threw himself at my feet and took me by the hand. 'My God!' he said, full of emotion. 'How cold you are!'

" 'I came on foot,' I replied, 'and I've been walking all night.' And I went to the fire avidly, for my strength was almost exhausted, and warmed myself for a full quarter of an hour without speaking.

" 'Poor Gretchen!' Herman murmured, fatuously. 'How she must love me!'

" 'Madame,' the Graf von Holdengrasburg said to me, 'are you not frightened by the role that has been destined for you?'

" 'Not in the least,' I replied. 'The role pleases me greatly, and I shall play it entirely naturally.'

" 'You think so?'

" 'I'm sure of it.'

"Herman burst out laughing. 'Good old Gretchen!' he said. 'Is she courageous enough?'

" 'I believe that I have proved that,' I replied, dryly. 'I've come from Heidelberg on foot, as a mendicant. Now, as I want nothing from you, since you left me alone and penniless, I shall come here every evening, remain until dawn, and then go away.'

" 'Where to?' asked the Graf.

" 'To the house of a parish priest, in a village a league from here.'

" 'On foot?'

" 'No, you'll lend me a horse.'

"I had told a lie in saying that I would go to the village priest's house, but it was necessary, in order to furnish myself with the right and the pretext to go away, to lie in a death-bed every morning. Hermann tried to insist; his father and brothers joined forces with him.

" 'Would you prefer it,' I said, 'if I were to go immediately and not play the role of the dead woman?'

" 'No, no!' they said.

" 'Let her do it,' Hermann said. 'It's a woman's caprice... it will pass.'

"The day was breaking; the Graf and his sons, who had forgotten the time as they sat by the fire, got up to go to bed.

" 'Until this evening,' I said to Hermann.

"He wanted me to stay; I was inflexible. I was given a horse–and I assure you that it was far from useless, for I was extremely tired. I got astride it and took the road to the village in whose cemetery I had spent the previous night.

"There were beautiful meadows all around the field of rest; I picked a few daisies and forget-me-nots,[41] so that I might breathe their perfume in my grave, and I tethered the horse to a hawthorn hedge. The horse began cropping the grass and I went back into the cemetery.

"The empty grave that I had occupied the previous night had been taken since nightfall. I wandered for more than an

117

hour without finding another, and was obliged to wait in a cypress bush for the gravedigger, who had been working since dawn, to finish excavating another and leave.

"That night, I found the horse again, remounted it, and galloped to the castle. The Graf and his sons welcomed me with open arms, and taught me my role–which I already knew, as you will understand, and they told me that a *znapan* would bring you from Marienwerder the following day.

" 'Come to my room, Gretchen,' said Hermann, 'It's necessary that I give you all the relevant instructions.'

" 'I'm cold,' I said. 'Let's remain here.'

"By the time he had finished talking to me, the time had come for him and his brothers to go, and he had to leave me. 'Oh!' he murmured, with angry annoyance, 'you're playing me, Gretchen, but tonight...'

" 'It will be the same tonight,' I replied. 'I want to punish you. I shall sleep side by side with you, but you will respect me... or I shall kill you.' And I showed him the dagger that Gretchen carried in her belt, which I had stolen from her.

" 'You're a strange girl,' he said to me. 'It shall be as you wish.'

"I have no need to tell you what happened that night–you know as well as I do. After the comedy, I retired with Hermann to his room, kissed him lightly on the forehead and put him to sleep. It was then that I came to find you. After leaving you, I returned to Hermann's room, and when he woke up, he saw me beside him. An hour later, I left my horse in the meadow, as on the previous evening, and went into the cemetery. On the threshold of the funeral field, I met a young dead woman who was on the way out, enveloped in her shroud.

" 'Where are you going?' I asked her. 'Don't you know that day is about to break? The Sun will soon be up.'

" 'I know that.'

" 'Are you not dead?'

" 'Of course.'

" 'The dead can only travel by night.'

" 'You're right–but today is Corpus Christi, and on that day, women who died virgins can wander until evening through the meadows and along the green hedges, to gather daises and whitethorn to make crowns. I died a virgin; I'm exercising my right.

" 'Where is your grave?' I asked her.

" 'Over there,' she said, pointing with her finger.

" 'Well,' I replied, 'I'm going to lie down in it for an hour, because I've been traveling all night. When I've slept a while, I'll come to join you. I, too, have a desire for daisies and whitethorn, and, like you, I died a virgin.' That was true, wasn't it?

"I did, indeed, sleep for an hour. Then, as I got up, I had the idea of appearing to you in broad daylight. Instead of re-joining the dead woman, I mounted my horse again, and I arrived, to general amazement, under the bower where you were breakfasting.

"Now, dear angel," the vampire concluded, "I'm warm and I'm strong. I'll leave you, and I'll come back tomorrow night. You'll see me beforehand, for I'll return from the cemetery at sunset. Adieu."

The vampire kissed the Baron again, on the mouth and the forehead, then it moved off, with its habitual slow stiffness. At the threshold, it turned round one last time, blew him a kiss, smiled at him and disappeared.

Immediately, the Baron felt himself possessed by a strange fever and a leaden sleep that strained and paralyzed his thoughts for several hours. When he finally woke up, he heard two voices close at hand, on the other side of the partition wall against which his bed was set, conversing quietly.

One of them was Wilhem's. The other was Roschen's!

The Baron had lied without knowing it when he had told the dead woman that he did not love Roschen, for he started violently, and jealousy bit into his heart when he heard her voice intermingled with Wilhem's.

XVII

Wilhem's voice caused the Baron to shiver profoundly. He was suddenly overcome by an inflexible curiosity. Perfectly certain in advance that he was about to hear things that would hurt him cruelly, he put his ear to the partition and listened with an avidity that was almost savage.

"I tell you, Roschen," said Wilhem's voice, "that you haven't been the same towards me for two days."

"You're mad!"

"Oh, I'm not mad–don't worry."

"You must be, to address me in such ridiculous terms."

"I have a heart, which senses..."

"Ah!" said Roschen, with a certain sarcasm.

"And eyes, which see..."

"Really!" Roschen's voice became mocking.

"Oh! Look here, Roschen–as I say, I see and I feel. Since that accursed stranger has come between you and me, since we've been playing this infernal comedy, you've taken your role so seriously..."

"Of course," Roschen said, with a burst of laughter that was not at all ingenuous.

"Do you love him?"

Roschen released an exclamation. "Oh! You don't believe that, do you, Wilhem?" she said, in a pleading tone.

"More than that," Wilhem said, dully. "I know it."

"That's madness!"

"I've divined it."

"That's a lie!"

"I feel it and I've divined it, I tell you. I feel it in the disordered beating of my heart. I divined it yesterday in the lascivious and indolent fashion in which you leant on his arm. I saw you grow pale and tremble when Gretchen appeared before him. Roschen, you're deceiving me–or you will deceive me..."

120

"Wilhem!"

"If you do that," Wilhem went on, his anger increasing, "woe betide you Roschen, woe betide you!"

"But I swear to you..."

"I picked you up out of the gutter, Roschen. You were a working girl in Heidelberg, a tailor's daughter... nothing more."

"Mercy!" murmured Roschen, tremulously.

"I made you the mistress of a student, and a gentleman student at that—more than that, I gave you money and jewels, fine clothes and..."

"You're a coward!" Roschen cried, interrupting him. "Your reproaches are an insult to me, and above all to yourself. Yes, I became, poor working girl that I was, a gentleman's mistress—but the working girl was pure, she was an honest girl, and, in the quarter where my father repaired old clothes, she was respected after her fashion. Today, you've changed my poverty into opulence, but I'm dishonored, and I hang my head in shame."

Wilhem let out a cry of rage. "Do common people have honor," he demanded, "do they speak of it as we gentlefolk do?"

"The common people, Wilhem, are more noble in their poverty and their hard labor than a gentleman like you, who dishonors his escutcheon in trying to redecorate it with ill-acquired gold."

"What do you mean, slut?"

"I mean, Wilhem, that no matter how much you've been paid, or to what end your conduct is directed, the job you've been doing these last several days is infamous."

Wilhem reddened with wrath. "Who told you," he said, in a choked voice, "who told you that there isn't a political purpose..."

"Oh yes! There's the eternal excuse of the gentlemen of Heidelberg when they do something cowardly..."

"Cowardly!"

"They claim," Roschen continued, calmly, "that they have a political purpose. And this woman, this Gretchen whom you've hired, whom you're directing–has she, too, a political purpose?"

"If you add one more word, Roschen," Wilhem said, interrupting as his fury mounted, "I'll kill you!"

Roschen released a cry of terror, and begged for mercy.

It is easy to understand what Monsieur de Nossac was going through during this dialogue–which, so to speak, tore away a corner of the mysterious veil that seemed to envelop the castle and his strange hosts. His indignation overflowed, however, when Wilhem threatened to kill Roschen, and he leapt off the bed excitedly, taking hold of his sword.

Immediately, whether by chance or because the noise he had made in quitting his bed had been heard in the neighboring room where Wilhem and Roschen were conversing, complete silence fell. Then a door opened, and a new voice resonated curtly and imperiously, speaking in the Slavonic language. "Hey, Wilhem," said the voice, which the Baron recognized as that of Samuel, Wilhem's twin brother, "when will you stop quarrelling–or, rather, pretending to quarrel–with Roschen... who is our sister and not your mistress, remember? Do you think that our guest hasn't heard you by now?"

"Oh, he must have!" Wilhem replied, jeeringly, in a low, almost stifled, tone. "He'll be jealous all night, poor Baron."

"And that's my bad faith," Roschen murmured, in a similarly low voice, "for he's noble and brave, my future husband, and you're treating him like a vile mercenary." She went on, laughing: "It must be confessed that my father has strange whims and very inflexible theories regarding bravery. No one other than the Baron would have been able to resist the terrible proofs to which he's been put."

"Which, it seems to me," Samuel continued, "implies no necessity for the bizarre dispute that Wilhem, who has been drinking all night, is inflicting on his ears. My God! To be able to sleep through the din you're making, he'd have to have spent 369 consecutive nights in a foxes' bazaar while the student king was being fêted there."

Wilhem laughed drunkenly.

"Let's go," Samuel added. "Go to bed, Wilhem. You come with me, Roschen–I'll escort you to your room."

"My little Samuel," Roschen murmured. "Can it be that your trickery with regard to my future spouse has not yet reached its end?"

"I certainly hope not!" Wilhem said. "I want to be sure–perfectly sure–that he's brave."

"You're drunk," Samuel said, sententiously, "and you're mixing in things that don't concern you. Go to bed, son of Noah, and sleep it off, if you can."

Monsieur de Nossac was dumbfounded by what he had heard. Which of the two flagrantly contradictory versions echoing in his ears was the truth?

Was it Wilhem's, calling Roschen a Heidelberg working-girl, and treating her in the cold-blooded fashion in which a student treats his mistress? In that case, it would be necessary to accept that the ingenuous smile and the virginal candor that shone from the young woman's face comprised an ignoble lie, a hideous antithesis, a disgusting paradox in action...

Or, on the other hand, was Samuel sincere in treating Wilhem as a drunk, and accusing him of wanting to excite the Baron's jealousy and put his love to the proof?

There were two reasons for Monsieur de Nossac to put his trust in Samuel's words. The first was that he could not, roué that he was and blasé as he was, bring himself to believe in Roschen's perversity, and see in her dignified manner, distinguished tone and frank noblewoman's gaze anything more than a working-girl from Heidelberg, apt to mangle her native language, to drink beer in broad daylight and to sip brandy from her lover's glass.

The second was even more reasonable. Wilhem and Roschen had spoken at first in French, proof that that they wanted to be understood. Samuel, on the contrary, had spoken in Slavonic, and Wilhem and Roschen had immediately switched into that language.

A long silence followed the altercation that had taken place between Roschen and her two brothers, and it became evident to the Baron that she had gone with them. He deemed it prudent to go back to bed, because he needed to reflect, to search for the solution and objective of all the mysteries surrounding him.

Among the extraordinary things that he had seen and heard, there were certainly some that might be rigorously explained–the story of the Black Huntsmen, the torch-lit hunt and so on. All that proved only one thing: the facetious humor of the master of Holdengrasburg. But what of Gretchen–which is to say, the late Hélène de Nossac, who had stolen Gretchen's clothes? Hélène, who, she claimed, had emerged from the tomb and covered 800 leagues on foot by night, sleeping every morning in a new cemetery, as a traveler stops every evening at the door of some hostelry–how could that be explained?

The Baron forgot about Roschen, Wilhem and their brothers for a moment, to think about the dead woman. In the same way that he had forgotten Gretchen while listening to the faint voices of Roschen and Wilhem resounding in the next room, he now resumed thinking about her, fixing his attention on his nocturnal memories with a desperate tenacity. With extreme care, he analyzed every sensation, and recalled every word that the dead woman had spoken, every detail of her incredible story. He ended up concluding that it really was his wife–the wife he had killed, and whom God had allowed to emerge from the tomb to torment her living spouse.

Suddenly, a strident voice became audible in the neighboring room, where he had heard Wilhem and his sister a little while before, singing the first verse of the ballad of the Black Huntsman. Then, when the verse ended, the same voice added: "Well, Milord Satan, my father, did I not play my role as castellan well yesterday? Are you not content with me? I extinguished the embers of my eyes and the gleam of my claws rather well, and—may God damn me if I'm not damned already!—if this petty Baron de Nossac does not believe me to be kneaded out of flesh and bone, like him..."

On hearing these strange words, the Baron thought that he was going mad, and he ran precipitately to the casement window, through whose panes the first light of the new-born day was filtering. He opened it and leaned out excitedly, as if to chase the terrors out of his mind. He wanted air and light—but he released a sudden cry of fright, and felt weak at the knees.

The grassland, the gardens, the forest and the village—the entirety of that ravishing landscape on to which his window opened, everything that he had seen the previous day—had disappeared, as if Satan himself had carried it away in a fold of his skeletal wing... and in its place, he saw nothing but a tormented, deserted, wild landscape, with a sinister torrent, a dark and silent forest on the horizon, and an uncultivated and desolate plain in between.

Satan had passed that way.

XVIII

In response to the Baron's cry, a door opened and the castellan of Holdengrasburg came in, with a friendly but slightly mocking smile on his lips.

"The Black Huntsman!" the Baron murmured.

"Finally!" cried the castellan, jovially. "Finally, my dear Baron, you're afraid!"

The Baron paled with anger. "Afraid!" he cried. "Me, afraid?"

"By the horns of Satan, my father, I believe so, my dear sir."

"Whoever you may be, mine host," replied Monsieur de Nossac, to whom the word afraid had restored all his self-assurance, "and whatever you may be, I call upon you to prove that I am afraid!"

"You released a cry just now that was charged with fear."

"You think so?"

"By God, yes!"

"Very well," said Monsieur de Nossac, "if uncertainty generated that fear, remove the uncertainty and show yourself to me in your true light, and you shall see whether I am still afraid! If you are Satan's son, say so–and then I shall fight you–me, a man, against you, a supernatural being! If you are a mere gentleman who amuses himself with trickery, say that instead, for I consider that these tricks have gone on too long, and my sword will put an end to them."

As he pronounced these words, Monsieur de Nossac leaned proudly on his sword, and looked the Huntsman in the face.

"My dear guest," the latter said, with a burst of laughter less mocking than benevolent, "I am in the wrong this time, and I humbly offer you my apologies. I ought to have restricted myself to yesterday's pleasantries and not renewed them today. If the apology is insufficient, my sword is at the service of yours."

"Ah!" said the Baron, coldly. "Have you not yet had enough of playing the role of castellan, Milord Satan?"

Another burst of laughter escaped the Graf. "You're mad!" he said. "I'm flesh and blood, like you."

"That's not what you said just now, though."

"Damn! So you believed that?"

"It seems to me," said Monsieur de Nossac, haughtily, "that it is quite believable."

"You think so?"

"Without a doubt. And for proof, I demand to know you what you have done with the countryside that was beneath my windows yesterday."

"Are you quite sure that it was beneath those windows?"

"Perfectly sure. I recognize the bed, the wall-hangings–everything, including that armchair on which I put my clothes when I went to bed."

"Very well," said the Graf. "Since you're as sure as that, come with me, and I'll convince you of the contrary."

He drew the Baron away. The Baron followed him, without a word. As he had on the previous day, the Graf von Holdengrasburg took his guest through several contiguous rooms and finally arrived in a bedroom, where he stopped.

"Look!" he said.

The Baron looked around in astonishment, and saw a room exactly similar to the one that he had occupied the previous night–and no less similar, in its size, furnishings and decorations, to the one that he had just left.

"You see," his host said, "that everything here is in the same order as it is over there. One thing alone is missing–your clothes. I took care to have them moved at the same time as you were transported, fast asleep, from one bed to the other. You sleep very heavily, Baron." As he spoke, the Graf von Holdengrasburg opened the window, and the Baron recognized his cheerful and picturesque landscape of the previous day: its flowery meadows, its shady gardens, its pretty village, its green forest. As on the previous day, he perceived a man and a woman walking beneath the castle walls, through thick grass still streaming with morning dew–except that it was not Roschen and Wilhem, but Gretchen and Hermann, her lover.

As on the previous day, the Baron shivered, and felt a cloud passing before his eyes. He was jealous of the dead woman, as if she were still living. "Monsieur," he said to the Graf, abruptly forgetting the hostile attitude he had adopted toward him, "are you quite sure that that woman is the mistress of your son Hermann?"

"Gretchen–but of course."

"Well, I assure that it is my own wife–my late wife–who has come back to torment me and to suckle at my neck every night."

"You're mad."

"No, I'm not mad; I'm in full possession of my reason, and I was not asleep last night. She came to me, moving slowly, as she had the previous night. She lay down beside me, and bit me, as on the previous night..."

"Hold on," said the Graf von Holdengrasburg. "The best proof I can offer you that she did not bite you is that the cut you made with the tip of your sword is half-healed this morning, and there is no other wound there."

"That's true," said the disconcerted Baron, having looked at himself in the mirror. "Nevertheless, everything I have told you is scrupulously exact."

"I doubt that."

"And if I were to repeat, word for word, the bizarre story she told me?"

"What story?"

Monsieur de Nossac, his eyes still fixed upon Hermann and Gretchen, who were leaning on one another with a voluptuous languor, related the tale of his wife's strange odyssey through the cemeteries of France and Germany, in a voice that was curt, jerky and punctuated by interruptions at every unusual movement of the two lovers.

"I bitterly regret my stupid jokes, Monsieur le Baron," said the Graf, mournfully, "They have definitely disturbed your mind to the point at which you're dreaming while awake."

Monsieur de Nossac looked at the Graf. The latter's face expressed profound pity–a commiseration so heartfelt that it could not be doubted. "Wait," he said. "I can convince you."

"We'll see."

"Do you know where Gretchen goes every day?"

"To the home of the parish priest."

"Are you sure of that?"

"Quite sure."

"You see, then, that I wasn't dreaming–that I really heard and saw–for neither your son nor you told me that detail, and yet I know it. You give her a horse, don't you?"

"Yes," said the astonished Graf.

"And she came here from Heidelberg on foot, as a beggar?"

"Yes, how did you know that?"

"I know many other things too," the Baron said, animatedly. "For example, you were by the fireside when she arrived. Hermann was embarrassed, and you asked her: 'Are you not frightened by the role you are to play?' "

"By my faith!" cried the Graf von Holdengrasburg. "You must be a sorcerer–and I'll end up believing in your vampires!"

While they were talking, the light had brightened, and dawn was fringing the blurred and bluish summits of the neighboring mountains with purple and opal.

"Hold on," said Monsieur de Nossac, leaning out of the window and drawing the Graf with him. "Look!"

Someone had just brought Gretchen a horse, and Gretchen had mounted it with the aid of Hermann's knee, after having given her lover a long kiss.

"Well," said the Graf, "what's extraordinary about that?"

"So you don't see anything yourself?"

"By my faith, no! It's Gretchen mounting her horse and going away. What do you expect? The woman is as proud as the true Bohemian she is. Hermann abandoned her; she followed him because she loved him, but she does not wish to eat his bread."

"And she's going to the priest's house?"

"Certainly."

"Very well! Me, I tell you that she's going to the cemetery."

"What foolishness!"

"Would you like to follow her with me?"

"I'd like that very much, my dear Baron, if only to convince you of your folly–but you're forgetting, alas, that I cannot."

"Why is that?"

"Because I am, from the viewpoint of the country, the terrible Black Huntsman. If some peasant were to encounter me at the village gates, he would not hesitate to say that he has seen the Black Huntsman without dying. That would do considerable damage to my reputation."

"Very well—I'll go alone."

"You're free to do so, but it's madness."

The Baron finished dressing in haste. Then, not wishing to listen to his host striving to prove to him that he was mad, he hurtled out of the room, descended the staircase and left the castle, with his sword in his hand. He ran to the path that Gretchen had just taken at a gentle trot.

The dead woman was riding at a leisurely pace between two florid hedges, seemingly breathing in the delightful aroma of the fields, with which the air was impregnated. The Baron walked behind her, shivering in spite of himself, not daring to catch up with her, even though it would have been easy for him to do so.

Suddenly, the dead woman—who appeared to be lost in a melancholy reverie—looked up questioningly at the eastern sky. Purple waves had succeeded the iridescent tint of opal, and the Sun was almost up. She seemed to understand that, and pressed her horse, which broke into a trot. In order not to lose sight of her the Baron had to break into a run. Within ten minutes, Gretchen and he had reached the village, she on horseback and he on foot.

Outside the village there was an enclosure of about a hundred square yards, surrounded by a hedge in full bloom, with clumps of cypresses planted here and there, sprinkled with black or white crosses, most of them devoid of inscriptions. This was the village cemetery.

The gate stood ajar, having not been locked overnight; the field of rest was open to all. Gretchen stopped at the gate, and got down slowly and stiffly from the horse. Then she consulted the sky again, which was increasingly tinted by the harbingers of the Sun. The Baron, who was close behind her, heard her murmur, with child-like joy: "Oh! I have time to gather flowers... I have the time!"

She released the horse–which, doubtless entirely accustomed to such freedom, went at a lively trot to a part of the meadow where the grass was lusher and more appetizing. Then she, in her turn, went to a little brook that ran babbling through the grass, knelt down awkwardly, and gathered a handful of forget-me-nots and blue convolvulus flowers. Afterwards, she went to the hedge and took a sprig of hawthorn therefrom.

A beam of light suddenly slid over the summit of a neighboring rock, and the opposite extremity of the valley reflected the first rays of the Sun. The dead woman released a cry, ran precipitately into the cemetery, fled to a small grove of fir-trees, into which she disappeared momentarily, then immediately reappeared, draped from head to toe in a white shroud–her own, doubtless, which she carefully hid every evening before going to the castle.

Monsieur de Nossac was still standing at the threshold of the cemetery, with sweat on his brow. He saw her go, thus clad, to a recently-dug grave and lie down in it, stretched out at full length. He felt his knees giving way beneath him. All of a sudden, though, the doubt that had assailed him so many times, and had led him so often to the conclusion that he was being tricked, took hold of him again, and he cried: "For the love of God, I must get to the bottom of this!"

He ran to the grave and halted abruptly.

The dead woman was immobile at the bottom of the grave, enveloped in her shroud, holding her flowers in her clenched fist. No breath lifted her bosom; no movement indicated that she had been walking just a short while before. Death had reclaimed her... She would sleep until nightfall.

The Baron bent down to take hold of a corner of the shroud and lift it up, but terror suddenly took hold of him and he went to lean on a nearby cypress, pale and near to fainting...

XIX

If Monsieur de Nossac was not always master of a re-flexive reaction of terror, at least he was easily able to famil-iarize himself with the terror in question. He leaned against the trunk of the cypress, almost fainting, for a moment, but soon collected himself. Making a violent effort, he returned to the edge of the grave and bent down again.

This time, he had the courage to take hold of a fold of the shroud, lift it up, and gaze attentively at the face of the dead woman. That face was pale, immobile, mute, like the true face of death that it was. Not a muscle twitched, no mysterious fluctuation of blood appeared to have taken place in the net-work of blue and swollen veins that extended capriciously beneath her fine translucent skin. Monsieur de Nossac studied her for a long time; then he grew bolder and, setting his knees on the ground, extended his arm and touched her face with his hand. It was as cold as the hand that the dead woman had placed in his two days before, and as the kiss she had given him the night before.

Becoming even bolder, the Baron then took his sword and pricked the cadaver's breast with its point. Blood immedi-ately sprang forth, pink, fresh and translucent, small droplets of which reached the shroud and marbled its dazzling white-ness with red stains. The dead woman did not flinch, and her blood continued to flow in a trickle.

Monsieur de Nossac was quite convinced that it could not be a trick of some comedy, that he really was dealing with a dead woman, and that the blood that he had just spilled was his own, which had been taken the preceding night. He imag-ined that, on the following night, the vampire would be even more exacting for having lost blood from its veins, and that he would end up dying of the continual loss, from which he had neither the will nor the strength to preserve himself.

Once his mind had accepted this reasoning, he was ashamed and regretful of what he had just done. He leaned over the cadaver again and put his finger on the wound while he searched for a means of bandaging it. This means he found, in the shape of his handkerchief, which he knotted securely to a corner of the shroud, and which he wound around the dead woman like a girdle.

When he had finished, he intended to get up, but he perceived that the dead woman's blood had run over his hands; he was afraid, and his hair bristled. He took a corner of the shroud and wiped it away. In taking that corner, though, he shifted the cadaver, and the dead woman's clenched lips parted. It seemed to the Baron that she was about to speak and say to him: "You are a blasphemer!" Then he felt himself being seized by that vertiginous numbness, that strange paralysis, which overcame him every night at the hour when the vampire was accustomed to arrive, and he shivered at the thought that he might be constrained to lie down in the grave and fall asleep–into that leaden slumber which took hold on him on the departure of his nocturnal visitor–side by side with her in the cemetery.

The Baron's terror became so intense that he made a supreme and heroic effort, stood upright on his stiff, near-frozen legs, and leapt out of the grave.

The first two steps he took were terrible; it seemed that an invincible force of attraction nailed him to that cadaver and to that yawning tomb–but finally, when those two steps had been taken, the paralysis diminished. He drew away, less slowly, then began to walk more rapidly. Eventually, he was able to run, and threw himself outside the cemetery gate with the celerity of fear, which nothing else can equal.

At the threshold of the cemetery, however, a young woman was standing, pale and tremulous with emotion. It was Roschen: Roschen, to whom her pallor and emotion lent even more grace and charm; Roschen, dazzlingly beautiful, her eyes full of a vague and delicate sadness, her mouth pleated by a bitter smile, with a hand on her heart as if to stifle its precipitate pulsation.

At the sight of her, the Baron cried out. "You, here, Roschen!" he murmured.

She took a step towards him, took him by the hand and said to him: "I'm risking my life in following you here, but that's not important... I have to speak to you."

"Oh, speak!" murmured Monsieur de Nossac, gazing at her admiringly and experiencing the rebirth of that love–spontaneously generated, but threatened several times over by Gretchen's strange and fatal ascendancy–which overwhelmed him entirely.

"Not here!" she said, in alarm.

"Why?"

"The dead are too near. Come..." And she drew him away.

As we have already said, the forest was close by. A sunken path, bordered by a burgeoning hedge as tall as a man, led directly to it, without overmuch possibility of anyone following it being seen, either from the castle or from the village. Roschen took it at a rapid pace, still holding the Baron by the hand.

As they went forward, the wan daylight that lit the forest became darker and darker. Soon, Roschen paused in the middle of a sort of clearing, where rocks formed a natural semicircular bench.

"Let's sit here," Roschen said.

The Baron sat beside her. Roschen turned her head to the right and the left, inspecting their surroundings with minute and prudent circumspection. "Are we really alone?" she murmured.

"Yes," the Baron replied, having looked around in his turn.

"Oh! It's just that if anyone were to hear us..."

"What?"

"He would kill me,"

"Who?" roared the Baron.

"Him!" she said, fearfully.

"Who's him?"

"Wilhem!"

The Baron tapped his foot on the ground in a sudden fit of temper. "Always this Wilhem," he murmured. "Always him."

The Baron's voice had taken on a tone so harsh that Roschen shivered, and her hand trembled in Monsieur de Nossac's. She opened her mouth to speak, but emotion choked her; she could only raise a supplicatory gaze to the Baron: a gaze that signified: "Spare me! For I love you..."

Scarcely sensible of that gaze, however, the Baron replied with the same irritation: "What is that man to you, then, and what fatal influence does he have over our destiny, that you should start at his name and tremble on hearing his voice?"

Roschen did not reply, and lowered her eyes.

"Tell me, Roschen," Monsieur de Nossac continued, "that the terrible words I heard a few hours ago–those infernal words which made me doubt the goodness of God, the virtue of women, and the candor of your smile–tell me..."

Roschen let out a stifled cry, let herself fall to the Baron's feet, and murmured: "Forgive me... I am entirely culpable."

Monsieur de Nossac felt his reason totter, his heart fail, his body grow weak. "It was true, then?" he murmured.

"Yes," Roschen said, in a faint voice.

"Then... you're not his sister?"

Roschen shook her head.

"But you're..." He stopped; she had thrown him an eloquent and suppliant glance.

"This marriage, then..." he went on.

"A lie!"

"But that's infamous!" cried the Baron, beside himself.

"Oh," said Roschen, "I know very well how infamous it is–but what do you expect? I was a poor working-girl in Heidelberg. Wilhem seduced me with a promise of marriage.

135

Wilhem had obtained a terrible empire over me; he dominated me completely. He left with Hermann, Conrad and old Berghausen..."

"Who is this Berghausen?"

"The one you call the Black Huntsman."

"So he isn't the father of Wilhem and his brothers?"

"No. Wilhem has only one brother–Samuel."

"And the two others?"

"They're students–friends of theirs."

"But this... Berghausen...?"

"He's an old student, in his 30th year."

"So this castle isn't his?"

"No."

"Whose is it, then?"

"I don't know."

"A mystery!" murmured the Baron. "A strange mystery!"

"Yes, yes," Roschen relied, shivering. "All five of them obey this Gretchen, God confound her! This Gretchen, be she dead or living–I don't know anything... but she exercises a strange influence over everyone... including you..." Her voice choked as she finished.

The Baron shuddered. "Over me?" he said, astonished.

"Oh yes!" Roschen went on, heatedly. "Over you...You love her..."

"No!" he exclaimed, forcefully.

Roschen released a cry of joy. "Are you telling the truth?" she said, joining her hands together.

"Yes," the Baron murmured. "It's you that I loved..."

Roschen lowered her head. "But you love me no longer?" she said, with an indescribable emotion.

"You belong to Wilhem!" the Baron replied, darkly.

Roschen released a feeble cry–a cry of stifled distress–spread her arms wide, stiffened and felt on to the grass, almost swooning. "I loved you so much...!" she said

That cry and its tone went straight to the Baron's heart, touching him profoundly.

"What if I loved you still?" he asked.

"Is that true? You're not lying to me?" she cried. "Isn't it only pity that draws those words from you?"

Monsieur de Nossac took the young woman's pale and quivering head in his hands, kissed it ardently, and repeated: "Roschen... I love you!"

"Very well," she said to him. "If you love me, follow me!"

"What do you mean?"

"Take me away from Wilhem, for Wilhem loves me, and will kill me. Take me far away from him, for I no longer love him, because I've been horrified by him since I saw you... since I fell in love with you!" Roschen got to her knees, pleadingly. "Take me away," she repeated, "And I will love you so much that you will forget that I once belonged to another, that I was a poor girl, a University working-girl!"

"I shall forget it," Monsieur de Nossac said.

"And you forgive me, don't you?" she said, taking his hands.

"Yes," he replied, giving her a second kiss.

"You forgive me for having participated in that infamous comedy of which you were the victim?"

"Yes, yes... but let's go!" cried Monsieur de Nossac.

"Oh, not now!" said Roschen. "But tonight..."

"Why?"

"I'll make all the preparations for our flight."

Monsieur Nossac felt himself shiver at a sudden thought. "The vampire will come," he murmured.

"Well," said Roschen, whose eyes flared, "if it comes..."

"Well?" the Baron queried.

"You'll run it through with your sword..."

"I won't be able to... It fascinates me..."

"This evening, at supper, throw away the last glass of wine that is poured for you."

This advice illuminated the Baron's mind.

"I understand everything now," he said, "and I shall avenge myself!"

"Silence!" Roschen said to him, suddenly. "Be quiet!" Listen!"

A voice was audible in the distance, calling: "Roschen! Roschen!"

It was Wilhem's voice.

XX

Roschen pressed herself against the Baron, pale and trembling.

"I'm afraid!" she murmured.

"There's nothing to fear–I'm with you."

"Oh, he'll kill me...!"

Monsieur de Nossac had a magnificent smile. "Only if I let him," he said, putting his hand on his sword-hilt.

"Roschen! Roschen!" repeated the voice, which seemed to have a hint of anger in it.

"Wait," said Roschen. "The wisest course is for us to separate."

"Already, child?"

She put her little hands on the Baron's shoulders, and smiled at him softly. "Shall we not be reunited tomorrow?"

"Oh, yes, certainly," he murmured, with the enthusiasm of love.

"We'll flee far away, won't we, my beloved?"

"Yes, my child."

"We'll rejoin the French army; we'll go to your homeland. I'll follow you everywhere, as a dog follows its master and a shadow its body..."

"Roschen! Roschen!" repeated the voice, for the third time. "Roschen, where are you?" This time the voice was furious, jealous, implacable.

Roschen grew pale. "Adieu!" she said. "If he comes this far, hide yourself, or pretend to be unconscious..."

They gave one another a long kiss, and she fled–but she had gone scarcely ten paces when she came back. "Don't forget... this evening... don't drink your last glass of wine... and kill her!"

"Yes," said Monsieur de Nossac, becoming pensive.

"When the hour of departure is nigh, I'll warn you. I'll have horses ready saddled; you'll only have to get dressed, and we'll go. Adieu."

She disappeared.

It was in the nick of time. Scarcely had the sound of her footsteps died away in the depths of the thicket when a noise made itself heard from the opposite direction, and Wilhem suddenly emerged into the clearing, where the Baron remained, feigning complete insensibility in accordance with Roschen's advice. Wilhem stopped at the sight of him, stupefied.

"Oh!" he said. "I'm beginning to believe that, brave as he is, our man has been greatly afraid for two days, and that instead of following Gretchen to the cemetery, he was seized by such a panic that he came to roll in the grass here, like a man who really had seen the Black Huntsman."

He approached the Baron, and shook him quite violently.

"For the love of God!" Wilhem murmured. "We're certainly going to kill him, but not for a while, and he mustn't die today."

Wilhem ran to a little stream that was running through the grass a few paces away, caught some water in the hollow of his conjoined hands, and came back to throw it in the Baron's face.

The Baron deemed that Wilhem was sufficiently convinced of his unconsciousness for him not to be obliged to prolong it indefinitely, and opened his eyes as the water made contact.

"Hello, guest," said Wilhem, cheerfully. "What are you doing here?"

"I was asleep," Monsieur de Nossac replied, heroically.

"What sort of sleep, if you please?"

"What do you mean, what sort of sleep?"

"Was it fatigue or terror, of course?"

"Terror?" said Monsieur de Nossac, disdainfully.

"Of course–you were sleeping very deeply."

"You think so?"

"Oh, I'm sure of it–I shook you vigorously."

"Then I must have slept badly the night before."

"Nonsense! Be honest, guest."

"I am."

"You've experienced some new trickery on the part of my honored father, Graf von Holdengrasburg, and fright overcame you–so you fled here, where you fell unconscious,"

"Oh well," said Monsieur de Nossac, feigning utter carelessness. "That's true–I admit it."

"Well, if there's one thing of which I'm sure," Wilhem said, "it's that I'll quarrel with my father if he continues his ridiculous practical, jokes."

"Me too!" cried Monsieur de Nossac. "I'll demand satisfaction from him."

"Tut tut! Calm down, my dear guest, please, and come with me."

"Where are we going?"

"To the castle, where breakfast awaits us."

"So much the better," said the Baron. "I'm hungry."

"And then we'll mount up and chase a red deer... we haven't hunted for two days."

"Will Gretchen be there?"

"I don't know. It's possible."

"Personally, I maintain the contrary."

"Why, if you please?"

"Because Gretchen is lying in her coffin in the cemetery–because I've seen her with my own eyes... and pricked her with my sword."

Wilhem shivered.

"And because," the Baron continued, "whatever anyone might say, she really is dead, and is a frightful vampire who has taken it upon herself to suck me and devour me every night, one drop of blood at a time."

"What madness!"

"Be incredulous–it doesn't matter. I know perfectly well what I've seen. I know what terror took hold of me, and made me flee to that place where you found me unconscious."

"You've been the victim of a hallucination."

"I swear to you that I have not."

"And I don't believe you... but come to breakfast." And he took the Baron's arm in a familiar manner.

At that contact, Monsieur de Nossac felt a start of anger, and he was tempted to squeeze Wilhem in his arms, to crush him to his breast, and to sink his sword to the hilt in the bosom of this man who had made love to Roschen...

Fortunately, the Baron had begun to comprehend that someone was making mock of him, and even had designs on his life, and he judged it prudent to contain himself.

They arrived at the castle, where Wilhem perceived Roschen in the gardens. He ran to her, saying: "Where have you been?"

"Into the forest," Roschen said.

Wilhem's forehead furrowed momentarily under the pressure of a suspicion, but the suspicion vanished immediately when Roschen added: "I went to see Werner, the woodcutter."

"To table, Baron, to table!" cried the distant voice of Hermann, who was running forward.

"And afterwards, to horse!" added Conrad.

"Well?" said the Graf von Holdengrasburg, taking Monsieur de Nossac aside.

"I was not mistaken. I saw her in the cemetery."

"You're mad!"

"Not at all, I swear to you." And the Baron repeated to the Graf what he had told Wilhem. The castellan shook his head doubtfully. Nevertheless, he added in a low voice: "I must get to the bottom of this."

"That's simple," the Baron said. "I'll take you there."

"No, not today–but tomorrow, we'll both follow her."

"So be it," said Monsieur de Nossac, negligently.

"By the way," said Hermann, arriving just then, "I asked that scamp Gretchen to come with us today."

"And?" the Graf asked, darting a significant glance at Monsieur de Nossac."

"She refused."

"Why is that?"

"Because she claimed that she was not in the habit of hunting all day without eating."

"What about the meal at the halt?"

"You know very well, father, that Gretchen is proud, and doesn't want to eat our bread."

"That's right. Oh well, to horse! We'll do without her."

XXI

The Baron and his hosts mounted their horses, and the tally-ho was sounded.

"Isn't Roschen coming, then?" Samuel asked Wilhem.

"No," said Wilhem, in an ill-humored manner.

"Why not?"

"Because I've forbidden her to."

Samuel shrugged his shoulders. "You're a despot to that child," he said.

"You think so?"

"More than that–I'm indignant about it."

William arched an eyebrow. "I'm jealous," he said.

"Imbecile!"

"I fear that she doesn't love me."

"Idiot that you are, Wilhem! Your stupid jealousy will end up betraying us. and all will be lost."

"Well, what does that matter?"

"It matters a great deal to us all, idiot! If we don't play our parts to the end, we're ruined. We have so little credit, and so much need of money!"

"Shush!" said Wilhem, pointing to the Baron, whose horse was drawing closer to theirs, little by little.

They parted.

The hunt was magnificent; the stag was cornered in eight hours. The horses, dogs and beaters performed marvelously, and Monsieur de Nossac surrendered himself to his hunter's instincts, telling himself that there would be time after the return for thoughts of Roschen and their means of flight.

The return was effected towards nightfall. The hunters found supper served and Roschen awaiting them in the dining-room.

Roschen found an opportunity to draw near to the Baron. "All will be ready," she said, furtively.

The supper was joyful. They joked with the Baron without acrimony; they mocked vampires–but not a word was said about Gretchen, either by the Graf von Holdengrasburg or by Monsieur de Nossac.

"Baron," said the Graf, as the supper drew to its close, "we'll empty, according to our custom, a flagon of Malvoisie.[42] Hold out your glass."

The ancient and dusty bottle was uncorked, and the Baron held out his glass. But at the moment when each of the diners lifted his elbow, he threw the contents of his glass under the table surreptitiously. No one saw him do it, except Roschen and a newcomer who had appeared on the threshold. This was Gretchen.

Gretchen raised an eyebrow and directed a penetrating glance at Roschen–whose eyes were furtively lowered–and her lips pursed in an expression of terrible hatred.

"Why, here's Gretchen." cried everyone.

Gretchen came in and bowed, with a broad and charming smile–but she was as pale as ever, and her slightly stiff gait betrayed the last vestiges of the torpor from which she had emerged.

Monsieur de Nossac shuddered at the sight of her, and felt his eyes drawn towards her, glued to that pale visage by an invincible and mysterious force. He did not, however, experience–as he had the previous night–that sudden numbness that had taken hold of him immediately after supper. Desirous in his turn, however, of making himself master of the situation by a ruse, he feigned tiredness and asked if he might retire.

As he passed close to Roschen, she gripped his hand furtively and said to him: "I will come to wake you... and if the vampire comes..." She stopped, surreptitiously darted a hateful and jealous glance at Gretchen, and concluded: "Kill her!"

The Baron shivered, and did not reply. But when he was in his room and had gone to bed, he began to reflect, and admitted to himself that he was the dupe of a terrible hoax, on which Roschen's revelations had cast much light. He arrived at the conclusion that Gretchen was an adventuress who was playing the role of his wife, hired by some personal enemy that he must have made, as everyone did. Having arrived at this conclusion, he sat up, making sure that his sword was in his hand, and said to himself:

"I am no longer in the mood to be made to suffer from nightmares and bitten by a false vampire."

He waited for a long time, but no one came.

Hours went by, and the Baron ended up falling asleep, clutching the hilt of his sword to his breast. Suddenly, though, he awoke with a start. The door opened and creaked on its hinges, even though it had been pushed very carefully, and the Baron saw a white form outlined in the midst of the darkness. At that sight, although he was still half-asleep, the Baron sat up straight, and drew his sword-hilt forcefully against his breast, as if he were in need of reinforcing his courage.

He had gone to sleep telling himself that Gretchen was nothing but a wretched girl in the pay of one of his enemies– but with the aid of sleep, his terrors regarding vampires had returned, and when he saw that white form marching towards his bed, he felt his hair stand on end. However, as he had not drunk his last glass of wine, he was in perfect command of his body and free of that paralytic numbness that had over-whelmed him on the preceding nights.

The further the white form advanced, the more the Baron's thoughts accelerated. Gretchen, woman though she was, had become a vampire again, and he hated and loved that vampire at the same time. He felt simultaneously attracted and repulsed, fascinated and irritated by her. He felt towards Gretchen, be she woman or vampire, an inexplicable and extremely violent sexual attraction–a sexual attraction that seemed unnatural, revolting him and rendering him intoxicated with fury, which was converted into hatred by the slightest reflection on his part.

He was, therefore, delivered to a terrible inner conflict by the appearance of the phantom–a struggle between his heart and his mind, which lasted ten centuries in two seconds. The heart was attracted, welcoming Gretchen with open arms; the mind confused and intoxicated him, murmuring in his ear: "Kill her!"

Throughout this struggle, he gripped his word convulsively, and felt the sweat of anguish and fear running slowly and coldly down his cheeks.

As for the phantom–which, the previous night, had opened the door noiselessly and marched towards the bed with stiff assurance, it had modified its gait oddly. The door had opened cautiously, and it had left it ajar. It advanced on tiptoe, stopping occasionally, listening anxiously, apparently timid and uncertain in its course, as if it were a stranger unaccustomed to the darkness and the disposition of the apartment, fearful of bumping into some hard-edged item of furniture at some unexpected angle.

Finally, the white form reached the bed, reached out its arms, and silently put them around the Baron.

The Baron extended his arms in his turn, and–shivering but determined, dominated by a feverish and vertiginous force–he cleaved the phantom's breast with a furious thrust of his sword.

The mind had vanquished the heart!

The phantom released a cry of pain, and collapsed in a heap with a gasp. That cry made the Baron shiver. Suddenly sober, he threw himself out of the bed.

"Gretchen! Gretchen!" he howled.

"It's not Gretchen..." murmured the phantom, in a faint voice.

The Baron cried out; his cry, joined with the one that had escaped the phantom's punctured breast, presumably woke the hosts of the manor of Holdengrasburg with a start. While Monsieur de Nossac bent down, breathless and beside himself, over the white form gasping at the foot of his bed, the doors opened and a faint light suddenly penetrated the apartment. Samuel and Wilhem came in, half-dressed, pale and shivering. In response to the light of the candles they were carrying, the Baron released a cry of despair and furious madness.

That form was not the vampire at all. It was not Gretchen the dead woman, the blood-sucker. It was Roschen!–Roschen, who had come, at two o'clock in the morning, to wake her lover and say to him: "Come...a saddled horse awaits us at the drawbridge."

After the Baron, it was the turn of Wilhem and Samuel to recognize Roschen and release a terrible cry of mournful exclamation.

Roschen was not yet dead. Her breath caught in her throat. Her eyes turned toward the Baron with sublime resignation. She wore an ineffable smile of forgiveness, which seemed to say to him: "All this is my fault, and I have killed myself–you mistook me for her."

Then, as the seconds were precious–because, before the demanding and furnishing of explanations, it was necessary above all to try to prevent fleeting life from escaping the unfortunate child's lips–the three men simultaneously bent over the dying Roschen. One of them supported her pale head; another staunched the blood that was flowing from her gaping wound with his handkerchief; the third threw himself out of the apartment, calling for help. That third was Samuel.

Wilhem and the Baron, two beings who hated one another instinctively, had silenced their hatred as they found themselves together, crouching over that unfortunate young woman, uniting their efforts and abilities to hold rapidly-approaching death at bay.

Samuel, meanwhile, had woken Conrad and Hermann, who were medical students and who made what haste they could. They arrived too late. Roschen had just expired, her hand in the Baron's, murmuring to him: "I love you."

Wilhem and the Baron both came slowly to their feet, pale, mute and overwhelmed. Their eyes had been glued to Roschen's discolored and contorted face for some time, but the arrival of Samuel and the two students interrupted that dolorous contemplation. Then they each took a step back and stared at one another, silently, coldly and menacingly.

The Baron, sensing the aggression of which he was the object, put his hand on the hilt of his sword.

Wilhem did likewise. "Monsieur," he said, "I don't know why, and by what strange fatality, you have just murdered the being I loved more than any in the world. I don't know how and why I find this woman in your room, at the foot of your bed, at two o'clock in the morning. I ought to be demanding terrible explanations from you–but I'm thirsty for your blood, and I would lose time I cannot spare. En garde, Monsieur."

And Wilhem, standing up straight, threw back his adolescent head, drew his sword and waited. The wait was brief, for Monsieur de Nossac drew immediately, without saying a word, and adopted the defensive position.

The Baron fenced like a pupil of the late Regent, Wilhem like a German student–which is to say, with an impetuosity, absence of calculation and promptitude of thrust and riposte that disconcerts an unskilled opponent, but causes a man of self-assurance and skill to smile.

If Monsieur de Nossac had fought a normal duel with Wilhem–which is to say, a combat separated from the challenge by a night's rest–or if he had not been able to see Roschen's corpse in front of him, or if his eyes, as they were lowered, had not encountered the red pool that his victim's blood had formed on the floor-tiles, Wilhem would have been a dead man. But the Baron was distressed and desperate; sweat was running down his forehead. He had a cloud before his eyes and a wall of ice around his heart. His self-assurance had fled; despair guided his arm, and he piled error upon error. Twice his sword, aimed at Wilhem's breast, barely grazed the young man's arm; twice he was struck by his opponent, and his blood stained his shirt, mingling with Roschen's.

Conrad, Hermann and Samuel were mute witnesses to this mortal combat.

Finally, Wilhem, profiting from a mistake, lunged with all his might. His blade struck the Baron's breast and was buried there to the hilt. The Baron released a stifled cry, spread his arms wide, staggered back and fell supine upon Roschen's corpse, dragging the sword embedded in his torso with him.

Wilhem then put his foot on his adversary, and drew out his sword. The flesh had already closed up on the wound.

"I am avenged!" he said.

Suddenly, the door opened, and Gretchen appeared on the threshold, pale, imperious and with eyes ablaze. She paused for a moment, madly, as if thunderstruck by the sight of the spectacle before her eyes. Then she knelt down by the Baron's body with a disquiet that could not be feigned, put her hand on his heart, examined the wound with the minute attention of a surgeon, assured herself that the Baron was still alive, and bandaged the wound. Afterwards, coming suddenly to her feet, with her lips pursed and her eyes burning, she studied the murderer and his three companions with supreme disdain and terrible anger. Pointing imperiously to the door, she said: "I've paid you. Now get out, and go as far away from here as the Earth can bear you!"

Three of them obeyed without saying a word, but Wilhem took a purse full of gold from his pocket, threw it at Gretchen's feet, and said: "You've killed my mistress with your infernal jokes and your subterranean purpose, which none of us has ever understood. Your gold is useless to me, since the woman I love is no more. Take it back–I want nothing from you."

He knelt over Roschen's cadaver and shed two burning tears, which fell upon the young girl's death-whitened cheek. Then he got up and took a step toward the door–but, as if he were too regretful and remorseful to leave the young girl's corpse in Gretchen's hands, he returned to it, took it in his arms and carried it away on his shoulder, like the most precious of treasures.

XXII

Terrible as it was, Monsieur de Nossac's wound was not mortal. When he regained consciousness, despite the fact that the terrible fever that burned in him, he was able to see that Roschen's corpse had disappeared, that the students were no longer in the room, and that he had been put back into his bed. At the head of the bed, sitting in a large armchair, a woman was preparing a dressing. The woman was Gretchen.

The Baron recognized her, and delirium took hold of him, instantly precipitating him into the fantastic and terrible world in which the imagination takes refuge when the body is injured and incapable of action. How long that delirium lasted the Baron never knew, but through the mists of the fever, in his rare moments of lucidity, he saw Gretchen, ceaselessly at his bedside...an anxious, attentive Gretchen, preparing all his potions and remedies herself, dressing his wound, sometimes planting a kiss on his forehead, sometimes smiling at him hopefully, putting up a camp-bed in his room every night, getting up 20 times a night to take his sweating hands in hers, to check the intensity of his fever and the rapidity of his pulse, the state of his maddened brain full of visions. And during the long, confused and clouded life of his malady, during that dolorous agony when Death approached so frequently, but always withdrew again, one single dominant and tenacious thought absorbed his mind and the vestiges of reason that occasionally returned to him.

That thought was that he loved Gretchen.

Finally, the fever diminished. The delirium disappeared, to be succeeded by sleep–and one morning, on awakening, the Baron found his room empty. Gretchen had disappeared.

Where was she?

Feeble as he was, the Baron had strength enough to get up and go as far as a table, on which he perceived a piece of paper folded in quarters. He opened it precipitately and read:

You are out of danger and I am leaving you. I wanted to amuse myself and profit by a strange resemblance. Forgive me the terrible drama that took place at my instigation. You will never see me again, so I will make you a confession: I love you. Adieu.

Gretchen Walkenaer

The Baron re-read the letter several times. Then, transported by love and the residue of is delirium, he threw himself out of the room and ran through the semi-denuded castle, finding it deserted.

At the gate was a horse, ready saddled, in whose saddle-bag he found his purse. The Baron had strength enough to put his feet in the stirrups and urge the horse forward, saying: "I must find Gretchen, if I have to go to the ends of the Earth."

And he set off in the direction of Heidelberg.

XXIII

Monsieur de Nossac arrived in Heidelberg, inquired everywhere as to the residence of Gretchen Walkenaer, and eventually found it. Instead of Gretchen, however, he only encountered an old tailor who, in response to his question, replied: "My daughter Gretchen has been dead and buried for two months." It was exactly two months, if the vampire's narrative was to be believed, since the late Hélène de Nossac had stolen the clothes of Gretchen, dead like her, and set off for the manor of Holdengrasburg.

All this was so extraordinary that Monsieur de Nossac wanted to convince himself of the tailor's veracity. He obtained, not without difficulty, an order for Gretchen's exhumation. He recognized his vampire readily enough, but the unhappy tailor cried out: "Someone has stolen her linen dress. her shroud and her golden cross!"

"Wasn't your daughter the mistress of a student named Hermann?" asked the distraught Baron.

"Never!" replied the indignant old man.

"That's strange!" murmured Monsieur de Nossac. "I'm beginning to believe that I'm mad!"

And he fled, bewildered–as if he wanted to justify the suspicion that he had just expressed as to the state of his reason.

Part Two

XXIV

"Have you consulted a physician, my dear Baron," said the Marquis de Simiane, after having listened gravely to his friend, the Baron de Nossac, who had just told him the strangest story.

"No. Why?"

"Because you appear to me to have gone mad."

"That's what I've begun to believe, Marquis. There are certain moments when, to tell the truth, I can't tell whether everything that happened to me might not have been a dream."

"For myself, I'm entirely persuaded of that."

Suddenly, Monsieur de Nossac struck his forehead. "Weren't you wounded a few months ago," he said, "in the vicinity of Heidelberg?"

"Yes. What of it?"

"And weren't you cared for by a student named Hermann von Holdengrasburg?"

"Indeed–a very clever chap, from a rather good family."

"Then you've seen his mistress–this Gretchen who resembled my wife so strongly."

"Not at all. Hermann had no mistress."

"I can't make head nor tail of it," murmured the Baron.

"There's the rub. And you weren't able to find this phantom–this vampire, which, after sucking your blood, converted itself into a nurse to care for you?"

"No," said the Baron, sadly. "I've searched everywhere. I've been scouring Germany, and Europe entire, for three months–three months of which I was hardly conscious, lost in a waking dream... three months of suffering... oh!" The Baron interrupted himself, placing his hand on his heart. "I suffered so much..."

"Idiot," said the Marquis. "We've had too many intimate suppers together, spent too many mad nights and run through too many back alleys for you to be carried away by some petty vulgar passion like some student, novice priest or schoolboy."

Monsieur de Nossac shrugged his shoulders. "My dear chap," he said, "love is like those American apples, so prettily-colored, so silkily smooth, which can keep a child busy for a whole day, throwing it from hand to hand–but if he has the misfortune to bite into one, it kills him. I have played with love all my life, but I took it seriously for a minute, and I have poisoned everything that remains to me."

"Nonsense!" said the Marquis. "There's an antidote to that poison."

"Which is?"

"To fall in love with someone else."

"I won't be able to..."

"Try."

"Madness!"

"And in the meantime, moreover, you've been a widower for nearly 18 months. If two years expires, your wife's fortune reverts to her heirs."

"I'm well aware of that. What does it matter to me?"

"My dear Baron," said the Marquis, with philosophical disdain, "persuade yourself of this: of all the incurable evils, the worst is poverty. It is difficult to cure. You were lucky the first time, and avoided the claws of your creditors with a certain skill. Believe me, don't test your luck any further. Luck is like women–it turns with every gust of wind."

"What do you want me to do, then?"

"To get married, of course."

154

"To whom? How?" the Baron murmured, with profound discouragement in his voice.

"My dear Baron," the Marquis went on, "there are three kinds of marriages for gentlemen like us. The first is the marriage of convenience—which is to say, a quite respectable and thoroughly tedious combination of people of similar rank, birth and fortune. That is out of bounds when we are slightly ruined, as you and I are. To regild one's escutcheon and provide hay for one's horses, one marries the daughter of a peasant, who brings you a fortune tucked into her chemise, whose father addresses you as Monsieur my son-in-law and detests you cordially, thinking that he is obliged to pay dearly for the honor of having you in his family. The third is the marriage of inclination. That is *ad libitum*; one takes one's wife from some country seat tottering in the wind, from the wings of the Opéra or the road to Porcherons—it hardly matters! No one will care or find fault with it. Now, the first is out of bounds to you for all sorts of reasons; you have made the second, and that furnishes you with the means to make the third. You are rich enough for your wife to have the right to be poor."

"Undoubtedly," murmured the Baron, in a tone that signified: What does any of this matter to me?

"However," the Marquis de Simiane went on, "it's necessary to make haste, my dear. In six months, if you haven't taken a wife, you'll be the poorest gentleman in France and Navarre."

"What does that matter to me?" the Baron said again, shrugging his shoulders.

"Even so," Simiane continued. "If I were to show you, in some corner of Paris or the provinces, a girl with the prettiest face imaginable—18 years old, ash-blonde, with the feet of a Chinawoman, the eyes of a virgin, and poor enough to become mad with love..."

The Baron raised his head.

"She's poor, you say?" he said

"Oh, I guarantee it. She spins yarn all night to support her old father."

"She's one of the common people, then?"

"On the contrary–the nobility, of ancient stock, for the love of God! But you know the proverb: great name, threadbare cloak! The father's taken 17 bullets, and hasn't enough pistoles to stop up the holes." [43]

"There's a poverty that smells sweet, having its own chivalric perfume, Marquis."

"Wait, my dear chap, that's not all. Last year, a tax-farmer arrived in his golden cart at the gates of our country seat. Actually, I shouldn't say country seat, for it's a fine old crusader's castle, with a rusty drawbridge, a muddy moat, mossy towers and a tottering belfry. The wind leads an infernal dance under the doors and through the corridors, the tapestries are hanging in tatters, the woodwork is rotting and the escutcheons have a venerable coat of condensed smoke heartily thickened through the centuries. And in the midst of that wretchedness, Baron, there is an old châtelain who would confront you with the lordly attitude that only the boldest possess, and a young châtelaine who has the poses and the gait of a queen. Then there are also three servants who no longer receive wages, who work even so to support their masters and have never lost the profound respect that vassals once had for their liege-lord. They are courtiers of misfortune in the most complete sense of the term. And finally, a young man–the châtelain's nephew, an orphan, the most handsome boy on Earth, a child of 18 or 20, as slim and blond as his cousin..."

"Ah!" said the Baron, arching an eyebrow. "She's in love with him, of course."

"No," replied the Marquis. "At least, I don't think so. He's applied for the guards, and doesn't give much thought to love."

"No more than you give, my dear, to the tax-farmer about whom you were started talking, but abandoned in order to give me a long description of the manor and its occupants."

"That's true. Let's get back to the tax-farmer. So, the peasant came to the castle gate one autumn evening. It was cold; the Sun was setting in a grey shroud stained with bloody wounds; the wind was sighing in the leafless hedges and brambles; the icy ground hadn't thawed out all day. The tax-farmer was warmly wrapped up in his Russian headgear, the windows of his *berline* were carefully closed and his feet were in a foot-muff. Even so, he felt chilly whenever a gust of cold wind got in, and his afflicted eyes were searching for some lodging appropriate to his importance when he perceived the grey towers of the manor.

"He ordered his driver to halt, and the *berline* stopped at the end of the drawbridge. Then, as the drawbridge had been lowered for a century or so, he crossed it and entered the courtyard. In response to the noise of the wheels and the horses' hooves, the door of the manor opened and a servant came running out. It was the oldest of the three. When the postillion told him that the stranger was asking for hospitality, the poor man started trembling. His master was so poor! He was just about to reply that his masters were not at home, when the châtelain appeared and said: 'Welcome, strangers!'

"The tax-farmer was received cordially–nobly, even–in spite of the manor's penury. Meager as the larder was, it was plundered; the last bottles of a vintage wine were pitilessly uncorked, the carved goblet of his ancestors was taken from the dresser where it was carefully conserved, and the young châtelaine gave up her apartment–the only one in the manor that was presentable.

"The tax-farmer perceived this profound poverty; he also perceived the dazzling beauty of the young woman–and, as he had been seeking for a long time to devulgarize himself somewhat by means of an alliance, he thought that an excellent opportunity had presented itself. The tax-farmer stayed at the manor for two days; on the third, he asked the father brazenly for the châtelaine's hand. The old lord bowed profoundly, took the tax-farmer by the arm and led him to a dusty gallery where smoke-darkened canvases were hanging on the walls. They were his family portraits. The oldest of them dated from the time of Philippe-Auguste, and depicted a knight armored in iron, cut down and mortally wounded at the battle of

Bouvines.[44] The most recent depicted a cardinal, the châtelain's uncle.

" 'This,' he said, 'is my daughter's only dowry. To obtain her hand, however, will require its near-equal.'

"The tax-farmer bit his lip, got into his carriage and left."

"By God!" cried Monsieur de Nossac, "I like the father so much that I'm beginning to grow fond of the daughter. Where is such a treasure hidden?"

"Two leagues away from your wife's tomb, near your château in Léonais."

"And the name of the châtelain?"

"The Comte de Kervégan."

"And his daughter?"

"Yvonnette."

"A pretty name!"

"Shall we climb into a carriage, then...?"

"What?" said the Baron, shivering.

"...And take the road to Léonais," the Marquis continued, imperturbably.

"But I haven't told you..."

"You haven't told me anything, but we should take our leave."

"That's impossible!"

"Why?"

"Because I love Gretchen."

The Marquis shrugged his shoulders. "You'll love Yvonnette," he said.

"I don't believe..."

"Me, I'm sure of it. Besides..." The Marquis paused. "Besides, you'll have a choice, for she's expecting a cousin."

"From where?"

"America. A sparkling creole, it's said, who seduced every Portuguese naval officer in Brazil."

The Baron shook his head. "All this is very seductive," he murmured.

"Well, then..."

"But I love Gretchen."

"Ah!" said the Marquis. "You're starting to become unbearable."

"So be it, then! I'll go... tomorrow..."

"No, immediately."

"Why immediately?"

"Because you might go mad again between now and tomorrow."

Monsieur de Nossac continued to hesitate. "I'll do it, then," he said. "Send for the horses."

"No need," said the Marquis, drawing him to a casement window. "Look."

A post-chaise was standing in the courtyard of the Hôtel de Simiane, already fully-harnessed, with a postillion in the driving-seat and grooms hanging from the straps. No objection was possible henceforth.

"Let's go, then!" said Monsieur de Nossac.

As he linked arms with the Marquis, though, a thought struck him. "But this cousin?" he said.

"What about the cousin?"

"Are you sure that she's not in love with him?"

The Marquis burst out laughing. "You see," he said. "You're already in love with her, without even having seen her."

"No," said Monsieur de Nossac, insouciantly. "But I'm jealous of all women, as a matter of personal principle."

"Pasha!" murmured the Marquis.[45]

The *berline* set off in response to two cracks of the postillion's whip.

Gretchen was vanquished!

XXV

Monsieur de Simiane had considerable difficulty chasing the memory of Gretchen away from the Baron's troubled mind, even temporarily. Throughout the first day of the journey, the Baron was pensive and melancholy, burying himself in his corner of the *berline*, watching the trees beside the road go by with the vague sadness that so often takes possession of travelers remorsefully fleeing some wound of the heart.

On the second day, the Baron permitted himself, after a satisfying meal at the hostelry, to listen to a few lewd stories which his friend related in a very serious manner. That evening, he no longer took account of the trees along the roadside, and began to find Simiane insufferable for not telling him any more about the châtelaine of Kervégan. Monsieur de Nossac, however, had not the courage to question him. He contented himself with burying himself in his corner to dream about the as-yet-unknown young woman with whom he was predisposed to fall in love.

At about eleven o'clock, as the *berline* crossed the border of Brittany, drowsiness took hold of him and he fell deeply asleep, not to awake until eight o'clock in the morning, at the moment when the chaise topped the little rise where, 14 months before, he had seen the spires of his wife's manor house for the first time.

"Well," said the Marquis, extending his hand. "There's your castle."

"I recognize it."

"We'll stop there first."

"Oh?" said Monsieur de Nossac, in a contrary mood. "Why not at the home of the dear Comte de Kervégan?"

The Marquis curled the end of his moustache in a mocking manner. "My poor friend," he said. "I was afraid I'd have a great deal of trouble getting you in an amorous mood, but I see that I was mistaken–you're already there."

"What do you mean?"

"It seems to me that it's patently obvious."

"What is?"

"That you can think of nothing but descending upon the Comte de Kervégan, who is poor–when you, Baron de Nossac, have a magnificent estate at your door. That would be to expose yourself to an exceedingly painful humiliation and embarrassment."

"That's true," said the Baron, pensively. "We'll stop at my house."

"And tomorrow, we'll get on our horses and pay a visit to the occupants of Kervégan."

"Why tomorrow?"

"Because we must have time to breathe, I suppose."

The Baron took out his watch. "It's eight o'clock," he said. "We'll arrive at nine."

"I know."

"We'll dine at ten. I don't see what there is to prevent us departing at midday."

"One very essential thing."

"Which is?"

"The dire need to sleep that I'm experiencing."

"You haven't been able to sleep in the carriage, then?"

"A fine question! As if such a sleep–jolted, interrupted, feverish–grants you much rest. We definitely can't go until tomorrow."

"But even so..."

"Even so, my dear friend, you ought to think a little about Mam'zelle Gretchen, to deceive yourself and help you to be patient until tomorrow."

The Baron bit his lip, and made no reply.

"Then again," the Marquis continued, phlegmatically, "it seems to me that you might just as well pay a short visit to your wife's tomb, and spend a few hours of regret..."

Monsieur de Nossac shivered, and did not dare reply–but the châtelaine of Kervégan ceased to populate the mists of his imagination for a few minutes. He began to think about that ravishing and pure young woman, whom he had scarcely seen, and whom his irresponsibility had killed.

Then, from the memory of that beloved dead woman, he passed on to the memory of Gretchen, who was her living image–and Gretchen, forgotten momentarily, having been effaced for a few hours from his memory and his heart, returned despotically to take sole occupation of them.

During this time, the *berline* had not ceased to roll onwards, and soon found itself at the gate of the ancient gardens within whose shade Madame la Baronne de Nossac, née Borelli, was resting in her final sleep.

The château's servants were the same ones that the Baron had found there a year earlier. They were sad and serious, still clad in mourning for their late mistress.

A feeling of inexpressible sorrow took hold of the Baron as he crossed the threshold of the manor-house. He climbed the staircase with his heart constricted, and went straight to the dead woman's bedroom–which, on his orders, had been left exactly as it was. He knelt down by the unmade bed, supporting himself on his elbows.

"Shall I love her forever, then?" he murmured.

And while Simiane plunged himself voluptuously into a bath of milk, the Baron went down to the gardens and made his way to the Baronne's tomb.

A little moss had sprouted in the interstices of the marble and fringed the tumulary inscription with green caterpillar-tracks. Above it, the chestnut-trees shook their huge crowns. Here and there, a patch of celestial azure could be seen through the foliage. A few Indian roses blossoming round about succeeded in giving a slight festival air of smiling tranquility to the tomb, which doubtless no longer sheltered anything but a worm-eaten skeleton.

Somber as it was, the Baron's sadness relaxed into a vague melancholy, and the summery perfumes, the blue sky and the green trees singing the wind's refrains, relieved the tomb of as much as possible of the funereal and the hopeless.[46]

As he sat down on it, he said, philosophically: "Gretchen resembled her so perfectly that to love Gretchen is to love her still. That is what I want–I shall find Gretchen again."

Then, as he yielded himself more and more to the serenity that surrounded him, as he opened his senses and his soul to the vague emanations of the Earth and sky that were spread around him, another thought struck him.

"If," he said to himself, "as I have already suggested to myself, my wife was not dead at all, and this tomb is empty. If Gretchen and my wife were one and the same... If..."

The Baron paused.

"My God!" he continued. "I've seen so many extraordinary things I can't say for certain that life, in certain scientific circumstances, cannot take on the appearance of death in the most striking fashion. Who can say for sure that she was dead?"

As he indulged himself with this thought, he was seized by a sudden idea.

"I must make sure," he said.

The gardener was passing through the depths of the garden, his spade in his hand. Monsieur de Nossac called him.

"Open that tomb for me," he said to him.

The gardener looked at him in astonishment.

"Open it," the Baron repeated, imperiously.

"I'll need pincers and a crowbar," the gardener said. "I'll go find them."

"Go," said the Baron. And he sat down on the tomb again.

Two minutes later, the gardener returned, armed with his tools, and set to work. The operation was difficult; the marble was sealed with iron nails welded with sulphur. As the work was not going fast enough to suit Monsieur de Nossac's impatience, he took up one of the tools himself and helped the gardener.

After half an hour, the leaden casket had been laid bare. A quarter of an hour after that, the oaken coffin was exposed. Finally, the maple bier in which the body was sealed made its appearance, apparently sealed in its turn.

At that point, the Baron hesitated, growing pale as his knees weakened.

"Must I open it?" the gardener asked.

Had Monsieur de Nossac been alone, he might perhaps have fled without daring to satisfy his bitter curiosity–but in the presence of this witness, he suppressed all emotion and overcame his scruples.

"Open it," he said.

The gardener took his crowbar and levered up the lid. A hideous and heart-rending spectacle was then laid bare. In the bier was a half-eaten cadaver, its face unrecognizable, having preserved almost nothing intact but an admirable head of ebony-colored hair, whose capricious curls spilled over the neck, the arms and the worm-strewn breast of the inert corpse–which, according to every appearance, had once been the dazzlingly beautiful Baronne de Nossac.

At this sight, the Baron became livid. He threw himself backwards with a cry of horror.

The Marquis de Simiane, who had run towards him while the coffin was being opened, caught him in his arms. "You're a madman!" he said to him. "Such shocks can kill." He drew the Baron back to the château and led him to the dining-room, where dinner was served.

"Let's eat," he said. "We'll go to Kervégan today."

But the brave Baron remained insensible of this news–which, two hours before, would have made his heart skip. He ate and drank silently. He did not recover his power of speech until the end of the meal, when–thanks to a few dusty bottles his butler had brought from the cellars on the orders of the Marquis–he unclenched his teeth and stammered a few words.

"Let's be on our way," said Simiane, lifting him up from the table and taking his arm. "In an hour, you'll have seen the marvel of the region, the fairy of Kervégan."

The Baron allowed himself to be led away and mounted his horse in a somber mood, allowing Simiane to set the pace for him and show him the way to go.

He scarcely remembered where he was going. He had forgotten the châtelaine of Kervégan. From time to time, he murmured distractedly: "I must find Gretchen... if I have to go to the ends of the Earth!"

Suddenly, when the spires of Kervégan were already visible above a little wood of larches and ash-trees, a clear and harmonious voice rang out from the bosom of the heath, full of youthfulness and melancholy, singing a popular Breton refrain:

You shan't go to balls any more, married lady;
You must keep to the house
While we go...

At the sound of this voice, so young and so pure, imprinted with a wild melodic quality, the Baron shivered and looked at the Marquis.

"What luck!" said the latter. "We'll have no need to go as far as the manor to see the châtelaine—that's her."

Indeed, the blonde head of a young woman appeared almost immediately in the midst of the heather, with a divinely angelic smile and those pure colors which God lets fall from his sublime palette on the visages of women who live amid woods and have not been etiolated by the corrupt and fatal air of cities.

The Baron abruptly reined in his horse, stunned and dazzled by such beauty. Almost immediately, though, another head popped up from the heather, no less beautiful and no less smiling, but more masculine. At the sight of it, the Baron cried out: "Wilhem! Wilhem or Samuel—one or the other!"

XXVI

The astonishment of the young woman, the Marquis and the person that Baron had taken for Samuel or Wilhem—the twin brothers who had played a role at the Holdengrasburg manor—was at least as great as the Baron's own stupefaction at the sight of the young man who had just appeared beside the châtelaine of Kervégan. That astonishment was followed by a moment's silence, which was finally broken by the Marquis de Simiane.

"Mademoiselle," he said, "I present to you Monsieur le Baron de Nossac–who has doubtless met your cousin somewhere..."

"It's Samuel," said the Baron, excitedly. "Wilhem's eyes were a shade more deeply-set."

"Samuel?" said the young man, staring at the Baron. "My name isn't Samuel, Monsieur."

"My cousin is called Hector," the châtelaine said, with a smile.

"It's Samuel!" the Baron insisted.

"Which Samuel?" Simiane demanded, impatiently.

"Wilhem's brother!"

"I have no brother, Monsieur," the young man replied, in a soft voice.

"Oh, I'm not mistaken!" the Baron cried, with a tenacity in his gaze and a tone that testified to his profound conviction.

"My name is Hector de Kerdrel, and I'm an only child–an orphan, the nephew of the Comte de Kervégan, in whose household I spent my childhood."

"And you've never left it?"

"Never."

"You were not at Holdengrasburg?"

"What is Holdengrasburg?"

"The castle of the Black Huntsman."

"Who is the Black Huntsman?"

"A German student by the name of Berghausen, who pretended to be the Devil's son."

The young man made a movement with his shoulders, which signified: "I don't understand any of this."

"Nor do I," said the châtelaine, replacing young Hector's shrug with a smile.

"Nor me," murmured the Marquis.

Monsieur de Nossac had fallen silent again. He looked attentively, by turns, at the dazzling young woman, the seemingly-petrified Marquis and this Hector de Kerdrel, who bore such a strong resemblance to Samuel. The smiles on the young man's lips and the young woman's rosy mouth were so ingenuous, no innocently astonished, and there was such candor in their replies, that it was difficult to suspect a further hoax. Then again, how could he believe that Samuel had come nearly a thousand leagues, quitting mountainous Bohemia for a valley in Brittany, with the sole purpose of continuing to play the same evil tricks upon the Baron that had been played in the Castle of Holdengrasburg–which had had such a fatal outcome, such a terrible dénouement?

Nevertheless, the resemblance was, in his eyes, striking and strange–as perfect as that of Gretchen for his wife, whose cadaver he had seen, two hours before, half-devoured by worms.

"My dear chap," said Simiane, in a profoundly compassionate tone, "I'm beginning to believe that you really do have some derangement in part of your brain, which makes you find resemblances everywhere."

This notion caused Monsieur de Nossac to shudder. Prepared to believe it, he looked at Hector de Kerdrel again.

Hector was so reminiscent of Samuel, and Hector and Samuel gave such a complete impression of being the same man, that Monsieur de Nossac became convinced that the accusation of madness he had carelessly let fall from his lips was true–that the Black Huntsman, the manor of Holdengrasburg, Gretchen, Roschen, Wilhem and his brothers must never have existed, and that it was a long and painful dream experienced one night in a bivouac or a trench, which he had mistaken for reality.

Monsieur de Simiane, the young woman and Hector followed the rapid emotions of doubt and anguish that were dividing his mind, having absorbed him anew and rendered him mute, by means of the expressions on his face. He felt their stares weighing upon him; he began to tremble as he thought that they were very close to accusing him of madness, and he suddenly lifted his head again, made a supreme effort, and brought a frank smile to his livid lips.

"Reassure yourselves," he said, "I'm not mad."

"We certainly hope so," Simiane murmured.

"It's just that Monsieur so closely resembles a young man I knew in Germany, and who had a twin brother who resembled him feature for feature, that I was alarmed–as my profound astonishment must have testified."

"I don't believe," Hector said, laughing, "that I have such pronounced German features."

"You're blond," said the Marquis.

"That's true."

"Mademoiselle," the Baron resumed, suddenly becoming the courtier that we have already seen, "I am ashamed that our first meeting has been marked by such a ridiculous scene, of which I am both the mediocre actor and the unfortunate author. Permit me to offer you my humble excuses..."

"I accept them," Yvonnette replied, blushing.

"My friend Simiane," the Baron continued, "has come to stay with me this very day, and, as I am not acquainted with any of my château's neighbors, wanted to introduce me to Monsieur le Comte de Kervégan, your father..." Yvonnette bowed. "When you met us, Mademoiselle, we were on our way to the château."

"You will be welcome there, Monsieur," Yvonnette stammered.

Monsieur de Nossac noticed that embarrassment, remembered Simiane's confidences on the matter of the Comte's poverty, and understood that Yvonnette was probably thinking that her father's self-esteem might suffer. Then, as members of the élite have a natural understanding of such things without the need of speech, he felt himself spontaneously drawn towards this child, who was so beautiful, so chaste, so dignified, so gracefully flirtatious and elegant beneath the simple linen dress and broad straw hat that she wore, in the style of the Tréguier region.

"Since my friend de Nossac deemed it appropriate to introduce himself, my beautiful cousin," Simiane said, "I no longer have an official mission to fulfill, and I shall reclaim my prerogative as an old relative. Give me your hand."

The Marquis dismounted, wrapped his horse's bridle around his arm, and offered his hand to the young châtelaine, who leaned on it nonchalantly, as one might lean on a father or an old friend.

The Baron felt a pang of jealousy, but he had wit enough not to show it. He followed Monsieur de Simiane's example, got down from his horse in his turn, and, while the Marquis led the way with Yvonnette, he linked arms amicably with Hector.

"My uncle will be delighted to meet you," said the young man. "He has wanted to do so for a long time, since he learned of your arrival."

Monsieur de Nossac shivered. Hector had Samuel's voice, just as he already had his face, his figure and his gestures. Doubt, that frightful and well-nigh incurable affliction, came back into his mind and took hold of it tenaciously. "Have you traveled?" he asked, in a tone closely akin to the one employed by a prosecutor extracting a confession from an accused criminal.

"Alas, no, Monsieur," Hector relied, sadly. "I have no fortune, and I am, fortunately or unfortunately, very proud. To travel in the manner appropriate to one's rank and birth requires money, and I have none."

"You have, at least, been out of Brittany."

"Never."

"Truly?"

"My most distant excursion has been a journey to Nantes, where I went to see the King's lieutenant."

"Do you know him?" Monsieur de Nossac asked, still interrogating Hector de Kerdrel's face, which was both impassive and innocent.

"Hardly—but my uncle, who was a Colonel of artillery in the same regiment, gave me a letter of introduction."

"What did you go to ask of him?"

"His patronage, Monsieur," Hector said, without humility or arrogance.

"Is it not Monsieur d'Aiguillon?" [47]

"Yes, Monsieur."

"I know him well, and if I can..."

"Oh!" said Hector "I asked so little..."

"What, then?"

"A uniform in the King's musketeers."

"And you haven't obtained it?"

"Not yet, but Monsieur d'Aiguillon added a warm recommendation to my letter, and I hope..."

"For the love of God, Monsieur! Hope! You'll make far too handsome a musketeer for the King not to accept you immediately."

"You're very kind, Monsieur, but I believe that my best recommendation is..."

"Is?" the Baron prompted.

"My father's name."

"Indeed," said Monsieur de Nossac, exerting his memory. "You're from a fine old family. The Kerdrels are well-known and well-connected in the West."

"My father was a Colonel in the Swiss Guards."

"I remember him now. I believe I even served with him on the Rhine."

"That's possible, Monsieur, for he fought in all the German wars." There was a ring of truth in the young man's replies; he cited names so well-known and honorable that one would have to have been mad to conserve any further suspicions regarding his identity with Samuel.

The Baron's final suspicions began to evaporate, and they had completely disappeared by the time that, on emerging from an immense stand of ash-trees, he saw the imposing mass of the old manor of Kervégan looming up before him. Monsieur de Simiane had not lied when he had advertised the castle as a construction of the era of the Crusades. It had the air of one of those knights who have seen centuries pass, but remain standing despite time's devastating flight.

It had massive towers, arches and battlements; its belfry was visible for several leagues around, and its moat was deep. But over the entirety of that proud aspect, tufts of lichen and Irish ivy had spread a vast cloak full of youth and bonhomie. Large woods, flowering meadows, hillocks covered with fruit-trees–a wholly inoffensive and natural rural landscape served to push it into the background, seeming to attest that its bellicose mission had been accomplished a long time ago. The intramural court, once the field where men-at-arms performed their maneuvers, was planted with chestnut-trees and acacias, which enlaced their branches around the windows, framing the arches with capricious festoons. Finally, to complete the scene and to conclude the mitigation of the old manor's appearance, young vines had been allowed to clamber up the walls here and there, promising marvels in spite of the harshness of the Breton climate.

The two gentlemen and their guides had no need to sound a horn outside the moat; the drawbridge had been lowered for a century and a half, and the chains supporting it had a rusty color that testified to their inaction. They went along a sandy path, found the door open, and went into a vestibule, which was as dilapidated as the rest of the manor, but in which the young châtelaine had placed a profusion of vases and baskets of flowers–beautiful wild flowers, none of which can be found in the beds planted by the gardeners of Chaillot or the Buttes Saint-Chaumont.[48]

Although the vestibule, the staircase and the dusty rooms to which the châtelaine led her guests–which served as a reception-room–had their rustic dress, they exhaled that cachet of fresh and innocent coquetry which only a young woman can give to an old dwelling or an old husband.

Finally, a door opened and a servant who was more than an octogenarian, but who still sported his livery, announced in a broken voice, with forced solemnity:

"Monsieur le Comte de Kervégan!"

XXVII

The Comte de Kervégan was a handsome old man of 70, still vigorous in spite of his white beard and white hair. He was tall, with a supreme majesty in his bearing and gestures. He had–at least, the Baron thought so–a vague resemblance to Berghausen, the German student who had played the role of the Black Huntsman so well. The resemblance was so slight, though, and the difference in their ages so disproportionate, that, despite his perpetual anxieties, Monsieur de Nossac did not give a second thought to the possibility that it might be him. Besides, whereas the face of the castellan of Holdengrasburg had been pleasant, friendly and sometimes lacking in dignity, the face of the Comte de Kervégan was austere, solemn and full of grandeur.

He came towards his guests at a slow and majestic pace, greeted them with a gesture of his hand, and turned to the Marquis. "My cousin," he said, "I thank you for not forgetting a old man; I've maintained so few links with the world, and the world forgets so quickly, that I am overjoyed when some relative or friend arrives to sit by my fireside."

"One sits down gladly beside the hearth of a man like you," Simiane replied.

The Comte turned to the Baron. "Monsieur le Baron," he said. "I thank my cousin Simiane for having conceived the fortunate idea of bringing us together. Our estates are neighbors, and I proposed to pay you a visit as soon as your arrival was made known to me."

"I am happy to have anticipated you, Monsieur le Comte."

"I have no need to introduce my daughter, Yvonnette de Kervégan, and my nephew, Monsieur Hector de Kerdrel, to you, for I see that my cousin Simiane has taken care of that."

The Baron bowed.

"But I hope to be more fortunate," the Comte continued, "in being the first to introduce you to my niece, the Marquise de Bidan, who is coming to France for the first time."

"A creole, I believe," Nossac said.

"The daughter of one of my brothers, who settled in the colonies."

"She's a widow," Simiane put in.

"Widowed at 26, Monsieur. Her husband was a wealthy plantation-owner. She has notified me of her arrival within a few days. She is coming to live with me."

"Ah," said the Baron, paying only slight attention to the Comte's words, and glancing sideways to study Yvonnette's charming face. She blushed as that gaze paused upon her.

"The ship on which she took passage," the Comte continued, "is expected at Brest any day now, and we–my daughter, my nephew and myself–are on the point of departing for that city to await the disembarkation."

"Excellent–I'll come with you!" said Simiane.

The Comte hesitated. "It's just that the means of transport are difficult..." he said.

Yvonnette drew closer to the Marquis. "Cousin," she whispered in his ear–loudly enough, however, for Nossac, who was close beside him, to hear–"spare my father's pride, and don't insist. We only have a wicker cart... you understand..."

"Monsieur le Comte," Monsieur de Nossac hastened to say, "I'm of the same opinion as my friend Simiane, but there's one difficulty that gives me pause–the fear of intruding upon a family reunion."

"Oh," said the Comte, smiling, "men like you never intrude upon anyone."

"In that case, Monsieur le Comte, permit me to put my *berline* at your disposal, and to invite you to dine with me on the day of your departure. My château is on the most direct route to Brest."

"I accept," said the Comte, simply.

"When would you like to leave?" Simiane asked.

"Why... tomorrow, if you can see no impediment."

"So be it!" said the Baron.

The conversation then turned to banalities–which suited the Baron marvelously, permitting him to devote himself exclusively to Yvonnette.

The two gentlemen stayed to dinner.

Simiane had not lied; the manor's poverty was long-standing. The crockery was scratched and cracked like ancient Sèvres porcelain; the tablecloth was threadbare. The food was meager, but well-prepared. As for the wine, the layers of dust covering the bottles attested to its antiquity and the parsimony with which it had been conserved. Monsieur de Nossac took no notice, however, thinking only of Yvonnette, seeing none but her. He was placed on her right; he sometimes brushed her hand. What did the rest matter to him?

Despite its frugality, the meal went on rather late; dusk was falling by the time the Baron and Simiane were ready to leave.

"Monsieur le Comte," Monsieur de Nossac said then, "I offer you, in my turn, hospitality at the château for the night, in order that we can make an early departure."

The Comte seemed to hesitate, but eventually made his decision. "So be it!" he said.

"Mademoiselle will take my horse, and you Simiane's, while we accompany Hector on foot."

"Oh no!" said Yvonnette "I prefer to walk across the heath."

"Me too," said Simiane.

"In that case," the Baron said, interrogating young Hector with a glance, "who will ride the Marquis' horse?"

Hector said nothing, doubtless out of timidity, but he looked at his cousin.

"That will be Hector," she said. "He's a poor horseman, and since he wants to serve in the guards, he needs the practice."

A spark of joy gleamed in the young man's eyes. "Is he very headstrong, your horse?" he asked the Baron.

"Ardent, but not headstrong."

Hector leapt into the saddle with unexpected pleasure, and–doubtless to give the lie to his cousin–proceeded to make the noble animal prance and caper with a boldness that might have lacked science, but had grace and coolness. "May I gallop?" he asked.

"If it pleases you, my young friend."

Meanwhile, the old Comte de Kervégan had put his foot in the stirrup, a trifle stiffly but with the method and science of a consummate horseman. Once he was in the saddle, he had, in the Baron's knowledgeable eyes, a proud and haughty attitude reminiscent of the knights of the Middle Ages, who seemed to be screwed to their saddles.

"Let's see," he said, "if I still remember my ancient *métier*." And he launched his horse after Hector, who was already disappearing into an ancient oak-wood.

Nossac, Yvonnette and Simiane remained alone.

Nossac gave his arm to Yvonnette.

All three of them plunged into the heath. Then, by a skillful maneuver, the Baron found a means of separating himself from the Marquis and walking alone with the young woman, hand in hand–still silent, but with a cloud of tumultuous thoughts in his head, and upon his heart, which only required some spark or jolt to set them loose.

It was a charming route that the two young people took, along florid hedges, across the fragrant heath, beneath a blue sky with a few glistening fleecy clouds drifting on the nocturnal breeze. Without any movement of their lips, without their voices springing forth from their oppressed bosoms, they spoke the mute and poetic language of love–which was awakening for the first time in Yvonnette, and which seemed to the Baron to be his first sensation of that genre, so different was it from the material and avid perfume that had presided over his previous *amours*.

Suddenly, the sound of a galloping horse was heard, disturbing them. It was Hector de Kerdrel, coming back at breakneck speed.

"Monsieur le Baron," he cried. "My creole cousin has arrived! We met her litter at the gate of your château, and my uncle has taken her in."

Monsieur de Nossac shuddered profoundly on hearing this sudden news–but why should he shudder?

XXVIII

Monsieur de Nossac had seen such extraordinary things in the last few months, had been both actor and spectator in such a strange drama, and had so recently been surprised by an astonishing resemblance, that he was ready to expect anything and fear everything.

He could not help being fearful in advance of this woman he had been told about, this creole who had arrived so abruptly and had been installed in his house, although he could not have explained why.

Besides, all women had had that effect on him since his return from Heidelberg. In all of them he seemed to recognize that fatal Gretchen whose image pursued him everywhere, after which he had run incessantly, and whose appearance he dreaded incessantly to see–that Gretchen beloved and hated at the same time, summoned and desired with every dream, every delirium, every fugue of passion, yet thrust away by reason, repulsed by an insurmountable aversion.

Momentarily fascinated, prey to a mysterious charm that she did not yet know how to explain, Yvonnette shivered as Monsieur de Nossac had shivered at the sound of Hector de Kerdrel's loud voice. And while the Baron was still under the sway of that bizarre oppression and that inexplicable terror of which we have just spoken, she blushed involuntarily, and abruptly withdrew the hand that he had been holding in his own–but then she let out a little cry of joy, and said, "Hurry! Quickly, Monsieur, quickly!"

And she increased her pace,

The charm was broken on the instant. The Baron obeyed. Like her, he accelerated his pace.

She did not take his hand then, nor did she lean upon his shoulder with languorous abandon; she contented herself with placing the tips of her fingers on his arm and walking beside him. Meanwhile, seemingly conspiring with the fatality whose messenger he was, the careless horseman reined in his horse and fell into step with the two pedestrians.

They arrived at the château a few minutes later. The young woman became so impatient that she broke into a run. The Baron, grumbling and cursing, followed her to the door of his own drawing-room, where the creole was already installed with her uncle, the Comte de Kervégan, and the Marquis de Simiane—who, thanks to another path and a short cut, had found the means to gain a quarter of an hour on the Baron and the young woman.

On the threshold of the room the Baron was seized once again by that inexplicable shivering, that sourceless terror that had previously invaded his mind and his soul, and he thought involuntarily of Gretchen.

"Come on, Baron," cried Simiane, from the back of the room. "Hurry—come and perform the honors of your hospitality."

That voice triumphed over the Baron' hesitation. Suddenly becoming once again the courtier and gallant gentleman we saw in the prologue of this story, he put his hat under his arm and advanced, his head thrown back and his stride decisive. In the middle of the room he bowed to the creole, who was half-hidden by a shadow.

The American got up immediately. As she returned the Baron's bow, she was struck by a ray of light from the candelabra, and her face was fully illuminated.

Monsieur de Nossac replied to the creole's dignified bow with a cry of anguish and stupefaction, almost of horror. "Gretchen!" he cried. "It's Gretchen!"

Astonishment was painted on every face, especially the creole's.

"Oh!" the Baron repeated, uncontrollably. "It's Gretchen!"

Instead of replying, the creole looked interrogatively at her uncle and the Marquis. The later exclaimed: "Until now I had not wanted to believe it, but there's no longer any doubt about it. Nossac is mad!"

Monsieur de Nossac reddened, threw himself toward the creole, seized her hands, drew her into the candlelight, and said to her: "Do you maintain that you are not that infernal and mysterious being who sucked my blood like a vampire in Germany–who, by night, called herself Hélène Borelli and said that she was dead, and by day bore the name of Gretchen, who..."

"Monsieur," said the creole coldly, "I don't know what you mean. You're accusing me of having sucked your blood in Germany, and I have never set foot there."

The Baron made a gesture of incredulity.

"If you doubt it," she went on, "you may read my surname and first names on my passport, and assure yourself that I have arrived from Martinique. I disembarked at Brest this very morning; if you have doubts as to the sincerity of the postillion, write to the Admiral in command of the port of Brest, who gave me his hand in order that I might descend to dry land..."

"There's one thing much simpler," said Simiane, "that will convince you that you are crazy, my good friend."

"Let's hear it!" said the Baron, frowning.

"Gretchen resembled your wife?"

"Feature for feature."

"Madame resembles Gretchen?"

"It's her!"

"So be it–in that case, she bears a similar resemblance to your wife?"

"Yes, yes! If I had not seen Hélène's half-eaten corpse, I would swear..."

"My good friend," the Marquis said, phlegmatically, "do you remember that I was the one who arranged your marriage?"

"Yes."

"Well, the only resemblance I can find between Hélène Borelli and Madame is so vague, so banal..."

The Baron recoiled.

"...That it was not apparent to me until now," the Marquis continued. "Do you doubt that?"

"Yes! Yes, I doubt it. In fact, I don't believe it."

"Your wife died here?"

"Yes."

"Your servants have seen her?"

"Yes."

"Summon them."

Monsieur de Nossac seized the tassel of a bell-cord and shook it violently. The gardener who had opened the Baronne's coffin that morning appeared.

"Look at Madame," said the Baron.

The gardener darted an astonished glance at the creole, then looked at his master in a fashion that signified: "Why did you want me to look at her?"

"Well?" demanded the Marquis, triumphantly.

Monsieur de Nossac was tenacious; he returned to his bell-cord and summoned all the domestics, one by one. None of them recognized the Baronne de Nossac in the creole. The Baron was crushed.

"You must see it," Simiane said. "You are mad–maddened by some disturbance of the brain. I recognize and admit that you are reasonable in every matter that does not concern Gretchen."

Monsieur de Nossac tottered like a man struck by lightning; he was suddenly seized by a delirium so extravagant that it resembled wisdom. "Well," he said, "I'm beginning to believe it. I'm mad! But that will not prevent me from extending to my guests the honors of my house, and we shall take supper by torchlight."

They did, indeed, take supper. Monsieur de Nossac, who needed to get drunk, drank like a cordelier, and placed the creole directly facing him. During the meal, his eyes were constantly fixed on her, studying the contours of her face, searching to discover a sign or movement that would betray Gretchen. The creole was impassive.

At eleven o'clock, Monsieur de Nossac retired, drunk and half-mad, to his apartment–but once he was alone, in the silence and the darkness of the alcove in which his bed was set, his terrors took hold of him again. Gretchen, momentarily set aside, recovered her despotic and fatal influence, and the Baron, beside himself and tremulous, sat up straight, with his hair standing on end, and murmured: "It's her! It's Gretchen!"

And while he was prey to that delirium, another thought struck him. She will come, he thought. She will suck my blood again, as she did out there...

This time, fascinated, dominated by a strange and furious fervor, he leapt from the foot of his bed, went to get his sword, and came to sit, near-naked, between his bed-curtains, saying excitely, in a voice that madness rendered sinister: "Oh, I shall see her clearly tonight, and Roschen will not be there to receive my blade... I shall strike... I shall strike a terrible blow!"

XXIX

The Baron remained sitting up in bed for a long time, his hair bristling, his eyes burning, clutching the hilt of his sword convulsively in his hand. His heart was gripped, as it would have been at the approach of any real danger, energetic action or criminal enterprise.

The large brass clock in its oaken case, which the former masters of the château had placed on the landing of an immense stairway, was the only thing that could be heard throughout the house, drawing lugubrious plaints from the manor's dormant echoes as it awoke them with a start. The Baron counted midnight, half past twelve and one o'clock in turn. Then his courage began to weaken. The cold of the night drew a shiver from him; the fever that burned him let up momentarily, and as his reason gradually returned, he could not help thinking about the fact that neither the Marquis, who was his friend, nor the domestics, had recognized Madame de Nossac in Gretchen. Had he, then, been tricked once again by his delirious imagination, and was the resemblance merely vague and indecisive, rather than being as strange and striking as he believed?

Once doubt had been set in motion in the Baron's mind, it became stronger and more tenacious. Then, his anxiety passed into anguish, and his fear of seeing Gretchen approach into the desire to have her close to him...

And, as the delirium returned, he began to call out to Gretchen with all the force of his will—except, however, that his lips could not open, nor his constricted throat release a cry...

The clock chimed two o'clock, and Gretchen did not come.

The Baron made a supreme effort, and an almost inarticulate sound contrived to emerge from his throat. "Gretchen!" he cried. "Gretchen!"

And, when there was no response, he continued: "Gretchen!... Gretchen...I love you!"

The same silence.

"Gretchen," he continued, "I wanted to kill you at first, but there's nothing to fear now... I love you! Come... you may take as much of my blood as you wish... drain all my veins one after the other! Gretchen, my beloved... Gretchen, come!"

Gretchen remained deaf to his entreaties, and no other sound troubled the mute echoes of the room but the Baron's feverish and broken voice.

"Oh," Monsieur de Nossac went on, "I understand that you're afraid, afraid that I might kill you... Well, there's no longer any fear of that, now... Look!"

181

And he threw away his sword.

Gretchen appeared to be insensible of this act of submission, for no white form emerged from the obscurity.

"I understand," the madman continued, after a moment's anxious pause. "You don't trust me... you fear that I'll pick up my sword again... well then, I'll break it!"

And he went, groping and bumping into the corners of the furniture, to pick up his sword. He set it on his knee, broke the blade in two places, and threw the fragments away, crying out anew: "Gretchen! Gretchen!"

The Baron was frozen, and while he waited for Gretchen, calling out his promises in his delirious voice, he got back into bed instinctively. As the fever, which calmed momentarily only to return to the gallop, continued to grip and burn him, he ended up losing all consciousness of his actions, rolled himself up in his bedclothes, and fell into a heavy sleep, murmuring: "My bed will be very warm, Gretchen, and you, who are always cold... Oh, come...!

Three, four and five o'clock sounded successively. Daylight came. Filtering through the shutters, it awoke the Baron, who was dreaming, and speaking in a loud voice in his dream, mixing up the names of Samuel and Gretchen, Roschen and Yvonnette. On opening his eyes, still oppressed by the visions of the nightmare, he must have believed that he was still at Holdengrasburg, for he leapt to the floor and ran to the window. He opened it, wanting to see whether the countryside had changed yet again, and whether he would see the forest and the meadows or the sterile plain and seething waters of the torrent.

Instead of all that, he saw the large trees of his garden, the flowering trees, through whose crowns the Sun slid its first rays, and whose every branch was an instrument from which a nascent concert of birdsong rose up. The morning air was pure and intoxicating. The Baron plunged his face into it with voluptuous avidity, and his last *frissons* fled on contact with it.

Suddenly, there was a noise behind him.

It was the Marquis. "Damn!" he said, coming in. "You're up early, for a man who went to bed drunk."

"I wasn't drunk."

"No, just staggering and raving."

"You believe so?"

"Absolutely! Moreover, I'll tell you by way of consolation, you're much more amiable drunk than sober."

"You think so?"

"You were charming yesterday evening, full of spirit and finesse. The creole found you ravishing."

The Baron shivered. "Don't talk to me about that woman," he said.

"Why?"

"Because I'm afraid of her."

"What do you mean?"

"I'm sure that she's Gretchen."

Simiane lifted his eyes heavenwards, compassionately, and murmured: "What a pity that such a fine gentleman should go crazy in some corner of his brain! The mental string that resonates to the name of Gretchen is definitely tuned far too high."

Monsieur de Nossac looked at the Marquis. Simiane's face was so distressed and full of compassion that once again he began to think that perhaps the Marquis was right and that he really was mad.

"Damn!" Simiane went on. "Here's the proof." He picked up the three fragments of the broken sword. "Did you smash it against the wall?" he asked.

Monsieur de Nossac did not reply. A sudden noise had drawn his attention back to the window, and his gaze, plunging into the garden, came to rest on a group composed of a man and a woman–a young woman and a very young man: Hector de Kerdrel and his cousin the creole. She was leaning on his arm with lascivious nonchalance, a lack of constraint that smacked of the hot countries in which she had been brought up–an abandon that made Monsieur de Nossac grow pale with anger.

"What's the matter?" Simiane asked.

"I don't know," the Baron replied. "But whether that woman is Gretchen or not, I'm jealous of her."

The Marquis burst out laughing. "And Yvonnette?" he said.

"Yvonnette?" murmured the Baron, like a man evoking a distant and almost-forgotten memory. "Who is Yvonnette?"

The Marquis sighed. "He's definitely mad," he murmured.

XXX

This was perhaps the tenth time in the last 24 hours that Monsieur de Nossac had heard that exclamation–"He's mad!"–spoken in his vicinity. At that moment, he certainly was. He ended up believing it himself when, with the phantasmagoric rapidity of which memory is capable, he remembered everything that had happened on the previous day.

Who was Yvonnette?

He had been able to ask such a question when, the day before, he had contemplated the young woman in a state of rapture–when, beneath the shadowy clouds through which the Moon had spread its tremulous light, he had shivered voluptuously at the sound of her voice, the touch of her hand, the whisper of her breath...

He had asked who Yvonnette was, when he had once been possessed by the thought that her love would be, for the man who might obtain it, the kind of happiness beside which the joys of Paradise are colorless and monotonous.

Remembering that, Monsieur de Nossac finally understood that his reason had taken flight, and that he was racing full tilt along the road to madness. He looked at Monsieur de Simiane then with a kind of dolorous astonishment, which seemed to demand both pity and advice.

"By my faith, yes, my dear," the Marquis went on, after a momentary silence. "You're going mad."

"I'm afraid so," Nossac murmured.

"So am I."

"What do you expect? That accursed creole resembles Gretchen so strongly!"

"Or rather, my dear, this Gretchen fills your imagination so completely that the least resemblance deceives you, and you see her everywhere."

"Can that really be true?" said Monsieur de Nossac, talking to himself but loudly enough for the Marquis to hear him.

"True enough that if Gretchen resembles your wife, the beautiful creole cannot resemble Gretchen very much, since the domestics..."

"My God! They might have forgotten Hélène's face."

"Nonsense," said the Marquis. "It's far wiser to admit that you must have a hole in the head." [49]

The Baron put his head in his hands and remained pensive for a few minutes.

"Whether I'm mad or not," he said, eventually, "I love Gretchen!"

"I can see that, damn it!"

"And everything that, for me, resembles Gretchen."

"Ah!"

"This creole resembles her..."

"And you're already in love with the creole?"

"I fear so,"

"But Yvonnette?"

"I loved her yesterday..."

"You'll love her tomorrow."

"Never!"

"We'll see..."

"It's the creole I love; she resembles Gretchen."

"Agreed. But the creole doesn't love you."

The Baron took a step back.

"She will never love you."

The Baron frowned and went pale.

"Because she's in love with someone else."

The Baron moaned. "Who is it?" he cried.

"Her young cousin."

"Hector? But she's scarcely seen him."

"What does that matter?"

"She didn't know him yesterday."

"She knows him today."

"But he's a child..."

Simiane burst into laughter. "All the more reason. A virgin beard, pink cheeks, blue eyes, blond hair, a slim figure, feminine hands and an angelic smile is more than enough to turn the head of a girl of 18–and he has all of that."

That's true, Monsieur de Nossac thought. But his pride prevented him from saying it aloud. "Well," he said, angrily, "I want that woman to love me... and she shall love me!"

"Madness!"

The Baron stood up straight, threw back his head, and said proudly: "I am the Baron de Nossac!"

"You were the Baron de Nossac."

"What do you mean?"

"That you're only a shadow of your former self."

The Baron shivered, and looked at his pale and weary face in a nearby mirror.

"You're only a shadow of the Baron de Nossac that all Paris and Versailles admired a year ago for the elegance of his costumes, the good taste of his house, the magnificence of his existence, the finesse of his mind and the extent of his good fortune..."

"Have I changed so much, then?"

"Look at yourself."

The Baron moved closer to the mirror.

"Your face is dejected, thinned out, withered; there are dark circles around your eyes; your lips are slack, your beard badly-cut. Your hands thickened during your last campaign, riding has made you knock-kneed, you've grown stouter, your cheeks are pasty..."

"You're exaggerating," said Monsieur de Nossac, momentarily recovering the lightly careless tone that he had once possessed. "I'll bet you a thousand *louis* that the creole will love me."

"I'll take the bet on behalf of my creditors. But first, if you don't want me to be on a sure thing, find a way of cutting short that sentimental promenade with which the creole and her cousin are honoring the paths of your garden." Still mocking, the Marquis drew his attention for a second time to the beautiful American, leaning nonchalantly on Hector de Kerdrel's arm.

A flash of anger lit up in the Baron's eyes. He moved his hand reflexively towards his sword and murmured: "I'll kill him!"

Monsieur de Simiane shrugged his shoulders. "Kill, my good friend, kill, and I'll answer for my thousand *louis*."

"How's that?"

"Oh, undoubtedly! She loves him, and he's her cousin. If you kill him, she'll conceive the most magnificent hatred for you that ever emerged from the heart of a beautiful, titled and amorous woman. Only a bourgeois woman can pardon a gentleman, her lover, for beating her husband to death in order to set her free."

"That's true," said Monsieur de Nossac, persuaded.

"In your place, I'd prefer to have him sent away, cunningly."

"But how?"

"Aren't you the Commander of the Royal-Cravate?"

"Of course."

"Give him a lieutenancy. When he's accepted his commission, order him to join his platoon immediately."

The Baron's frown suddenly cleared. "That's a great idea," he said. "Run down and tell him that I want to speak to him."

"Why don't you go yourself?"

"She makes me afraid."

"Yours is a strange kind of love! You're afraid of the woman you love."

"Yes, but I'll harden myself."

"God willing."

"And she shall love me!"

"God will make sure of it! But you're not handsome any longer. Now, to touch a woman's heart requires good looks, intellect or courage. Your good looks have fled, your intellect is experiencing a terrible somnolence under the oppression of Gretchen's memory, and as for your courage..."

"What?" said the Baron, arching an eyebrow.

"I know that's still the same–but it's necessary to find an opportunity to display it."

"You know the country, don't you?"

"Like Versailles."

"Then you must find me some over-refined and taciturn local popinjay with whom I can pick a German quarrel, whom I can convert into a scabbard."

"What!"

"What do you expect? Serious maladies require serious remedies. Love makes cruel demands."

"My dear," the Marquis said, philosophically, "dueling is a joke. Everyone fights, even rogues. My butler fights, my perfumer fights at daybreak, and your valet, if the opportunity presented itself, would issue a challenge to your coachman. A duel to offer proof of your audacity? Get away!"

Once more, Monsieur de Nossac was obliged to persuade himself that the Marquis was right. "Well," he said, "suppose I were to fight hand-to-hand with a bear before her eyes."

"There are no bears in Brittany."

"With a wild boar?"

"That's possible. That would be more ingenious, especially if you have the good fortune to break a leg. Lame suitors are infernally lucky."

"Mock away–I'm decided!"

"And when will this spectacle take place?"

"This very day."

"Your madness is lessening, Baron. my friend–you're regaining your wits."

"I'm trying," said Monsieur de Nossac, modestly.

The Marquis went to the window again. "Good!" he said. "There are our two lovers, disappearing into the bushes."

A spark of jealousy lit up in the Baron's eyes. Leaving Simiane stunned, he threw himself towards the staircase, went down four steps at a time and ran into the garden.

XXXI

The creole and young Hector had come to a small verdant enclosure, a thick arbor whose trellis the sunlight attempted to penetrate in vain, which interlaced its meandering foliage above a little spring bubbling up from the ground and running away through the bushy green grass.

When the Baron, guided by a secret instinct, arrived at the arbor, the creole was half-lying on a bank of grass, distractedly passing her hand through Hector's curly hair while he sat at her feet.

Monsieur de Nossac started, and felt a violent pain in his heart–but this pain had a salutary effect, for it renewed the inexpressible emotion that he had felt the previous evening in the creole's presence, to which he was once again subject, without any doubt.

At the sound of his footsteps, the creole withdrew her hand abruptly, then turned her head languidly, while young Hector got up, blushing with embarrassment.

"Madame," said the Baron, bowing, "I was looking for you..."

"You're a thousand times too kind, Monsieur le Baron."

"It's my duty as châtelain, Madame; I came to renew my humble apologies..."

"What apologies, Baron?"

"For my stupid conduct yesterday."

The creole allowed a nonchalant smile to glide over her lips. "Do I resemble Gretchen so very much?"

"Oh!" said the Baron. "You're her!"

"What madness!"

Monsieur de Nossac made a gesture of impatience. "That word madness again!" he murmured.

"I beg your pardon, Monsieur. I meant to say that there are bizarre resemblances."

"Yes, Madame, very bizarre. You resemble Gretchen so closely that you have the same wrinkles in the corner of your mouth, the same fingers on your hands, the same dimple in your chin..."

Hector had taken a step back, and he darted a jealous glance at the Baron, who continued to press the creole's hands in his own. Monsieur de Nossac noticed that glance, and his anger, momentarily appeased, returned, causing his eyes to flash.

"Are you a hunter, Monsieur de Kerdrel?" he asked.

"Yes and no, Monsieur."

"Why yes and no?"

"Because I have all the instincts of the noble science, without the means to practice it."

"Why?"

Hector blushed. "Because my uncle is poor, and we have neither beaters, nor outfits, nor horses."

The creole blushed in her turn at the confession the young man had just made. He, noticing her distress, raised his head proudly and seemed to drape himself in his poverty like a king's cloak.

Monsieur de Nossac went pale; everything was turning against him, even his rival's humiliation, which love had transformed into glory. "Well," he said, through clenched teeth, "you shall hunt today."

"Today?"

"I came to invite Madame to participate in a boar hunt that Simiane and I have planned."

"With pleasure," said the creole.

"We'll depart after breakfast. I have excellent horses."

"So much the better!" said the creole. "Give me the most headstrong."

"And me the most unmanageable," Hector said.

The creole released a little cry, a mixture of fright and almost-maternal love. "I don't want that!" she said.

"Why not?" asked the young man.

"Because you'll break your arms and legs, you silly fool!" And she passed her hand through his hair again.

Monsieur de Nossac howled internally, and became livid. "Be tranquil, Madame," he said, with sudden irony. "Monsieur de Kerdrel is a fine horseman; he'll have my horse broken in less than in hour."

Hector made an angry movement in his turn.

"And I'll want to punish him for it." the Baron continued, disdainfully.

Hector struck the pose of a man awaiting a provocation.

"I'll make you a gift of the poor animal, and you'll be obliged to keep it, my young friend." The Baron's tone was heavily patronizing.

"I accept it," said Hector, in the same sarcastic tone.

"And as it's necessary for a Lieutenant of Dragoons in the Royal-Cravate to be suitably mounted, you'll permit me to offer you a second."

"I'm not a Lieutenant of Dragoons!" said the young man, stupefied.

"Don't you know that I'm the Commander of the Royal-Cravate?"

"Absolutely."

"And that I have a blank commission for a Lieutenant?"

Hector's eyes lit up.

"Now," Monsieur de Nossac continued, playing the role of a generous man rendering a favor, "there's nothing but a name to write thereon–and, if you will permit it, that name will be Hector de Kerdrel."

The young man let out a cry of joy–but the cry was immediately suppressed by the creole.

191

"I don't want that," she said, in a small voice that was imperious and peevish.

"Oh, cousin!"

"When you're a Lieutenant, Monsieur le Baron will send you away to be killed."

"Or be promoted to Captain," said Hector, enthusiastically. "I accept, Monsieur le Baron."

"If I allow it..." said the creole.

"Oh, my little cousin," murmured Hector, setting himself on his knees again before the American, "be very kind, my little cousin... permit me..."

"Well," she murmured, emotionally, "we'll see..."

Monsieur de Nossac trembled with fury. He understood that it was necessary to break off temporarily, in order not to be flatly refused.

"So be it," he said, "we'll talk about it another time. Now, let's go to breakfast, and find Monsieur de Kervégan and his daughter."

"They left this morning," Hector said.

"And why is that?"

"To get my cousin's apartment ready–but they'll wait for us until this evening." Hector paused, then continued: "Well, have you a good pack of hounds?"

"Only a dozen dogs."

"That's not enough to bring down a wild boar."

"We shall not be bringing it down."

"What are you intending to do, then?"

"I intend to kill it with my hunting-knife," the Baron said, with superb self-assurance."

An expression of admiration passed over the creole's face, and instead of taking Hector's arm, she took the Baron's–and leaned on it, as one leans on a strong man's arm!

XXXII

The indolent abandonment with which the creole leaned on him gave the Baron a first scent of victory, and he went on: "In addition, my young friend, I shall give you pistols to ensure your personal safety."

Hector was undoubtedly about to refuse.

"And," the Baron continued, suddenly, "a horse whose mouth isn't overly sensitive."

Hector stirred impatiently, and frowned.

"Because, as a bold but inexperienced horseman, you tend to cut your horse's mouth."

This time Hector reddened all the way to the forehead, but he kept silent, contenting himself with darting a sideways glance at the creole, doubtless in search of encouragement. The creole was walking with her eyes lowered, however, and the Baron went on: "That will be a guarantee, besides, for Madame's near-maternal tenderness—which will soon take fright on seeing you mount an ardent horse."

The blow was direct and decisive. The creole bit her lip and replied, dryly: "After what you have just said to me, Monsieur le Baron, I understand that my young cousin is a bold horseman, if not experienced—and as audacity is worth as much as wisdom in certain cases, it would be quite puerile and ridiculous to inhibit his pleasures, like some morose tutor."

Hector undoubtedly had a full understanding of the advantage that these words, delivered in a tight-lipped fashion and a protective tone, gave to Monsieur de Nossac, and—whether by calculation or out of resentment—he fell behind in order to recover his self-composure, preferring to retreat temporarily rather than lose the game irrevocably.

Monsieur de Nossac and the creole hardly exchanged a word as they walked to the château, but the Baron still sensed the moist pressure of her arm on his, and walked slowly to prolong the sensation. They arrived thus in the dining-room, where the Marquis was waiting for them.

"I say, Nossac," said the latter, on seeing them enter, "it appears that the pack is in disarray."

"Bah!"

"And that you've no more than a dozen healthy dogs."

"I know."

"That will scarcely enable us to run down a young boar."

"You believe so?"

"I'm sure of it."

"Well, I'll corner a nursing sow and take her on with a knife."

"Madman!" said the Marquis.

"That's very imprudent, Monsieur!" the creole put in.

"You think so?"

"It's very dangerous."

"Not," he said to her, in a low voice, "if you follow me, and I feel your gaze upon me at the decisive moment."

The creole lowered her eyes, and blushed.

Good! Nossac thought. *She's in love with me already.*

Hector came in at that moment. "Monsieur le Baron," he said, "on due reflection, I don't want pistols."

"Why not?"

"Because you won't be carrying any."

"Is that all?"

"But of course."

"And like me, you want..."

"To kill the boar with a knife," he said, resolutely.

The creole raised her head and looked at him with satisfaction and an imperceptible glimmer of joy, which did not escape Monsieur de Nossac. Hector was gaining ground.

"My dear chap," said Monsieur de Nossac, coldly, "it's awkward that you should want to do that."

"Why awkward?"

"Because you'll be putting my life in great danger."

"How is that?"

"Very simply. If you try to kill the boar with a knife, as I want to do it first, you'll force me to throw away the knife and choke it with my bare hands, just as if it were a roe-deer."

This time, the victory was certain. Bold as he was, Hector shivered involuntarily, and dared not reply: I wish to do as you do. He lowered his head, blushed, and remained silent.

The creole was undoubtedly very annoyed by this retreat, for she said in a half-indulgent, half-mocking tone: "It's not generous of you, Monsieur, to lead my young cousin on to such ground. He's too frail, too delicate..."

Hector opened his mouth, doubtless to reply with some impertinence that might rebound to the Baron's advantage, but a furtive glance from the creole shut him up.

Monsieur de Nossac had won.

He was generous, guiding the conversation on to neutral terrain, which he maintained throughout breakfast.

XXXII

At eleven o'clock precisely, the hunters mounted their horses.

The creole was supplied with a superb white stallion with a fiery star on its forehead–a bold and vigorous animal with hooves of iron and muscles of steel, which did not balk at bushy hedges, crumbling walls or muddy ditches.

"Madame," the Baron said to her, "if I had not noticed a sparkle in your eyes, I probably would not have dared to offer you such a mount, but you have both the boldness that braves all and the will that dominates. You may set yourself in the saddle." And, like some gallant knight of the Middle Ages, the Baron offered his left hand to the lady and placed his right knee beneath her foot by way of a stirrup.

The creole scarcely put the extremity of her foot on the Baron's suede *culotte*, and leapt briskly into the saddle with the grace and self-assurance of a consummate horsewoman.

The Baron bowed, and went to Hector, who was frowning and grimacing as he idly twisted the shaft of his riding-crop, unable to help admiring the elegant group formed by three fully-harnessed horses held by hand, pawing the ground impatiently. They were all the same size, but were variously colors—one was white, the second was black as ebony, the third dark chestnut—but they were so beautifully conformed, and shook their heads so proudly, and dribbled so nobly on their bits, that one truly did not know to which of them to give preference.

"My young friend," said the Baron, "here are three horses, all of the same age, the same breed and the same bloodline. Choose whichever you please."

Hector was humiliated and joyful at the same time: joyful because the Baron had reverted to his first decision in giving him a horse of his choice and not one that was worn out, humiliated because this new decision resembled a pardon. He looked at the three horses in turn, examined them attentively, hesitated for a few minutes, then decided on the dark chestnut, whose legs appeared slimmer and more muscular, and its withers bonier and more refined.

"My dear friend," the Baron said, phlegmatically, when Hector had made his choice, "you've just selected the most headstrong of my horses, and also the most vicious. Hazard has favored you—but beware of one thing..."

"Which is?"

"Don't take your first fall on too steep a slope—you'll make it impossible for us to reach you and give you the necessary care."

"I shan't fall."

"Are you quite sure of that?"

"Oh, you'll see!" Hector said, launching himself on to the horse and gripping his mount's flanks tightly with his knees. He handled the horse confidently enough to reassure the most fearful.

"*En route, Mesdames et Messieurs!*" said the Marquis. "We'll hasten to the woods, and while we eat lunch, the beaters will send a magnificent nursing sow our way—large and lean—which won't have much trouble getting its teeth into our dogs."

"If I don't choke it beforehand," the Baron said.

They set forth.

Monsieur Simiane, who was the only one who knew the country well, led the cavalcade, and the four hunters trotted through a heath that grew as tall as a man to the hunt-rendezvous established a league away, in a clearing. It was at the bottom of a valley in the middle of a gigantic forest, interrupted periodically by a pastureland, a stream or a pool. The Baron's head beater was at the rendezvous with the kennel-grooms and the hounds.

The beast they were to hunt was ensconced in her lair a quarter of a league away, and its spoor indicated that she would follow the edge of a stream, engulf herself in a profound valley and drown herself therein, if she were not killed beforehand, in a pool six or eight leagues away, in the direction of the plains of Morbihan.

"Untie the horses," the Baron said, "and let's hunt!"

The tally-ho was sounded; the dogs launched themselves forward and disappeared into the thicket; the horses, electrified, bounded after them. Hector de Kerdrel, who had a reputation to make and a disadvantage to redress, threw himself ahead, hot on the heels of the pack.

A magnificent chorus executed by a dozen bass-tenor voices soon resounded from the covert, which the hunters' horns could scarcely overcome. Forgetting the hunt's primary goal for a few seconds, the Baron, overwhelmed by that imperious enthusiasm which is born in the heart of a hunter as the horn sounds, remembered the terrible fanfare executed in the woods of Holdengrasburg by the Black Huntsman. He sounded it with all the might of his lungs, with such vigor that one might have thought it a distant echo of the infernal voice that had so strongly impressed the *znapan* at the beginning of that story.

Even the creole–that nonchalant child of a tropical country, who traveled in a palanquin and had herself fanned during the burning days by obedient slaves–was electrified, fascinated by that powerful air. She gave her generous animal a smack on the rump with her riding-crop; whinnying with pain, its nostrils dilated and its eyes ablaze, the white stallion precipitated itself after Hector's horse, which was flying after the pack, striking sparks from pebbles and crushing fallen branches and dead leaves beneath its brazen hooves.

As for Monsieur de Nossac, he did not stimulate his mount with either whip or spur, but he continued his fanfare with a savage energy, and lost not an inch of ground on the creole, galloping side-by-side with her.

The hunt, as the beaters had foreseen, was engulfed by a profound valley, wild and studded with bizarre rock-formations, and led to a torrent, which flowed across a bed of pebbles and the trunks of fallen trees with an unexpected clatter.

A scarlet tint had appeared in the creole's cheeks. Overcome by enthusiasm, she glanced sideways at the Baron, who was glued to his saddle like a bronze knight, his fist on his hip and his horn to his lips–possessed, at that moment, of an energetic and masculine beauty that left Hector's feminine graces and infantile impetuosity far behind.

All of a sudden, the somber vault of foliage under which they were racing abruptly opened out; the forest encased by the valley was succeeded by a broken green plain with a thick mantle of pasturage, in the midst of which the beast and the pack appeared for the first time to the hunters' eyes.

The beast was a sow about three feet tall, striped with grey and fawn bands, a long head, thin, wiry legs, a bristling mane and bloody foam on her fangs. The pack was pressing ardently upon her, united in a huddle, so close together that a riding cloak could have covered the whole lot. The jaws of the first dogs were nipping the beast's tail at every instant; they were drinking her, as hunting terminology has it.

Hector was 150 paces in advance of the creole and the Baron. He was flying through the tall grass, oppressed and out of breath, sometimes crouching low over his horse's mane in order to turn his head and dart a triumphant glance at those who were following him. Suddenly, though, he felt his horse sag and sink beneath him. The grass came to head height, then higher still as he sank further down; then muddy water covered him, as it had already covered the animal.

He released a cry of alarm–but the horse lunged vigorously with its back and legs, and reappeared two seconds later to the anxious eyes of the hunters, who had seen it sink without being able to bring help. It was filthy with mud and covered with yellowish scum, as was its unfortunate rider–whose clothing, hands and face had disappeared into the same envelope, and who therefore resembled the man kneaded from clay which Prometheus attempted to bring to life.

Hector had encountered one of those pools that are called death-traps. The anxiety that had overcome the Baron and the creole at first was succeeded by mad and jeering laughter.

"The hunt's over for you, my friend," said Monsieur de Nossac. "Return to the château and have the servants provide you with a new set of clothes."

Hector was petrified, and blushed with shame and anger beneath his mask of mud.

"Since you're ugly enough," the implacable Baron continued, "to give anyone a fright in that strange costume."

"Go," said the creole, disdainfully, in her turn. "you look a fright..."

And while the pack continued to bay, as the beast attained the extremity of the plain and was swallowed up by a new thicket, the creole whipped her horse and resumed her course with lightning speed.

The Baron followed her.

As for the Marquis, he had taken another route to cut ahead of the pack and gain ground. The Marquise de Bidan and Monsieur de Nossac continued at the gallop, after having skirted the death-trap and gained the edge of the forest. Then the Baron took up his horn again and sounded the third couplet of the ballad of the Black Huntsman, which corresponded with the French fanfare known as the Forest Variation. But the fanfare came to a conclusion and, having passed the edge of the forest, the Baron and the creole could no longer hear the chorus of the hounds and the beaters' horns within the woods.

They cocked their ears in vain; the wind brought then neither the sound of baying nor the sound of horns. They had either lost track of the chase or–more probably–they had taken a wrong turn that they would have to rectify. The two hunters veered at hazard toward the south and continued to gallop, hoping at every instant to hear a shout, a sounding horn or barking, which would permit them to rejoin the chase. None was to be heard, and the horses continued their course.

As they came into a clearing, the Baron brought his mount to a halt, and immediately leapt to the ground. He had seen recent tracks on the damp and chalky ground; they were the footprints of a wild pig heading southwest–where, in all probability, it would reach a pool. Everything indicated that it was the beast they had been pursuing, save for one thing: the complete absence of dogs.

The Baron was not mistaken. "They've taken a wrong turn," he aid. "The beast's gone this way–we must look for it."

Remounting his horse, he set off again with the creole.

They ran thus for more than an hour, sometimes finding the beast's spoor on sand or moist ground, sometimes losing it on pebbles or rock, then finding it again. They reached a new plain, then a funnel-shaped valley, at whose entrance they perceived further spoor. The horses were out of breath, but the Baron's spurs and the creole's riding-crop came into play, and the pain renewed their exhausted strength.

The new valley into which they now ventured was wilder still, more deserted and more horridly splendid than the other.

Suddenly, Monsieur de Nossac stopped again, and extended his crop to indicate a white rock, on which a dark mass was moving. "Hold on," he said to the beautiful huntress. "There's our beast."

The creole shivered, following the direction of the whip, and perceived the sow. Cornered and out of breath, with her fangs bloodied, she was sitting on her tail, seemingly awaiting the firm tread of the pack she had wrong-footed.

"Madame," the Baron said, then, "I promised you that I would kill a pig with my knife, but our cousin Hector had the audacity to want to imitate me, so I shall undertake to strangle it with my bare hands."

The creole let out a cry of fright. "You're mad," she said. "I don't want that!"

"I always do what I have said."

"Kill it with your knife."

"No. Hector boasted of doing as much."

"He would not have done it."

"I don't know about that—but he said it, and that's sufficient for me."

"My God!" said the creole, going pale. "Are you so determined to surpass him in courage?"

"Yes, for you love him."

The creole started. "Who told you that?" she asked.

"I've seen it; I've divined it... I've deduced it..."

"What folly!"

"And," the Baron said, coldly, "I want you to love me!"

He got down coolly, threw away his hunting-knife and advanced towards the animal at a slow and measured pace, his head back and his stride arrogant, like a man going to a triumph rather than a certain death.

"Monsieur! Please, Monsieur! Stop!" the stunned creole cried after him.

He turned towards her, and said, "God forgive me! I believe that you love me already."

And he continued his march toward the sow, which stood up in her turn, released a dull grunt and took a step to meet him.

XXXIV

Monsieur de Nossac was beautiful at that supreme moment—as beautiful as the Roman knight who threw himself fully armored and on horseback into a chasm to propitiate the gods and save his fatherland.

He marched with a terrible slowness and cold self-assurance towards the monster that awaited him, standing firm, having taken a single step towards him. It would have been difficult to say which of them had a more menacing attitude: the horrible animal, which awaited its enemy with bristling mane, bloody mouth and bleakly ferocious eyes, or the man, who went towards it bare-headed, without weapons, with the intention of strangling it with his hands, as white and supple as a woman's.

The creole remained on her horse, petrified, fascinated and stunned by such audacity. She followed the Baron with a stupefied gaze, full of terror, doubtless thinking that she was dreaming, so unexpected was the spectacle to which she was a witness.

Eventually, two paces separated the monster from the man. The man had covered all of the intervening distance. He turned then to look at the creole. The creole seemed to be cast as a statue of Terror. Vainly, she wanted to cry out; vainly, too, she tried to climb down to the ground and run to the Baron's aid. Her throat was constricted; her saddle appeared to be an iron clamp, which screwed her to the horse and held her motionless and paralyzed.

The Baron's eyes fixed upon her for a moment, and this rapid glance enabled him to assure himself of the all-powerful effect that his boundless courage produced in women. Then he turned his flashing eyes back to the monster, and took another step.

He folded his arms across his breast then, and waited, seeming to say: "Must I come the whole way, then?" But the monster did not budge; the monster dared not advance. On the contrary, she recoiled, and seemed desirous of cornering herself on the rock that she had quit, employing it as a final rampart. Seeing that, the man took one step more, and was upon her.

Their breath–the man's cold and cadenced, the animal's halting and jerky–intermingled. The former's calm and terrible eyes met the latter's ferocious stare. Then, as two athletes measure one another before the contest, they contemplated one another and embraced one another with their gaze for one last moment before the arms of the one uncrossed and the jaws of the other opened.

And, as the monster still hesitated, scraping the rock with its stiff mane, trying to recoil one more step without being able to, the man extended his arms, more rapidly than thought, and seized the sow's gaping jaws–from which her terrible tusks projected–in his slender and aristocratic hands, whose satiny tissue overlaid muscles of steel. He gripped it so strongly that he shut the mouth violently, stifling a grunt of pain within the monster's throat.

The sow reared up; her muscular neck stiffened. Then with a brusque thrash, she tried to release its snout. If she had succeeded, the Baron would have been lost, for her redoubtable tusks would have disemboweled him–but his hands did not release their grip; they squeezed the foaming mouth more powerfully still, crushing the nasal fosses and inhibiting all respiration.

The rock against which the monster had backed up became fatal, by rendering all escape impossible. When she was stood erect on her hind legs, with her back to that unbreakable wall, any movement of that sort was paralyzed. Then, as the Baron's hands seemed to be converted into a vice, and as strangulation weakened his adversary, he thought that one hand would suffice, and put the other on the animal's throat.

It was a terrible struggle between that implacable and calm man, whose fiery gaze was riveted to the monster's frightful eyes, and the monster, struggling convulsively, trying in vain to extract herself from that gigantic pressure–to escape that agony of strangulation, which proceeded slowly and inexorably, blurring her eyes with a cloud of blood,

How long did the struggle last? Perhaps five minutes in objective terms, but an hour for the man, a century for the animal and an eternity for the creole–whose horse, an intelligent spectator of an unprecedented combat, pricked up its ears and quivered beneath her.

Finally, a last death-rattle and a last stifled grunt were emitted through the Baron's iron fingers from the strangled throat, from the monster's crushed snout... and the monster subsided little by little, still accompanied by that redoubtable grip, until it was half-lying on the ground.

The Baron continued squeezing for one more minute–a minute in which he seemed to be intent on burying his ivory hands in his adversary's quivering flesh–then, finally, one of his hands abandoned the throat to seize one of the sow's hind legs. Holding it thus, he lifted her up, held her over the valley– whose final plane was six or eight feet below the ledge that had served as a theatre for the tragic duel–and threw her down, still convulsing but with no more force, on to a heap of stones, where she fell inert and rendered up her last sigh.

Then the horrific charm that fascinated the creole was broken, and–exhaling a cry that no pen could describe, perhaps which no human voice could ever reproduce–she urged her horse towards the Baron. He had refolded his arms across his breast. With a triumphant smile on his lips, as calm as he had been before the struggle, but pale after the supreme effort he had just made, he stood motionless on the rock that he had immortalized, waiting for her.

Ten paces away from Monsieur de Nossac, the creole precipitated herself from her mount and ran to him, pale and panting, almost as exhausted as he was by the moral effort with which she had accompanied his actual effort.

"My God!" she murmured, in a faint voice. "Aren't you wounded?"

He smiled, tried to speak, and could not.

"Oh, you are!" she said, distraught. She had just noticed the bloody sputum which the monster had dribbled on the Baron's white hands.

He shook his head negatively, and pointed to the animal. Then he got his voice back. "It's hers," he said.

Then this man, so strong until then, who had neither paled not trembled in the face of mortal peril, felt himself overcome by a strange weakness and an extraordinary emotion in confrontation with this woman, who fixed such an ardent gaze upon him, and he staggered. She caught him in her arms.

"I beg your pardon," he murmured, "but I squeezed so hard, so hard..." He fainted, and subsided upon her.

The creole reached the trickle of water that ran through the bottom of the valley in a single bound. She took her Amazonian hat, whose plume had broken in coming through the thicket, converted it into a vase and filled it up. Then she returned to the Baron, and threw its contents in his face. Then, as the water was powerless to reanimate him, she sat down beside him, took his pale head in her arms, set it upon her knees and pressed her ardent lips to his forehead, which was streaming with cold sweat.

The contact of that mouth caused the Baron's eyes to open instantaneously. He released a cry of joy on seeing the emotional and fearful face of the woman for whom he had braved death looming over him.

The creole blushed then; after helping him to sit up, she got up with dignity, and withdrew to a distance.

"It's too late, Madame," Monsieur de Nossac murmured.

"What do you mean?" she said, anxiously.

"I've caught you—it's futile to try and hide from me..."

"What do you mean?" she murmured, becoming increasingly emotional.

"You love me!" said the Baron, triumphantly.

Monsieur de Nossac waited for one of those phrases or outbursts of emotion which spring from the heart at impassioned moments, which nothing seems able to arrest, but none came. By means of one of those sudden reactions of which only certain women possess the secret—and which are, in them, irrefutable proof of the despotic dominion of reason and self-assurance over the heart—the creole looked at the Baron calmly, and said to him: "You're mistaken, Monsieur."

The Baron recoiled, stupefied.

"The danger you have just run, Monsieur," she continued, "impressed me vividly. I have suffered on your behalf, I have brought you help because it was my duty. I shivered, because you undertook such a folly in order to please me. Can one say, however, that that anxiety, that concern, that solicitude, amounts to love?" The creole trembled slightly as she pronounced the final word.

"Oh, don't deny it, Madame," said the Baron, studying her attentively. "Don't deny it."

She shrugged her shoulders. "Conceited ass!" she said. And as this epithet made him frown, she went on: "Are you quite certain of being loved by me?"

"Yes, for I love you, with all the power that passion can produce."

The creole burst out laughing. "Is that because I resemble Gretchen?"

"No," he said, resolutely. "I love you because I love you."

"And do you love me a great deal?" the young woman said, still mockingly.

"As I have never loved any woman."

An ironic smile pursed the young creole's lips. "Monsieur le Baron," she said, "yesterday evening, after the supper that you offered us, when you had returned to your room, dulled by the fumes of wine, your friend the Marquis de Simiane told us about your marriage and the bad turn that the Duchesse did to your wife, and then something of your implausible adventure in Germany, and your simultaneous love for Gretchen and Roschen."

Monsieur de Nossac shivered. "I did not love them as much as you," he said.

"What proof do I have of that?"

"But what I've just done," he stammered.

"A trifle. You'd have risked something similar for this Gretchen, of whom I'm jealous."

"I did not love her as much as you... Now, she horrifies me!"

A glint appeared in the creole's eyes, but the Baron did not notice it. He was entirely in the grip of passion, and covered the young woman's white hands with burning kisses.

"Monsieur le Baron," she went on, "I am, unfortunately, neither your wife nor Gretchen, despite the resemblance that you wish to attribute to me. In consequence, at least have the courtesy not to speak to me of a love which is, in your own eyes, nothing but an amour by proxy."

"I love you for yourself."

"Still because of my resemblance to Gretchen,"

"My God!" cried Monsieur de Nossac, with ill-contained impatience. "I've already forgotten Gretchen. Why do you keep on talking about her?"

"You have forgotten Gretchen?"

"Yes, Madame."

"Monsieur, permit me to put the opinion of your friend, Monsieur de Simiane, to you."

"What?"

"You are mad."

Monsieur de Nossac knelt down and seized her hands. "Believe me, Madame," he said, in an emotional voice, "I love you..."

"How can I believe that?"

"Have I not proved it to you, then?"

"You have proved to me that you love Gretchen."

The Baron stamped his foot on the ground. "Hold on," he said, running to his horse and taking a pistol from its saddle-bag. "If you say to me once more that it is Gretchen and not you that I love, I shall blow my brains out."

And as there was a cold and desperate resolution in his tone, which implied that he would do as he said, the creole ran to him, put her lovely hand on his arm, pulled the pistol down and said to him: "I believe you."

The Baron released a cry of joy.

"And," he said, trembling, "you love me..."

The danger was past, for the pistol was back in the saddlebag. The creole emitted a little burst of laughter, mocking and ironic. "I haven't told you that," she said.

"But... I love you... me..."

"I believe it."

"Are you made of marble then?"

The creole glanced down at her shoulders, which her low-necked hunting costume left slightly exposed, and then at her hands, pure of form and possessed of the irreproachable whiteness of a statue, and replied to the Baron with one sublime word: "Flatterer."

Monsieur de Nossac had counted on overwhelming her with the rejected lover's ultimate insult, but she welcomed that insult and wore it like a compliment. That response disconcerted the Baron momentarily.

"Hold on," she continued, extending a hand towards the southwest. "Have you noticed how dark the sky is becoming?"

"Eh? What do I care?"

"We shall have a terrible storm."

"So much the better!"

"So much the worse! For I see no house or cottage in the vicinity where we can shelter."

"We'll easily find some grotto or cave..."

"But I prefer a cottage. Let's go, my handsome knight—get into the saddle and let's be off."

"Already!" said the Baron, darting a regretful glance at the wild spot where he had braved death for this woman, and in the middle of which she had the courage to mock him—for he strongly suspected that the feeble prestige he had obtained, with which he was still surrounded, would vanish when the cadaver of his victim had been left behind and they had both returned to real and prosaic social life.

"We must," she said. "I'm afraid of lightning."

As if the lightning had taken that as a kind of challenge, though, the sky—which was now entirely black—split, and an immense bolt of lightning sprang forth, striking so close to the two hunters that they were dazzled by it. The creole threw herself upon the Baron's bosom.

"Oh!" she said. "I'm afraid.. save me... protect me..."

"You see–you love me!" he said, triumphantly. "You lean on me like ivy on an old fort!" Monsieur de Nossac looked around in every direction, searching for a shelter in the midst of that wild and disordered landscape. The valley was deserted, devoid of habitation, without the smallest woodcutter's hut or shepherd's cot.

A second lightning-flash cleft the clouds, however, and another explosion of thunder resounded; the creole released another cry of anguish and said: "My God! Let's go! Hide me... I'm afraid!" And she pressed herself against him.

Monsieur de Nossac did not hesitate any longer. He took the young woman in his arms, put her in her saddle and leapt up behind her, as if he had forgotten that he had a horse of his own.

The creole was no longer thinking about that. A third flash of lightning shut her eyes, and then she abandoned herself, utterly distraught, to her cavalier–who, under the pretext of keeping her safely in front of him, pressed her to his bosom forcefully enough for her to feel the precipitate beating of his heart, and for him to feel hers. For her heart was hammering; she shivered, and she squeezed the Baron's hands with such force that he feared she might suffer a nervous fit at any second.

Was it only fear that was agitating her thus? Perhaps the Baron had hit the target in saying to her a short while before "You see–you love me already!" Might it not be the chagrin and secret humiliation of admitting her defeat that had thrown her into such agitation?

Monsieur de Nossac, doubtless still forgetful of his own horse, launched the one he had mounted into a fast gallop, retracing his steps along the route they had followed an hour before.

Large raindrops began to spatter the off-white stones of the valley, falling with a curt, almost metallic noise on the green domes of the trees, which interlaced their branches here and there above the path through the valley. Then the drops fell more precipitately and closer together, soon falling in an avalanche.

As the thunder resounded continually, making it dangerous to continue galloping and thus open up a current of electricity,[50] Monsieur de Nossac's eyes darted incessantly to the right and left, still searching for a shelter. That shelter he finally perceived. A rock, partly hollowed out, extended its superior part sufficiently over its base to offer a sort of roofed grotto. The Baron steered his horse in that direction, leapt to the ground, and carried the half-swooning creole to that natural awning.

The creole curled herself up as best she could, draping herself as warmly as possible in the mantle that the Baron had detached from the saddle-bow in order to cover her. Her teeth clenched in terror, her eyes attached with frightful fixity upon the lightning-split sky, she remained immobile and cold beside the Baron, who studied her with respectful pity.

"I'm cold!" she said, suddenly.

He took her in her arms and pressed her to his heart.

"You're hurting me!" she murmured.

His arms relaxed and set her at liberty–but shortly thereafter she repeated: "God, I'm cold!"

He took her in his arms again, and this time–whether because she really was cold, or because she was no longer conscious of her situation–she offered no resistance to that pressure, let her pale head and disordered hair fall back on Nossac's shoulder and shut her eyes.

XXXV

The Baron looked at her contemplatively for a minute, exhausted and collapsed in his arms. For that minute, he hesitated between respect and passion–then, carried away by passion, he put his quivering lips to the young woman's lusterless forehead.

At that contact, she shivered and opened her eyes.

"What are you doing?" she said.

"I love you," he murmured.

"Let go of me!" She pulled away abruptly, and looked at him angrily.

He knelt down then, took hold of her hands again and said to her: "I love you so much... forgive me!"

The flash of irritation that glittered in her eyes disappeared. She looked at this man, so strong, so admirably manly in the face of the most real and terrible perils; she saw him humble and suppliant before her–before her, trembling with folly and fright, before her, terrified by the lightning, chilled by the rain...who, on her own, would have found it impossible to flee, or even to take a few steps, so much had the storm frightened, not to say petrified, her...

She gave him her hand–her beautiful hand, tremulous and chilly–and said: "I forgive you..."

He started with joy, and replied: "Love me!"

A lightning-bolt struck so close to them at that moment that she threw herself into the Baron's arms again. He thought it a tacit avowal, and he brushed the disordered curls of her black hair with his lips. She shivered, as she had the first time; as she had the first time, she stifled a cry–but she did not try to pull away from his embrace.

"One word!" he said to her, in a prayerful tone. "Just one..."

"You can see perfectly well that I'm cold!"

He clutched her more strongly to his heart. "For mercy's sake!" he went on. "Just one word!"

"But...what word?"

"Oh! You know very well..."

"I swear to you..."

"Tell me. Tell me that you love me."

"Very well," she sighed. "So be it!"

He shivered with hope; his heartbeat faltered.

"So be it," she went on. "Monsieur le Baron de Nossac, Gretchen loves you..."

He cried out. "So you admit it?" he exclaimed.

"Admit what, if you please?" And her tone became cold and curt again.

"You admit that you are Gretchen?"

"Not at all," she replied, with an ironic smile. "I wanted you to prove to yourself that it was Gretchen that you loved in me."

The Baron reddened and shuddered. He looked at the woman: the woman smiling at him with the icy malice of a demon. The woman, weakened for a moment by terror, got to her feet, disdainful and cold–and he had no right to complain, for he had just offended her cruelly.

She took off he mantle and threw it at him. "Keep it for Gretchen," she said. "I don't want anything from you."

"If you know a prayer," he said, "say it."

She recoiled in terror. "Are you going to kill me, then?" she cried.

"Yes, Madame."

"But what have I done to you?"

"Nothing."

"So..." And she read so much anger and determination in his eyes that she threw herself to her knees, and lifted her hands in supplication.

"So," the Baron went on, "I shall kill you, and then kill myself. We shall have this deserted valley for a tomb, and the vultures for gravediggers. Pray, Madame..."

"But... what have I done to you?" she said, chilled and bewildered. "Why do you want to kill me?"

"Because I love you."

"And if I loved you too," she said, "would you still kill me?"

"Yes, if you tell me so–for tomorrow, perhaps, you would love me no longer."

She got up joyfully, put her arms around his neck, and said to him: "Kill me now. Kill me... I love you!"

He raised his weapon again and aimed it at her, but the weapon slipped from his hands and fell to the ground.[51]

"I don't want to! I haven't the strength to kill you..."

After that brief embrace, however, the creole blushed, and took a step backwards. "Monsieur," she said, "will you listen to me...?"

He shuddered. This woman's hesitations were terrible.

"Will you?" she continued.

"Speak, Madame."

"Monsieur, I'm 27 years old. I'm a widow. I have 50,000 *livres* a year. If you want me to love you, you must marry me!"

Monsieur de Nossac almost died of joy.

"You're an angel!" he cried.

"An angel, no. But I'll be your wife in a week's time."

And as the storm slackened, and dusk was already casting its first veil upon the misty hills and the chilly valley, she added: "Come on–the rain has stopped, the thunder's fallen silent. Let's go back."

They forgot about the second horse, giving it no further thought. They made their way back to the château on foot, entwined with one another.

It was, for the Baron, a repetition of that delightful promenade of the previous evening through the golden gorse, the perfumed heather and beneath the tall Breton hedges–a promenade in which nature spoke to the heart with a thousand whispers. One thing alone had changed: the idol!

The previous evening, Yvonnette had been leaning on him. Today, it was the creole.

XXXVI

When they arrived in the drawing-room, four people were waiting for them: the Comte, Monsieur de Simiane, Yvonnette and Hector.

Hector's eyes were charged with anger; he looked at the Baron with a fiery expression. Yvonnette went pale on seeing the creole on his arm, then a vivid scarlet mounted to her cheeks, and a tear hovered on the tips of her long eyelashes.

Monsieur de Nossac noticed Hector's distraught face first, and met his fierce stare. A feeling of ferocious joy gripped him, and he let a triumphant smile wander over his lips–but then his eyes, leaving Hector, fell upon Yvonnette. The Baron went pale in his turn, and he felt remorse penetrate his heart.

Yvonnette gazed at the Baron with resigned sorrow. The Baron shivered before that gaze, as he had already shivered at the sight of her pale face, and the remorse that was now welded within his heart assumed greater proportions. He went to her, without affectation, and took her hand. She withdrew the hand–not abruptly, but she did withdraw it.

"Why are you annoyed with me?" he asked her, in a low voice.

The young woman was pale, but she had courage enough to reply: "You're mistaken, Monsieur. Far from being annoyed with you, I am, on the contrary. infinitely pleased with you for bringing my cousin back safe and sound."

"Monsieur le Baron," said the Comte de Kervégan, interrupting Monsieur de Nossac's conversation with the young woman, "where did you take refuge during the storm?"

"Under a rock, Comte."

"And that was the most interesting episode of your hunt, I'll wager."

"Oh, dear God, yes," the Baron said simply.

"I beg your pardon, Baron," said the creole, with the voice of an enchantress, "but you're forgetting the wild pig."

"Oh! Yes, a mere trifle..."

"Brought down?" asked the Comte.

"No," she said, enthusiastically. "Killed on the spot!"

"With knife-thrusts, perhaps?" Hector said, sarcastically.

"Not at all, my young lord," said the Baron, darting a tender glance at the creole. "I simply choked it."

214

There was but one cry from the four people the Baron and the creole had found in the drawing-room.

"Impossible!" said the Comte.

"A joke!" said Hector, his teeth grinding in wrath.

"What imprudence!" murmured Yvonnette, tremulously.

The Baron heard that word, and was touched. He was momentarily inclined to go back to the young woman he had just quit, to take her hand and thank her with a glance, but the creole prevented him by leaning on his arm. "Baron," she said, in an adorably languid tone, "would you permit me to play Homer and sing your exploits?"

In any other circumstances, Monsieur de Nossac would have excused himself gracefully, but Hector was there—Hector, who, that morning, had knelt before his cousin, insolently kissing her hands and darting little glances full of triumph and impatience at him, the Baron de Nossac.

"Please do, Madame. One is proud to have a Homer like you, whose eyes are so beautiful—which is more than the Homer of antiquity could have had, being blind."

The creole immediately took up her lyre, and recounted the Baron's chivalric combat with a fine attention to detail, a vivid coloration and a lively imagery, which made him shiver with pride. The woman must love him very much to recall it so well, he thought—to highlight the least incident of the struggle, and to speak of it with such enthusiasm.

Hector's physiognomy expressed furious chagrin. "Well," he said, "if Monsieur le Baron wishes to make a fresh start tomorrow, I'll play his part."

"You'll choke a wild boar?" asked Simiane, who had been mute and careful until then.

"Yes," Hector said, resolutely.

"Child," the creole replied, with slightly ironic maternal tenderness. "I'll have one brought from Nuremberg; it will be made of cardboard, so you can choke it and torture it without any danger."

Hector went pale. He tried to speak, but anger and distress gripped his throat, and no sound could come out.

"Baron," the Marquis said, then, "you've forgotten one essential thing."

"Which is?"

"That Monsieur le Comte desires to return to Kervégan, and that it would be as well if your butler could have dinner served."

"Return to Kervégan?"

"Yes," said the Comte.

"It's pitch dark."

"Bah! The roads are familiar."

Monsieur de Nossac threw a suppliant glance at the creole. She understood it, and hastened to say: "Indeed, it's not very comfortable traveling by night."

"The roads are safe, niece."

"And muddy, uncle."

"You think so?"

"It's been raining."

"Thank you!" Monsieur de Nossac whispered to her. Then he raised his voice: "So you'll stay, won't you?"

"Of course, if my uncle wishes it. For myself, though, I'm horribly nervous..."

"Indeed–the storm frightened and exasperated you."

"Totally. Tomorrow, however, my dear uncle, I'll be quite ready to make an early departure."

"I'll take you back after breakfast," said the Baron.

"Agreed."

"Dinner is served, Monsieur le Baron," cried the butler from the doorway.

Monsieur de Nossac went to offer his arm to the creole, but Simiane got there before him. The Baron reverted to Yvonnette, but Yvonnette took her cousin's arm, and Monsieur de Nossac bit his lip.

"Well," Simiane whispered to his companion, "are you content?"

"Not yet."

"Are you not sufficiently avenged?"

"No."

216

"Will you kill him?"

She smiled, and made no reply.

The dinner was cheerful for the Baron and the creole, worrisome for Simiane, sad for Yvonnette, and pure torture for Hector.

Monsieur de Nossac went to bed early. He needed to be alone, to converse with himself for a few minutes, to put his head in his hands and to still the precipitate beating of his heart. His night was restless, his awakening belated. Who ever said that love does not sleep?

The Sun was streaming through the curtains when he woke up. He leapt briskly from the foot of his bed, spent a few minutes breathing in the morning air, still impregnated with the stormy vapors of the previous evening, and rang for his valet to help him dress.

The valet appeared with a letter in his hand. The Baron opened the letter precipitately, and read:

My dear Baron,

A night of wisdom has made me reflect seriously on a day of folly. You fascinated me yesterday, and I really loved you for an hour. I believe, may God forgive me, that in a fit of fever and fright, I promised you my hand.

My hand is not free, Monsieur; I promised my dying father that I would marry his nephew. It is necessary that Hector will become my husband. If I stayed in your house any longer, you might perhaps fall in love with me, and I would be culpable then, rather than merely overwhelmed, as I have been. I have therefore eloped with my husband, whom I shall take to Brest with his uncle and his cousin, where we shall embark on the Esperanza, which is setting sail for the West Indies.

Thank you, Monsieur le Baron, for your gracious hospitality; I shall always remember you kindly. I hope you will be able to forgive my thoughtlessness.

Adieu; Gretchen will console you. Kiss my hands, and then forget me.

The Marquise de Bridan.

217

Monsieur de Nossac recoiled, thunderstruck, and the letter slipped from his hands.

XXXVII

The Baron demanded to know where the Comte de Kervégan was. The Comte had departed for Brest with his family. He found no one but the Marquis, who was still asleep. They both mounted horses, and raced full tilt across country on the track of the fugitives. They rode all day and all night, but the storm had flooded the roads, and the distance was great. At every relay-station and every village they learned that a carriage had passed through a few hours before, headed for Brest.

Finally, at eight o'clock the following morning, they crested a little rise, from which Brest and the approaching road could be seen. The post-chaise was still ahead of them. At midday they entered Brest and made for the port. A merchant brig had just raised its anchor, and was setting out to sea, They asked the name of the brig; it was the *Esperanza*. The Baron demanded a boat to go after her, but he was told that the ship had the wind behind her, and all her sail on, and that it was impossible.

Then, seizing upon one last hope, the Baron thought that the fugitives might not have arrived in time to embark, and that the *Esperanza* had left without them. He ran to the office of the brig's owner and was shown the passenger-list–and read there, with sweat on his brow, the names of the Comte, his daughter and his nephew. The creole was lost to him, like Gretchen. Monsieur de Nossac then had a fit of despair and delirium, which obliged him to remain in bed for several days at a hostelry in Brest. Then, when the crisis was past, he asked for horses to return to his château in Léonais. But the Marquis, who had never left his side, opposed that, and said to him: "Let's go to Paris. There, if anywhere, you'll be able to find distraction."

Part Three

XXVIII

Six months had gone by.

The last warm days of summer, during which we left the Baron de Nossac taking the road from Paris to Brest, had been followed by the autumn months, the nebulous winter and the first *frisson* of spring. It was the end of March, the eve of mid-Lent.[52]

The day was mild and clear by the standards of old Paris; a colorful masked crowd had been swarming along the quais and boulevards since morning, sparkling with gaiety, abuzz with witty remarks. Its members marveled at one another, having been to Longchamp–which was then newly-born–to admire, with the naive astonishment of the Parisian populace, so clever and so stupid at the same time, the last pearls of frost shining upon the first shoots of spring.[53]

The laundresses of Paris were parading in the streets in carts and *calèches*, dressed like ladies of the court; it was their right on that day, which was their feast-day. The ladies of the court, meanwhile, found it amusing to disguise themselves as laundresses, and to greater and lesser Porcherons in wicker carts whose horses were decked out and beribboned like *rosières*.[54]

His Majesty Louis XV, nicknamed the Beloved, was then a child of 12,[55] dark-haired but a trifle pale in complexion, wearing his hair in curls, with cherry-red lips, beautifully slender hands and widely-spaced blue eyes. His Majesty Louis

XV, we repeat, had not disdained to take part in the *fête*. He had come from Versailles, accompanied by Monsieur le Duc de Bourbon, the Prime Minister, Monsieur de Villeroi,[56] his Governor, and the young Duc de Richelieu, Colonel of the Swiss Guards,[57] whose frequent incarcerations in the Bastille under the late Regent, involvement in the Cellamare conspiracy and intimacy with the Duchesse du Maine and the coterie of Sceaux had brought him into considerable favor since the death of the Duc d'Orléans.

The King, who had arrived in Paris the day before, had slept at the Tuileries. On the following day, he showed himself in the boulevards and at the Hôtel de Ville, where the merchants' aldermen and provosts were holding a daytime ball. There, he danced with the prettiest girls in the capital, and when he climbed into a carriage to take the road to Versailles, the ball having finished at five o'clock, he found an enthusiastic crowd lining his route, which greeted him with frenzied cries of "Long live the King!"

While the King was dancing at the Hôtel de Ville, a party of courtiers–fashionable ladies, rakes and young hotheads–was dancing in Porcherons. The King was the hero of the Hôtel de Ville; a simple gentleman filled that role at Porcherons. The gentleman in question was scarcely 30 years old, handsome–despite his pale face and the ardent fever of his expression–elegantly-dressed, witty to the point of audacity, and magnificent to the point of folly. His name was the Baron de Nossac: the same Baron de Nossac we left broken and crushed on the road from Brest to Paris; the same Baron de Nossac who had almost gone mad following the creole's departure, and who had returned to court in search of distraction.

He had succeeded. For six months, no one had seen any gentleman more magnificent, more extravagant or more cleverly mad in Paris or Versailles. For six months, no one had talked of anything but the bizarre and splendid feasts he held, the daily eccentricities of his intellect, and his unprecedentedly original lifestyle.

Monsieur de Nossac had become the Alcibiades of Versailles.[58] One thing alone seemed lacking in his glory–a dog whose tail he might cut off, like the Greek hero, to awaken public attention–until one of his friends had made it known, incontinently, that the Baron had sworn to cut off the ears of all the bears in the Jardin du Roi: a task which he had executed with the marvelous self-assurance and terrible audacity that he had displayed in Brittany in his hand-to-hand struggle with the wild pig.

Today, Monsieur de Nossac was in disguise, like the majority of his companions in extravagance. While everyone else had prepared their disguises several days in advance, the Baron had found his at the last moment, and had not thought about it until then.

A Chinese diplomatic mission had arrived a short while before, composed of four mandarins of the highest order, charged with offering the amity of the Celestial Empire to the King of France. The evening before, the Ambassadors had been presented at Versailles, and had received a grand audience with the King. The Baron had been present in his capacity as a commanding officer.

One of the mandarins had a moonlight-colored robe which occasioned a fit of hysterical laughter at Versailles–a contagious success that reached Paris and attracted mocking crowds of street-urchins and guttersnipes when the mandarin's carriage went along the Champs-Elysées. From that moment, the Baron's choice was made. He decided that he must have a moonlight robe for the following day–a robe absolutely identical to the mandarin's. One difficulty presented itself, however: there was no tailor capable of running it up, and no draper who had a single bolt of cloth in an identical shade. The Baron clung to his idea, though; he must have a moonlight-colored robe to wear to Porcherons on the following day,

"Let's take the Moon in our teeth," he said to his furnishers, "and use a piece of it to make your robe." The Baron showed his furnishers the door, and did not hang around kicking his heels.

That evening, the mandarins went to a performance at the Opéra, which was then showing *Didon* by the late Monsieur Quinault.[59] The mandarin in the moonlight robe was invited to visit the wings, and set off into a labyrinth of dark corridors and forests of cardboard, in the midst of a crowd of Phoenicians and Trojans whose enticing faces compromised the gravity of the Celestial Empire's representative more than once. Suddenly, a trapdoor opened and the ground disappeared beneath his hesitant feet; he uttered a cry and disappeared. The Mandarin had fallen into the third understage, on to a pile of mattresses.

There was general astonishment the next day, at Porcherons, when the mandarin was seen dancing the minuet with a mask on his face and his moonlight-colored robe on his back. Then, the mandarin having taken off his mask, there was ringing applause, as everyone recognized Monsieur le Baron de Nossac. What had become of the real mandarin? Was he still in the third understage? No one knew for sure.

There was a dinner with 200 place-settings at Porcherons. Then, with the dinner finished and dusk falling, everyone set out for Paris or Versailles. A group of young and pretty women–all masked–half-drunk lords, three-quarters-drunk officers and enriched peasants stifling in their fancy coats formed around the Baron.

The Baron took each of the women aside and whispered in her ear: "Whither are you bound, beautiful unknown? The court or the Opéra?"

To those who responded indignantly "The court!" he said "I'm holding a ball a week hence–I'll expect you." To those who confessed with proud humility that they belonged in the wings, he breathed in a whisper: "Supper tonight, at midnight, at my house in the Rue Saint-Louis, in the Marais. Silence!" Then finally, he did the same with the men; to those who had once enjoyed the intimacy of the Regent's fine suppers he said: "Supper, tonight, my place," To the others he spoke of the ball the following week, as he had done to the ladies of the court, recommending all of them to profound silence.

Then he climbed into his carriage, in his moonlight robe, and departed at the gallop along the road to Paris.

XXXIX

At a quarter to midnight, the Hôtel de Nossac was as dismal and deserted as if no human being had come through its doors for half a century. No light shone from its windows, no carriages stood in its courtyard. The street was deserted and silent in its vicinity, and the placid bourgeois residents of the Île Saint-Louis were profoundly asleep.

Suddenly, a post-chaise pulled by four dusty and breathless horses arrived, pulling up in front of the gate. A man in traveling clothes got down. It was the Marquis de Simiane, returning from Saint Petersburg, where he had been sent a few days after his return from Brittany to fulfill a secret diplomatic mission.

His manservant had to sound the bell three times before the gate opened, but it finally swung on its rusty hinges, without any human being, master or servant, appearing in the courtyard. The main door opened just as mysteriously. The Marquis, still alone, went into a vast ill-lit hallway, at the far end of which an old domestic was waiting, as bleak and mute as a statue.

Oh! oh! thought the Marquis. *Can the poor Baron be dead?*

"What does Monsieur le Marquis desire?" asked the domestic, recognizing him.

"I'd like to see your master," the Marquis said. "Isn't he here?"

"He is, Monsieur le Marquis."

The domestic got up. Going to the left of the master stairway that led to the grand apartments, he took a service stair and led the Marquis to a little bedroom, where the Baron was sitting pensively beside a meager fire, with his head in his hands, still wearing his moonlight robe.

The bedroom was no better lit than the hallway, and the Marquis did not notice the bizarre design of his friend's eccentric dressing-gown. What he did notice were the Baron's pale face and feverish eyes, and his dejected, defeated attitude of suffering.

"My God!" he said to him, offering his arm. "Are you ill?"

"Oh, it's you!" the Baron said. "How are you?"

"What about you–you're suffering, ill, aren't you?"

"Me? Not at all!"

And the Baron made a concerted effort, recovered a youthful smile, and straightened himself up politely. "I'm perfectly well, Marquis," he said. "Sound in body and mind."

"Are you quite sure?"

"A fine question!"

"Hold on," said the Marquis. "That's a singular dressing-gown you're wearing."

"It's a Chinese ambassador's robe..." And the Baron recounted the story of the third understage at the Opéra.

Monsieur de Simiane looked at him in stupefaction. "You're mad," he said.

"No, but I'm dying, and I'm dying happy."

"You're dying?"

"Alas."

"Of what, if you please?"

"Ah," said the Baron, "it's a sad and quite implausible story."

Bah! thought Monsieur de Simiane. *It's the Château de Holdengrasburg all over again.* And he added, in a low voice: "I'm beginning to repent the role I played; that woman will kill him..."

"Imagine, my dear friend..." the Baron went on. But at that moment, midnight chimed, and he interrupted himself. "I'll tell you the tale tomorrow. In the meantime, I'm hosting a supper tonight, and it's midnight."

XL

The Marquis reacted with profound astonishment. "You're giving a supper?" he said.

"Yes."

"To whom."

"To a select, though numerous, society," the Baron said, "composed of our old acquaintances from the Regent's suppers and demoiselles from the Opéra."

"Here?"

"But of course."

"I see no preparations, though..."

"Come on," said the Baron. "You'll see." And he opened a door, took Simiane by the hand, and led him through a dark corridor to another door, which he opened immediately, and from which sprang a flood of light. The Marquis looked in, and uttered a cry of astonishment.

The room was hung with black drapes spangled with silver tears. In the middle stood a table, sumptuously dressed. In the room's four corners perfectly motionless skeletons held torches in their hands; these served as candelabras. The place recalled the dining-room in the Castle of Holdengrasburg. Only the coffin was missing.

Monsieur de Simiane was rooted to the spot.

"I've seen similar decorations in Germany," the Baron said, calmly, "and they pleased me so much that I've imitated them here. Did you come up by the main staircase?"

"No."

"It's similarly decorated."

"What madness!"

The Baron went to a casement window and opened it. "My guests are late, it seems," he murmured.

"Indeed–the street is deserted."

"Oh well," the Baron went on, "while we're waiting for them I'll tell you that sad story that's causing me to die..."

Monsieur de Nossac invited the Marquis to take a seat and sat down himself with the indifference of weakness and discouragement. "My dear friend," he said to the Marquis, languidly, "I have but a week to live..."

"You're joking!"

"Don't you find me very pale?"

"Indeed."

"I no longer sleep."

"Why?"

"Because it's impossible for me to do so. I remember a certain story told to me by my uncle, the Bishop of Marmande, about a missionary that the Cochinchinese caused to die by depriving him of sleep." [60]

The Marquis looked at the Baron in astonishment. "And what prevents you from sleeping?"

"A phantom."

The Marquis shivered. "Your mind is still disturbed."

"Not at all. I really see a phantom every night."

"I'll wager that it's your wife's?"

"Yes," said the Baron, sadly.

The Marquis burst out laughing. "Still the same story," he murmured.

"You're mocking me–but you're wrong. It's true..."

"Who tells you that it's not Gretchen?"

"Gretchen!" said the Baron, shivering. "No, Gretchen's not here... It's not Gretchen."

"How, then," asked the Marquis, "does this phantom manifest itself to you? How does it prevent you from sleeping?"

"Ah," murmured the Baron, despondently, "that's what I was about to tell you. The phantom inhabits my bedroom, and it wakes me when I go to sleep."

"You believe in phantoms, then?"

"Since I see them!"

The Marquis shook his head. "You're demented," he said.

The Baron smiled sadly, and continued: "The first time I slept in this house after my return from Brittany, I was seized by an inexpressible anguish–a sort of superstitious terror that it was impossible for me to overcome. I saw my wife everywhere: in the ballroom, in the corridors, on the staircases, in the nuptial bedroom where I abandoned her so fatally to follow that accursed Duchesse to whom I was enslaved by my word...

"I had sufficient self-control, however, to summon my reason and tell myself that death is something irreparable and that eternal regrets are impossible. We had been traveling for three days in a post-chaise, I was ground down by fatigue, so I went to bed early and fell profoundly asleep. In the middle of the night, a noise–monotonous, slow and slightly jerky–awoke me. I opened my eyes with difficulty, and thought I saw something white moving at the opposite extremity of my room, dragging its feet on the floor-tiles with a sort of rhythm. I sat up and called out, but the white form continued to walk back and forth. Then a ray of moonlight suddenly fell upon it, and I saw a pale face, inundated by black hair falling all the way to the ground–a pale, sad face, which had a heart-rending smile and hollow, blazing eyes...

"I recognized that poor Hélène Borelli, who never had any other name but Madame de Nossac."

"You were dreaming, my friend."

"I thought so. Delirium took hold of me. I went back to sleep under the oppression of a nightmare and, when daylight came to wake me, the phantom had disappeared. I thought I had been dreaming. The day sped by for me, in various preoccupations. I went to see the King at Versailles and renewed my relationship with him. I gathered the means of distracting myself. Evening came; I was as exhausted as I had been the previous evening, and I went to sleep just as promptly. At midnight, I was woken up by the same noise as before. I perceived the same white form, and, with my teeth clenched, my eyes haggard, my breast oppressed, I watched it walk back and forth, not daring and not being able to move, paralyzed by

227

terror and trying in vain to close my eyes. The phantom walked until four o'clock in the morning. At the moment when the first ray of daylight filtered, indecisively, through the shutters and the curtains, I saw it draw away, as if the walls had recoiled before it, then suddenly disappear, without it being possible for me to ascertain how or by what means it had gone."

"That's bizarre!" murmured the Marquis.

"The following night, the same apparition."

"Again!"

"Always. It comes back every night, at midnight, finishing at four o'clock in the morning. Anguish grips me and wakes me at midnight; from midnight to four o'clock, terror prevents me from closing my eyes..."

"With the result that you never sleep?"

"Yes, but a feverish, nightmarish sleep, as fatiguing as staying awake."

"And you don't think... You can't get up to chase the phantom away!"

"No, for it loves me." The Baron's tone was broken-hearted.

"It loves you?"

"Yes, often, while walking back and forth it passes close to my bed, and then it looks at me with an expression of love and sadness, which makes me ill."

"Does it speak to you?"

"Never."

"Have you never tried leaving your lamp lit?"

"Yes, of course."

"Well?"

"At a given moment, without my being able to explain how, it goes out."

"This is too much," the Marquis murmured. "You're the victim of a hoax."

Monsieur de Nossac shook his head. "It really is my wife," he said.

"Or perhaps Gretchen?"

"No, for Gretchen was my wife."

"God! You're madder than ever!"

"I don't expect you to believe me, but I know full well that nothing is more true than that I'm not mad."

"Perhaps it's the creole, then?"

The Baron shivered, and passed his hand over his forehead.

"The creole?" he said. "The creole was my wife."

"Again?"

"My dead wife, who came to Germany under the name Gretchen, to Brittany under that of the Marquise de Bridan, and here under her own name, to avenge herself, my friend–to avenge herself on me."

"Perhaps she isn't dead."

The Baron cried out. "Oh! What an idea!" And he was pensive for a minute. "Madness!" he went on. "I saw her dead in her bed; I found her again, eaten by worms, in her coffin..."

The Marquis frowned. "What day of the month is it?" he asked.

"March 12."

Damnation! Monsieur de Simiane said to himself. *I'm not disengaged from my promise until tomorrow. I can't speak! What if he dies before then?*

"What are you thinking about?" the Baron said.

"I'm telling myself that it's a hoax."

"You don't believe in the dead, then?"

"Scarcely–and very much in the living."

"You see," Monsieur de Nossac went on, "I haven't slept for six months, and every day I wake up weaker, more worn out, nearer to my grave."

There was such a ring of truth and hopeless conviction in the Baron's voice that Monsieur de Simiane was profoundly shaken and greatly impressed. He said to himself: "So much the worse! I'll be breaking my word, but I'll prevent him from dying. I'll tell him everything!" And, after a momentary hesitation, he said: "Would you like me to give you some advice?"

"Go on."

"If the phantom appears tonight..."

"It won't come tonight, because I'm not in bed, and won't go to bed until dawn."

"Well then, the next night..."

"All right. What should I do?"

"If it comes, you should leap from the foot of the bed, take it by the arm, and say to it..."

The Marquis stopped, quivering. He had just glanced into an immense Venetian glass, and in that glass he had perceived a pale head looking at him with stern eyes and a finger placed to its lips, as if to command him to be silent.

"What should I say?" the Baron asked.

"Well," the disconcerted Marquis said, "you should ask it to go away and let you sleep."

Monsieur de Nossac shrugged his shoulders and did not reply. "Here are my guests," he said. "We'll have a joyful supper."

"You don't seem very joyful to me, though."

"Ah, there you are," murmured the Baron, with a heart-broken smile. "Mine is a double life. By night, I die; by day, I get drunk on pleasure."

The Baron had no time to say more; the door opened, and his guests came in.

An exclamation of stupefaction mingled with alarm escaped them at the sight of the room's funereal decorations, the women almost swooning and the men bursting into laughter as they found the joke charming. Everything about the Baron was charming.

The Marquis stared at Monsieur de Nossac then.

XLI

Monsieur de Nossac was no longer the man that he had been a few minutes ago: the sick and stooped madman with the dull eyes and the slow, sad voice, whose movements were weary. This was a gentleman standing upright, with his chest out, a smile upon his lips, shining eyes, curt and witty speech, whose movements were rapid and graceful.

He peeled off his mandarin's robe and appeared to the eyes of his guests dressed in a stylish cherry-red doublet with blue ribbons and slashed sleeves, scarlet cuffs and a ruff of fine silk. He was wearing makeup, with a beauty-spot like a marquise, and stood with one hand on his ruff and the other on the golden hand-guard of a little ceremonial sword clasped to his waist.

"He is ravishing!" murmured the women.

"To the table! said the Baron, joyfully.

Despite the room's funereal decorations and the skeletons fulfilling the role of candelabras, it was a merry feast. The flagons of Aï, Xérès, Malvoisie and Constance, the venison pâtés, the pheasant suprêmes, the jellied eels, the crayfish buissons, the partridge bisques, the fowls and the truffle terrines disappeared as if by enchantment.[61]

As the faces became heavier, the conversation became more excited. The women took off their masks—with one exception.

"Beautiful mask," the Baron said to her, "show us your pretty young face."

"I am pale," the mask said, coldly.

"But even so..."

"The glare of candlelight makes me ill."

"Please, my beautiful mask," insisted several men, joining in with the Baron.

"If that is what you want," the mask said, calmly, "I shall retire."

Hmm! thought the Baron. *I've been cheated. It's some woman of the court who has insinuated herself here.*

"Baron," the Marquis exclaimed, suddenly, "how much did this supper cost?"

"Ask my steward."

"Baron's you're ruining yourself."

"That's all the same to me."

"In that respect, you're right."

"Why is that?"

"Because two days hence, whether you have an income of 100,000 *livres* or three million in debts, you will be neither rich nor poor."

"Bah! How is that?"

"Do you remember a paragraph in your wife's will?"

"Which one?"

"The one that obliges you to remarry within an interval of two years in order to keep your fortune."

"Damn–that's true! I hadn't thought of that. Well, the interval..."

"Expires the day after tomorrow, Baron. You have only 24 hours to find a wife."

"I don't want to get married."

"You don't say! Why?"

"Because I love my wife," the Baron said.

Everyone laughed.

"The dead don't count," murmured the masked woman.[62]

"You think so, beautiful mask?"

"Undoubtedly." And the woman laughed mockingly beneath the black velvet of her mask.

"It's sad, Baron," the Marquis went on. "Very sad, I assure you, to see a fortune like yours return to an imbecile father-in-law and his unknown nephews."

"Damn! That's true."

"In your place, I'd prefer to marry anyone at all...or anything at all."

"In that case," the Baron cried, "I shall have to find a wife right away. I'll be dead in a week, and I'll make her fortune by dying."

There was a general murmur: "Superb!"

"Who wants to marry me?" he went on.

The women looked at one another, then cried out, all at the same time: "Me! Me! Me!"

"We're not in Turkey," the Baron murmured. "Permit me to make a choice. Let's go, Mesdames–show yourselves. I'll choose the prettiest."

The masked woman alone had said nothing, and still kept her mask on.

"Lower the mask, Madame!" the Baron said to her.

"Monsieur," she replied, in a mocking voice, "if you want to marry me, you'll marry me with my mask. If not... no." A fiery glance darted through that same mask.

"So be it!" said the Baron. "You shall be my wife. It's you that I'll marry."

"Thank you," she said. And she extended her hand.

As he touched that hand, the Baron shivered, without knowing why.

XLII

Despite the Baron's reputation for eccentricity, his guests could not help suppressing a start of astonishment.

"What!" came the cry from all around. "He chose the masked woman!"

"Why not?"

"What if she's ugly?"

A gaze more scintillant than lightning sprang from the unknown's mask, while she shrugged her shoulders and let out a dry and mocking laugh ripple from her white teeth.

"With such a gaze and teeth like that," the Baron murmured philosophically, "no woman is ever ugly."

"Well said, Baron," replied the domino. "When is the signature of our contract?"

"Tomorrow, of course," said the Baron.

"It's the only time," Simiane added.

"Except," Monsieur de Nossac objected, "that as it's appropriate to have some slight acquaintance, I ask you one favor, Madame."

"Speak, Baron."

"You'll grant me an hour's private conversation after supper."

"So be it, Baron."

"In that case, let's finish supper."

The end of the supper was joyful, sparkling with wit, scintillant with quips. Afterwards, the joyous crowd ran tumultuously though the staircases and corridors, leaving behind them bursts of laughter, wine-stained napkins, heady perfumes and withered flowers.

Then the Baron offered his hand to the domino, and in a sad and serious voice, which contrasted starkly with the artificial gaiety of the night, he said to her: "Come, Madame."

The room to which the Baron led the domino was a vast hall hung in blue velvet, furnished in old oak, with large and heavy gilded candelabras, Venetian glasses of the highest dimension, and a thick carpet from the Gobelins factory, representing a scene from *Les aventures de Télémaque*.[63]

This room was austere without being cold; the heart did not shrink and one breathed quite easily, but the soul did not expand there. A poet might have found it subject-matter for a reverie; a lover would have experienced a frisson within it. The domino was presumably seized by some such thought, for she said to the Baron: "This room is rather sad."

"You think so?"

"Yes—for a conversation...of love."

The Baron arched an eyebrow. "Who told you that I wanted to talk to you about love?"

The domino shivered. "Oh!" she said, emotionally.

But the Baron had second thoughts, for he took her hand again, led her silently to the far end of the room, opened a door, and introduced her into a little boudoir decorated in white and gold, filled with a humid atmosphere charged with delicate perfume, illuminated by the dull light of a Venetian lamp with multicolored glass.

The Baron sat the domino down on the cushions of the sofa; then, instead of sitting next to her, he leaned his back on the mantelpiece of the chimney-breast, leaned his head on the rococo clock, placed the tip of his foot on the copper tritons of the fireplace, and seemed to collect himself momentarily.

The domino examined him attentively, curling herself up on the sofa with the lissome and coquettish nonchalance of a pretty woman.

"Madame," the Baron said, finally, "Will you deign to listen to me?"

The domino opened her lips indolently and let fall an adorable; "Will it take long?"

"No," he said. "Just a few words."

The domino put her chin in her beautiful hand and her elbow on her knee. "I'm listening," she said.

"Madame," the Baron went on, "I'm very rich today; in two days, if I don't marry you..."

"You'll be ruined, won't you?"

The Baron nodded his head affirmatively. "I shall marry you, therefore, in the eyes of the world in general, and our guests in particular, to conserve my fortune. I don't know whether you are rich, of the nobility or the bourgeoisie, from the court or the Opéra."

"Does that matter to you?"

"Absolutely not. Do you expect me to make love to you?"

"Why not?" said the domino, in a mocking tone

"Because it's impossible."

"In truth?"

"I love another."

"Charming! In that case, Baron, let's renounce our marriage."

"That's folly!"

"Not at all. Perhaps I'm as rich as you. I want love, not money."

A bitter smile pursed the Baron's lips. "Do you believe that I could love you?" he murmured.

"I dare to hope."

"You're cruelly mistaken, Madame. You're also mistaken in supposing that I'm marrying you to conserve my fortune."

"Bah!"

"The dead don't need anything."

"Are you dead, then?"

"I shall be, within a week."

The domino started in astonishment, almost in terror. "You're mad!" she murmured.

"I have been, but I shall die sane."

"Why and of what are you dying?"

"Of an incurable malady."

"What is this illness?"

"I love a dead woman."

A shiver more visible still took hold of the domino.

"Listen," the Baron continued. "I sense my life ebbing away; my last breath and my last hour are drawing near. I shall die laughing, though my laughter is poisoned, but I shall confide my secret to you; only you shall know it, and perhaps only you will shed a tear upon my tomb."

The domino was no longer mocking; she listened.

"Until a little while ago," the Baron went on, "I gave no thought to snatching my fortune from the avid collaterals who have nothing for me but hatred and resentment. One thought occurred to me, though–the idea of sowing a little happiness along my route, although my own happiness had fled...so I offered my hand to an unknown, and that unknown is you. You will not refuse a regret for my memory..."

The Baron stopped, and appeared to be waiting for a reply. The domino continued to keep silent.

"I love a woman who died two years ago," Monsieur de Nossac continued. "That dead woman is my wife."

The domino shrugged her shoulders.

"In Germany, I met a young woman who resembled her, and I fell in love with that young woman; in Brittany, I found a creole who resembled her equally, and I fell in love with that creole–but in the young woman and the creole I only loved my wife."

"Really?" said the domino, mockingly.

"On my honor, Madame."

"Do you know, Baron, that your wife has suffered a misfortune?"

"In what respect, Madame?"

"In that you have only loved her in death."

The Baron let out a dull moan. "That's not true!" he said.

"What do you mean?"

"I loved her the moment I set eyes on her."

"What happened, Baron, was that you went to spend your wedding night in the arms of a mistress. That's a singular kind of love."

"How do you know that, Madame?"

"I know it–that's sufficient."

Monsieur de Nossac became suddenly sad and solemn. "What would you think, Madame," he said, "of a gentleman who, having given his word, trampled that word underfoot?"

"I would say that the gentleman was a dastard."

A glint of joy shone in the Baron's eyes. "Well," he said, "listen then, listen! I had a mistress, I was ruined; the Regent had just died. I had never seen the woman that I was to marry; I was marrying her without love, and to save me from poverty. But it was necessary for me to get rid of my mistress, and I was weak enough to make her a sworn promise. I promised her one night of her choice, after the day of my marriage..."

The domino got up. "After?" she said, hotly.

"When I saw my wife, I fell in love with her. Alas, it was too late to revoke my oath. On the evening of my marriage, at the moment when I had just led my wife to the nuptial chamber, when I was just about to enjoy a kind of happiness that I no longer deserved–a virgin's love–a domestic presented himself and whispered a few words in my ear, and I followed him. There was a carriage at the door of the house; in that carriage was my mistress. She claimed the fulfillment of my promise, and I was constrained to obey. Oh, what an infernal night that was! The nameless tortures and mortal regrets I suffered during those few hours are impossible to describe.

"When the hour of my deliverance sounded, I ran to the Borelli house; my wife had departed for Brittany. I climbed into a post-chaise and chased after her. En route, I was met by my mistress's new lover. He was a handsome youth, as amorous and chivalrous as one is at 20. He struck me a furious blow with his sword, which laid me up in an inn for a fortnight. When I was able to resume my course, when I arrived at my wife's home, she was dead!"

The Baron stopped, and put his hands convulsively to his forehead, where sweat was pearling in icy droplets. The domino had drawn closer to him, little by little. Suddenly, she took his hand, and said to him in an emotional voice: "Monsieur le Baron, are you quite sure that your wife is dead?"

Monsieur de Nossac shivered profoundly. "Yes," he murmured. "I have seen her cadaver, eaten away by worms."

"You're mistaken–that wasn't her."

The Baron recoiled. "Who told you that?" he cried.

The domino tore off her mask. The Baron cried out, and slumped against the chimney-breast. "Gretchen!" he murmured.

"Not Gretchen, but the creole... Not the creole, but Hélène."

"You!"

"The woman you saw was my foster-sister. As for me, I wasn't dead, and I left the night preceding my interment." The domino continued in a choked voice: "Baron, I thought myself offended, I wanted to avenge myself. I beg your pardon!"

Monsieur de Nossac, pale and tottering, took his wife in his arms, but was unable to utter a word, choked as he was by emotion.

"The Castle of Holdengrasburg," the Baronne went on, "the Black Huntsmen, the Château de Kervégan, Hector, Roschen and Yvonnette–all that was nothing but a detestable and terrible comedy that I put together with floods of money, some wretched German students I purchased body and soul and who served me..."

The Baron finally contrived an exclamation: "But...Roschen?"

"That one was worth more than the others...she was a poor ignorant girl who played her role out of love and fell victim to it."

"And...Yvonnette?"

"Yvonnette was Samuel's mistress–he called himself Hector in Brittany–as Roschen was Wilhem's."

The Baron lifted his hand to his forehead. "I am mad!" he murmured.

"No," said the Baronne, throwing himself at his feet. "You are not mad, and you shall live, for I love you."

They spent a delightful night together, hand in hand, forgetting the rest of the world, letting the candles go out and the first kisses of dawn brush the shutters.

At the moment when the first ray of sunlight penetrated the boudoir, the door opened and Simiane came in.

"Madame," he said, coldly, "you have demanded two years of silence from me; the two years are up and I shall speak."

"There's no need," said the Baronne. "He knows everything."

The Baron looked at her, astonished. "What do you mean?" he said.

"Listen," Madame de Nossac went on. "On the first night after your duel, you were delirious and your restless sleep was intermingled with terrible dreams. I bribed our host with a little gold, I came into your room, I put a pistol to your head, and, transported by fury and drunk with vengeance, I made ready to kill you. A man had run after you. That man appeared on the threshold and cried out. On hearing that cry, I hesitated; an idea occurred to me, and I said to him: 'The Baron's life belongs to me; if you take another step, or call out, I shall kill him!' And while terror nailed him to the spot I went on: 'I will grant you his life on one condition.' "

" 'What?' he asked.

" 'I wish to avenge myself,' I went on. 'For two years, you must obey me blindly; you will be mute.'

" 'And you won't kill him?'

" 'No. Give me your word.' He gave it to me, and became my accomplice to save you."

The Baron extended his hand to Monsieur le Simiane. "You're mistaken, my friend," he said. "You thought you had saved me..."

"Well?" two tremulous voices said.

"Well, all these emotions have broken me...I'm dying."

The Marquis and the Baronne cried out in unison.

Monsieur de Nossac took his wife's pale face in his convulsive hands, planted one last kiss upon it, murmured an adieu and promptly fell backwards. "One should not play games with the imagination," he said, in a faint voice. "The seat of life is in the brain."

And he died.

For a long time afterwards, on cold and foggy evenings, the peasants of Léonais sometimes saw a pale woman dressed in black, her eyes bright with madness, walking with an unsteady and rapid gait beneath the leafless trees of the park or through the yellowed meadows: a kind of phantom that no one dared approach, and who sang, with outbursts of heart-rending laughter, the ballad of the Black Huntsman:

The old castellan with furrowed brow,
Is still sitting up as midnight passes,
In his huge antique armchair.

And if anyone asked one of them who the woman was, they replied in a terrified fashion:

"It's the ghost of the Baron's dead wife."

Afterword

The narrative resolution of *La baronne trépassée* follows the standard pattern of its day; most of Paul Féval's novels employing Gothic and folkloristic materials insist on rationalizing the greater part of their substance, explaining away their apparent supernatural intrusions as hallucinations or the result of imposture. It was not until the 1860s that Féval became willing to feature explicitly supernatural material in his plots in a relatively extravagant fashion; even then, his works of that sort tended to be novellas rather than novels, and he seems never to have felt entirely comfortable, always tending to undermine his own efforts with slightly embarrassed humor.

In adopting the policy they followed before 1860, Féval and Ponson were following the precedents established by the most successful of all the English Gothic novelists, Ann Radcliffe, who was also tremendously popular in France. Although her plots relied heavily on seemingly-supernatural events, Radcliffe always provided naturalistic explanations in her conclusions and narrative codas. On occasion, these naturalistic explanations were far more implausible than a straightforward intervention of supernatural forces would have seemed, but Radcliffe was very conscious of living in an Age of Enlightenment, in which superstition was supposedly obsolete, and evidently considered it something of a moral duty to make such rationalizing moves–in stark contrast to such wholehearted supernaturalists as Matthew Gregory Lewis, of whom she disapproved. Many of her followers similarly thought it a point of honor and principle to do likewise, although they must have realized–as must she–that such moves were intrinsically anti-climactic, and sometimes absurdly bathetic.

Although Gothic motifs made a considerable comeback in the latter part of the 19th century, establishing supernatural horror fiction as a significant modern genre, a Radcliffean subgenre of mystery fiction did survive alongside it into the 20th century, in which authors exercised their ingenuity to set out events that seemed to have no other possible explanation than a supernatural one, before demonstrating their virtuosity as well as their virtue by providing a convincing naturalistic one. Maurice Renard's *Les mains d'Orlac* (1920; tr. as *The Hands of Orlac*) is a classic of the subgenre, and the most elaborately ingenious constructions of this sort are perhaps those produced by the collaborators who signed themselves Boileau-Narcejac; they include the oft-imitated *Celle qui n'était plus* (1952), filmed as *Les Diaboliques* (1954), and *D'entre les morts* (1954), which provided the basis of the famous Alfred Hitchcock film *Vertigo* (1958).

When the American pulp magazines were indulging in the reckless experimental invention of new fictional genres in the 1930s, they produced a small subset of magazines hosting this kind of formula, nowadays known as "weird menace" pulps–*Horror Stories*, *Terror Tales*, *Thrilling Mystery* and *Dime Mystery* were the key examples–and the formula also crops up in British pulp fiction of that period, but it has almost faded into extinction since then. Its last significant manifestation was the children's animated TV series *Scooby-Doo*, but any modern reader familiar with that series will have had no difficulty following the storyline of *La baronne trépassée*, and will not have been in the least surprised to discover that the wife was never really dead, or that her impostures were supported and sustained by the supplementary efforts of the Baron's best friend.

Readers who are able to recognize *La baronne trépassée* as a significant historical precursor of "weird menace" fiction– are likely to be forgiving of the essential implausibility of its narrative contortions, while those who recognize it as a typical example of the make-it-up-as-you-go *roman feuilleton*–are equally likely to be forgiving of the number of loose ends left dangling in the course of its development.

It is probably unnecessary, in this context, to raise such questions as how the Baronne financed her extraordinarily elaborate operations when her apparent death would have forbidden her access to her fortune, what drugs she used to produce the Baron' various altered states of consciousness, how she managed to contrive such convincing simulations of deathly coldness and blood-sucking, why she bothered to steal the clothes from poor Gretchen's body, and how on Earth she found the patience to walk up and down in the Baron's bedroom for four hours every night for six months, pretending to be a ghost. When we have set questions of that trifling sort aside, however, more interesting questions still remain regarding the method and reliability of the narrative, and its precise subgeneric status.

The Marabout line that reprinted *La baronne trépassée* in 1975 advertised itself as *Marabout Fantastique*, the latter term being commonly used in French as a generic description roughly, but not exactly, equivalent to the way "horror" is used in English. The English generic description is, of course, rather untidy, and it is often politic to draw distinctions between "psychological horror fiction" on the one hand and "supernatural horror fiction" on the other, as well as to characterize other border-crossing exercises such as "dark fantasy" and "horror-sf" and to identify a species of "physical horror" on which crime and thriller fiction draws heavily. The French *fantastique* cuts across the borderline that might be drawn between psychological and supernatural horror fiction, but in a strangely deliberate fashion, analyzed by Tzvetan Todorov in *Introduction à la littérature fantastique* (1970; tr. as *The Fantastic: A Structural Approach to a Literary Genre*).

Todorov narrows the definition of the *fantastique* in such a way as to make it intermediate between two other genres, which he calls the *merveilleux* [marvelous] and the *inconnu* [rendered as "the uncanny" in the English translation, which links it–not entirely appropriately–with Sigmund Freud's identification of a fictional genre of the *unheimlich*, which is also conventionally rendered into English as "the uncanny."] The point Todorov attempts to make is that literary characters confronted with seemingly-impossible events are, at least in a post-Enlightenment era, logically required to hesitate between two alternative accounts of what is happening to them. Either the events really are happening, in which case the generally-accepted modern world-view is mistaken in ruling the supernatural impossible, or they are not, in which case the character must be deluded, either by his own madness or deliberate deception practiced by others. In Todorov's scheme, a plot that is resolved in the former fashion belongs to the genre of the *merveilleux*, while one that is resolved in the latter belongs to the *inconnu*; when the ambiguity is preserved all the way to the end, however, and never resolved by authorial *diktat*, the story remains within the genre of the *fantastique*.

The main difficulty with this definitive scheme, clearly demonstrated by *La baronne trépassée* and other instances of "weird menace" fiction, is, of course, that the ultimate resolution is often a matter of secondary importance to the whole story, sometimes seeming–as in Ann Radcliffe's classic Gothic novels–to be an intrinsically anticlimactic and rather cursory matter. Even if the ambiguity is ultimately resolved, it is the ambiguity that provides most plots of this sort with the greater part of their dramatic tension. Indeed, as Todorov realizes, the very fact of the ambiguity supplies these stories with a particular kind of horror: that arising from a character's increasingly-anxious inability to decide whether he is mad or really in the grip of diabolical agencies–an inability whose anxiety is further augmented by the fact that it is not obvious which of the two alternatives is the more dreadful.

It is in the context of the evolution of the *fantastique* that *La baronne trépassée* is a highly significant contribution to the development of modern horror fiction. More intently and more enthusiastically than any previous work, it plays upon the Baron's inability to figure out what on Earth is happening to him in the Castle of Holdengrasburg, and, more importantly, on his simultaneous inability to decide which of the interpretations would qualify as the lesser of the two evils. He appears to be one of the most fickle characters ever devised, in his abrupt see-sawing between Gretchen and Roschen, and later between Yvonnette and "the creole," but his emotional incontinence in falling in and out of love, like his perpetual shivering, shuddering, quivering and trembling, is merely symptomatic of a more deep-seated and quintessentially horrid uncertainty.

Within Todorov's scheme, *La baronne trépassée* belongs to the genre of the *inconnu*, and most modern readers will have spotted that at a relatively early stage, but all its narrative energy and effect derives from its affiliation to and intense extrapolation of the *fantastique*. The horns of the Baron's dilemma are exceedingly well-pointed; unlike the great majority of his predecessors, he finds it very difficult–and ultimately impossible–to believe that the naturalistic explanation of the remarkable occurrences he suffers is the preferable one, not merely because it would condemn him as a madman, but because he really does have grounds for thinking that he might be better off if he were being entertained by the Devil's son, or if the vampiric Gretchen really were in the process of devouring him.

Ponson's development of his material is far from perfect. Writing three years before the publication of Gustave Flaubert's *Madame Bovary*, he was not party to modern debates about the propriety of different kinds of narrative viewpoint, and automatically employed an author-omniscient viewpoint that is, alas, entirely inappropriate to his subject-matter. The idea of placing the narrative viewpoint within the consciousness of a protagonist, even while writing in the third person, had only just begun to occur to a handful of writers as a possibility in 1853, and none of those who recognized its scope and utility had yet come close to perfecting the technique. Ponson deserves due credit for almost getting there in much of his narrative–to the point at which the narrative is bound to seem glaringly mistaken to the modern reader on the few occasions in Part One when its viewpoint does exit from the Baron's fevered consciousness (as, for instance, when the Baron is lying unconscious after Wilhem has run him through). It is worth remembering that Ponson came that close by virtue of instinct alone–and that in this respect, as in so many others, he exceeded Paul Féval's similar attainments.

In the same way that he was not in a historical position even to consider setting the author-omniscient viewpoint firmly and completely aside, Ponson was not in a position even to consider the Todorovian alternative to the resolution he attached to his story. If he had been able to anchor his narrative viewpoint more firmly within the Baron's consciousness, then he could have maintained the story's ambiguity to the bitter end, but no matter how many information-withholding games an omniscient author has played in the course of telling a story, he cannot leave the central ambiguity of a plot unresolved without seeming deliberately perverse. From Ponson's viewpoint, the prospect of providing his story with an ending had to be a straightforward matter of either/or, and it was probably inevitable that he plumped for the *inconnu* rather than the *merveilleux*. Even in this respect, however, the modern reader–with the benefit of educated hindsight–can see how close he came to another kind of resolution, which would actually have suited his plot much better, and would have neutralized the effect of some of his accidental errors.

Perhaps, given that Ponson came as close as he did to contriving something radically new and different, it is worth wondering whether the Baron's story actually did end in the way that Ponson's allegedly-omniscient narrative viewpoint supposes, and whether what really happened might have been something that voice, by virtue of its primitive historical situation, was unfortunately unable to consider.

Among the many subgenres of modern fantastic fiction that had not yet been invented in 1853 was the subgenre of "posthumous fantasy," defined and elaborately discussed by John Clute in *The Encyclopedia of Fantasy* (1997) which he

246

edited with John Grant. Posthumous fantasy is, in essence, a variety of afterlife fantasy in which a story's protagonist does not realize that he is dead, but embarks upon a long hallucinatory odyssey—which he takes for lived experience despite its manifest and increasing peculiarity—whose sum is a kind of rite of passage that puts his life, and especially the events leading up to his death, into some sort of moral and existential context.

In the most primitive versions of the formula—including its archetype, Ambrose Bierce's "*An Occurrence at Owl Creek Bridge*" (1891) and its most familiar modern example, the movie *The Sixth Sense* (1999)—the protagonist's eventual realization that he is dead is sprung on the reader as a "surprise ending", but in more sophisticated versions, such as William Golding's *Pincher Martin* (1956) or the movie *Donnie Darko* (2001), the journey of discovery is far more important than the revelation itself, and no particular emphasis is placed on the mere fact of the ultimate revelation.

If we look more carefully at the events narrated in *La baronne trépassée*, more intently and more than its own narrative voice is able to do, we can easily see that it bears a very strong resemblance to subsequent posthumous fantasies. All the clues that the author of a posthumous fantasy might be expected to plant are there. Even if the Baronne de Nossac's final explanation had not revealed her presence at the Baron's sickbed following his first fateful duel, the reader would have been perfectly entitled to suspect that, in fact, the Baron had never recovered from that wound, and that the subsequent events of the novel were entirely a product of a terminal delirium suffered at that time. When the Baronne tells the Baron (and the reader) that she actually put a pistol to his head, with the intention of blowing his brains out, the reader is not merely entitled but encouraged to believe that perhaps she really did shoot him. The almost-immediate result of her revelation is, after all, that the Baron drops dead on the spot, mirroring the effect of realizing the truth on the protagonist of many a posthumous fantasy—which is often akin to the effect on a character in an animated cartoon when it is belatedly brought to his notice that he has run off the edge of a cliff.

The Baron's adventure makes far more sense as a posthumous expiatory rite of passage than it does as actual experience. If he really were suffering a delirium, that would explain why he is perpetually feverish, without quite knowing why. It would also explain, far better than the Graf von Holdengrasburg's lame account, why the day-long hunt through the forest in Part One was so phantasmagoric, and how it came to be attended by all manner of human and canine servants that the Baronne could not possibly have acquired, even if she had had any money. It would even explain, after a fashion, how the Baron could be present, in 1724, at historical events that did not occur until 1734, how Louis XV could still be 12 years old in 1726, and why the plot jumps forward by three months, losing all coherency in the process–because another common feature of posthumous fantasies is that the protagonist periodically finds anomalies in his experience arising from attempts made by his subconscious mind to let him know, indirectly, what his true existential situation is.

It is true, admittedly, that the novel's narrative voice does not tell the reader that this is what has happened–but the most sophisticated of all modern posthumous fantasies do indeed belong to the genre of the *fantastique*, and leave it up to the reader to make the deduction unaided; two notable examples are Ruthven Todd's *The Lost Traveller* (1943) and Michel Bernanos' *La montagne morte de la vie* (1967; tr. as *The Other Side of the Mountain*). It seems highly probable than Ponson did not know, any more than his narrative voice did, that *La baronne trépassée* is a posthumous fantasy, but the deduction is nevertheless possible and rationally plausible. Indeed, I am prepared to go so far as to declare *La baronne trépassée* most definitely is a posthumous fantasy, and is a much better book for it.

My readers might, I suppose, think that I am exceeding my warrant as a mere translator in making this declaration, but translation is not and cannot be a purely passive process, so I feel perfectly entitled at least to offer the suggestion, and I believe that there are good reasons why the reader ought to take my word for it. How much more satisfying it is–is it not?–to realize that the Baron's dropping dead was not an arbitrary intrusion evoked to put a swift end to a text whose author had run out of inspiration, but a cleverly precorroborated consummation of an inevitability established in its prologue! What a relief it is to know that the Baron's dalliance with the misfortunate Roschen was not the moral atrocity that it first seemed, but a self-accusatory symbolic re-enactment of the Baron's epiphanic insight into an essential weakness of his character! You, dear reader, may thank me, if you wish, for pointing this out, but the real debt is most definitely owed to Ponson, who put all the materials in place. I am merely extrapolating his logic to its intrinsic end-point; I hope and trust that he would approve, and be grateful.

Brian Stableford

Notes

Introduction

[1] An article on Rocambole, including a complete bibliography of the series, is included in *Shadowmen: Heroes and Villains of French Pulp Fiction* (ISBN 978-0-9740711-3-8). Two Rocambole plays translated by Frank J. Morlock have also been released by Black Coat Press as *Rocambole* (ISBN 978-1-932983-57-9).

[2] Translated by Brian Stableford as the title story of the Black Coat Press collection *The Vampire Soul and Other Sardonic Tales* (ISBN 978-1-932983-02-9).

[3] Translated by Frank J. Morlock and released by Black Coat Press as *The Return of Lord Ruthven* (ISBN 978-1-932983-11-1).

[4] Translated by Frank J. Morlock and released by Black Coat Press in the collection *Lord Ruthven the Vampire* (ISBN 978-1-932983-10-4).

[5] Translated by Brian Stableford and released by Black Coat Press as *Revenants* (ISBN 978-1-932983-70-8).

[6] Translated by Brian Stableford and released by Black Coat Press as *The Vampire Countess* (ISBN 978-0-9740711-5-2).

Prologue

[7] A contemporary French reader would immediately have identified this as a reference to Philippe II, Duc d'Orléans (1674-1723), who became Regent after the death of Louis XIV in 1715, when Louis XV was only five years old. The Regency officially came to an end in February 1723, when the 13-year-old Louis was deemed to be old enough to take the throne in his own right, but the Duc d'Orléans retained considerable influence and became Prime Minister in August of that year before dying in December. His government was deeply unpopular, and the court of the period acquired a reputation for decadence unameliorated by the innovative splendor of Louis XIV's era; the Regent's own conduct was subsequently held up as a model of depraved morality.

[8] Porcherons was once a hamlet northeast of Old Paris, which was eventually swallowed up by the expanding city. Its drinking-dens were very popular in the 17th and 18th centuries.

[9] Giulio Mazarini, known as Cardinal Mazarin (1602-1661) succeeded Cardinal Richelieu as Louis XIII's Prime Minister and continued in that role when the young Louis XIV succeeded his father, thanks to the affection of the widowed Queen, Anne of Austria. Rumors of a secret marriage did circulate at the time and long afterwards, but were never substantiated.

[10] Anne, Duchesse de Montpensier, nicknamed *La Grande Mademoiselle*, was Louis XIV's first cousin; her family hoped at one time that she would marry him, but she became involved in anti-Royalist rebellion instead and was deeply distrusted thereafter. She married a Gascon whose family name was Puyguilhem, but who had become famous as Antonin Nompar de Caumont, Duc de Lauzun, a sometime Maréchal de France. Louis XIV secretly married his favorite mistress, Françoise d'Aubigné, Marquise de Maintenon (1635-1719), in 1684.

[11] There was an actual Marquis de Simiane at the French court in 1723, although he remains fairly obscure in terms of the historical record; his father, who had died in 1718, owed his own moderate celebrity to having married Pauline de Grignan, (1674-1737), the grand-daughter of Madame de Sévigné, who published her grandmother's correspondence. It is unlikely, however, that Ponson attached the name to his character for any reason connected with the historical individual's biography.

[12] The Baron's *grande maison* would, of course, have been his château. Louis de Rouvroy, Duc de Saint-Simon (1675-1755) published a famous series of memoirs between 1691 and 1723 which gave future generations (including, one presumes, Ponson) a uniquely intimate insight into the court of the period and its chief characters, although it revealed very little of his

own life, leaving Ponson quite free to invent an imaginary mistress.

[13] Aï, or Ay, is a region on the river Marne not far from Rheims, which was famous for the quality of its sweet champagne wine. Voltaire penned a tribute to the wine in verse and it was also highly complimented by Léon Gozlan, who presumably included it in the ill-fated cargo of champagne he attempted to export to the colonies–thus ruining himself–before turning to a literary career.

[14] Louise de Bourbon, Duchesse du Maine (1676-1753), whose husband was the son of Louis XIV and Madame de Montespan, presided over an important political salon at her Château de Sceaux; there she formed *L'Ordre de la Mouche-à-miel* [The Order of the Honey-bee], which took its name from a device on her family's coat-of-arms; its members were deeply implicated in a conspiracy against the Regent named after Antoine de Cellamare (1657-1733), the Spanish Ambassador to the French court, who was expelled in its aftermath. Guillaume, Cardinal Dubois (1656-1723) was Prime Minister at the time of the plot.

[15] The Duchesse de Phalaris was the last in the long sequence of the Regent's mistresses; almost nothing is known about her except that the Regent died in her arms. The first edition of Larousse was unable to specify her first name or her maiden name, but estimated her birth-date as c.1700 and observed that her husband, a *mauvais sujet* (bad lot), owed his title to the fact that he was a Cardinal's *neveu* [literally "nephew"–a term used euphemistically for the *protégés* of cardinals, whether they be illegitimate sons or catamites]. Her name was included in the pornographic scandal-literature with which pre-Revolutionary radicals blackened the reputation of the Ancien Régime, but nothing said about her there, or in the *romans feuilletons* that used such source-material, can be trusted.

[16] Jeanne Agnes Berthelot de Pleneuf, Marquise de Prie (1698-1727) was the recognized mistress of Louis-Henri, Duc de Bourbon et d'Enghien, Prince de Condé, during the troubled

period when he was Prime Minister of France after the death of the Duc d'Orléans. The couple were exiled in 1726 after attempting to remove their great rival Fleury (see the following note); the Marquise committed suicide shortly thereafter.

[17] André Hercule, Cardinal de Fleury (1653-1743)–who was also the Bishop of Fréjus–was 70 when the Duc d'Orléans died, and did indeed stand aside to allow the Duc de Bourbon to become Prime Minister, although he remained the King's closest confidant. When the Duc attempted to remove him in 1726, Fleury came out best in the struggle, thus licensing Ponson's judgment–made with the advantage of hindsight–that he would lose nothing by waiting.

[18] This play on words does not translate very well. *En plein jour*, here translated as "in broad daylight," carries the metaphorical meaning of doing things openly, with nothing hidden. The fact that the wedding will, take place *en pleine nuit*, here translated as "in complete darkness" (because it will be celebrated at midnight) thus implies that there is something shady about it.

[19] A Marquis de Villarceaux was a notable courtier in the days of Louis XIV; this one is presumably imagined to be his descendant. The name of Mirbel, though familiar by 1853, did not become prominent until the latter part of the 18th century, when there was a celebrated botanist of that name and an unrelated Madame de Mirbel became famous as a miniaturist painter.

[20] A sutler–*cantinière* in French–was a camp-follower who sold liquor to soldiers on campaign.

[21] Léonais, or Liones, was the birthplace attributed to Tristan, a popular tragic hero of chivalric romance. The initial reference may, indeed, have been to a province of Brittany, but the name became associated in later writings with a land that had once allegedly lain between Brittany and Cornwall but had been lost to inundation. In addition to the apparent reference to the prose Tristan, the legend of the drowned land was also referenced, in passing, by the Brittany-based writer Marie de

France, whose *lais* [lays] were among the most notable products of 13th-century French romance. English *littérateurs* mostly followed the example of Thomas Malory in dressing the term up as Lyonesse, but French recyclers of the legend usually preferred the de-lionized Ys or Is. The legend of the drowned land was repopularized in France by the publication in 1839 of T. Hersart de Villemarqué's annotated collection of Breton ballads, *Barzaz Breiz* (whose authenticity need not be taken entirely for granted); a prose version was adopted into Paul Féval's *feuilleton* novel *Les Belles de nuit ou Les anges de la famille*, serialized in *L'Assemblée nationale* in 1849-50, which Ponson had presumably read. A later and much shorter version of Féval's story will be included in the Black Coat Press collection *Anne of the Isles and Other Legends of Brittany*, scheduled to be released in 2007 (ISBN 978-1-932983-92-0).

[22] D is presumably intended to stand for *Dieu* [God] and P for some derivative of the verb *protéger* [to protect], or their Latin equivalents, but this part of the inscription remains ambiguous in more ways than one.

[23] I have transcribed Ponson's *mânes* directly into English rather than substitute the more familiar "spirit" or "shade" because it is almost certainly intended to carry an extra layer of meaning. Although the Latin-derived word had come to be almost synonymous with "ghost" by the 19th century, its original reference was to the gods and ancestral spirits of the Underworld.

Part One

[24] The title of Comte de La Motte was famous in French naval history, one holder of that title having distinguished himself during the American War of Independence. Its wearer in the year in which this part of the story is set was presumably in the navy, but I can find no evidence of his being present at the siege of Danzig.

[25] Ponson's time-scheme is ten years out of joint at this point. Stanislaus I (1677-1766) had been elected King of Poland in 1704, at the instigation of Charles XII of Sweden, but had been forced to leave the country in 1709 after the intervention of the Russians; although the power-struggle continued through December 1724–one year after the death of the Baronne de Nossac. The actual events forming the basis of those described in this chapter took place in 1734, following the death of Stanislaus' great rival, Friedrich August (1670-1733)–who had first been elected King of Poland in 1697 and was reinstated in 1709–and prior to Stanislaus' abdication in 1735. The "Prince August" to whom the passage refers is Friedrich August II's son, Friedrich August III, who was installed as King of Poland at the instigation of the Russians in 1733. The Russian forces besieging Danzig were commanded by an Irishman named Peter Lacy (1678-1751), whose son, known as Frantz Moritz, Graf von Lacy was also a successful Russian commander. Danzig is now Gdansk.

[26] The Rennes-born French diplomat Robert, Comte de Plélo (1699-1734) died at Danzig, while taking a volunteer force to the aid of King Stanislaus, acting on his own initiative.

[27] Antoine-Félix, Marquis de Monti (1684-1738), the French Ambassador to Poland, rendered Stanislaus considerable assistance, and certainly helped him get into Danzig, but does not appear to have helped him get out again. General Steinflich is fictitious.

[28] The town Ponson calls Marienwerder is presumably one situated 26 miles southeast of Danzig on the Nogat; it was subsequently integrated into Prussia as Marienburg but has since been restored to Poland as Malbork.

[29] Ponson provides this invented "Slavonic song" with a French scansion and rhyme-scheme, rendering its grammatical organization rather tortuous in the process. Because it is impossible to conserve the rhyme and scansion in English while also conserving the meaning, I have taken the liberty of revising the lines to conserve a slightly better grammatical order.

[30] Nicolas Boileau-Despréaux (1636-1711) was a poet, satirist and critic who termed himself (ironically) the *Régent de Parnasse*, thus entitling himself, rather perversely, to be reviled as the rule-maker of French Classicism–the school to which the Romantic Movement opposed itself. He was really nothing of the sort, although he formed a significant bridge between the contrasted work of the friend of his youth, Molière (who allegedly based the central character of *Le misanthrope* on him), and the friend of his later years, Racine. Boileau was always insistent that as a satirist–and, to the extent that he attempted to be one, a rule-maker–his sole objective was to be the scourge of bad writing. Ponson was perfectly well aware that Boileau would have considered him a bad writer, but it did not prey overmuch on his conscience.

[31] The term "Jansenist" was often used as a label for any kind of heretic, and is used as a synonym of "Satanist" in the Paul Féval novel translated in a Black Coat Press edition as *Revenants* (see Note 5), which was probably one of the works that motivated Ponson to write *La baronne trépassée*. Nicolas Boileau had, however, been a Jansenist in the strict sense–his alleged misanthropism provided a model of the sect's gloomy philosophy–and undoubtedly considered it to be a form of Christianity preferable to orthodox Catholicism.

[32] Chambertin is one of the finest French vintages, Johannisberg one of the most famous Rhenish wines.

[33] In the text, the Baron concludes at this point that the Black Huntsman has three sons rather than four; perhaps the mistake is his rather than Ponson's, but there seems little point in leaving the error unaltered–the huntsman has said quite plainly that he has four sons.

[34] There is some peculiar wordplay in this section, in which the remarkably-named sons report traces of some implausible quarries. *Brisée* [spoor] is phonetically reminiscent of *brise* [breeze]–a theme continued by *buffle* [buffalo], which recalls *bouffée* [gust] and perhaps by *ours* [bear], which might suggestive of *ouragan* [storm-wind]. The twins' names are more

similar in French than English, but not quite symmetrical; the former is called *Bise-d'hiver* and the latter *Brise-de-nuit*. *Elan* [elk] is much more familiar as a term for a bound of enthusiasm or a spirited temperament.

[35] Chiens Céris were a breed of hunting-dog ancestral to the modern Poitevin breed. Saintonge was an ancient French province whose capital was Saintes; it is now part of the département of Charente-Inférieure.

[36] The *glebe* and the *corvée* were two of the more burdensome institutions of Feudalism. The former term refers to a plot of land which peasants had to work on behalf of the Church, the latter to labor on roads and other estate fixtures undertaken (without salary) on behalf of a liege-lord.

[37] A day's ride from Marienwerder–or anywhere else on the river Nogat–could not possibly have brought the Baron anywhere remotely close to the Hungarian border, even with the aid of a diabolical mount and guide. The text subsequently identifies the castle's geographical location as Bohemia, which presumably implies that what Ponson means by "the Hungarian border" is the border of the Austro-Hungarian Empire, but that was also a very long way from the Nogat. It is conceivable that Ponson had confused Marienwerder/Marienburg with Marienbad, which is in Bohemia (nowadays part of the Czech Republics), but whether or not that is so, he obviously did not bother to consult a map.

[38] Jean-Pierre Claris de Florian (1755-1794) was a French fabulist, second in reputation only to La Fontaine, whose work had something of the satirical bite of his great-uncle, Voltaire.

[39] The Régiment de Royal-Cravate was one of many colorfully-named regiments of the *Ancien Régime*; its name is directly transcribable into English.

[40] The first word of the French version of this sentence is *où*, which usually means "where," but can also mean "what," "when," "which" and "how," and therefore carries a generous ambiguity difficult to convey in English. I have used "how"

because it retains an element of double entendre relevant to the crucial ambiguity of the narrative.

[41] Ponson gives the name of this flower in German, as *vergissmeinnicht*, in order to emphasize a metaphorical meaning that its usual French equivalent, *myosotis*, does not carry.

[42] Malvoisie is a sweet dessert wine from Greece or Cyprus, roughly equivalent to those the English called malmsey.

Part Two

[43] This is a common item of wordplay, exploiting on the similarity of *pistole* (a Spanish coin) and *pistolet* (pistol).

[44] Philippe II, known as Philippe-Auguste (1165-1263) defeated the English king Richard the Lionheart in battle before undertaking the Third Crusade with him. After Richard's death, following the resumption of hostilities between England and France, Philippe scored a long sequence of victories against King John's armies and allies, of which his victory at Bouvines in 1214 was the most outstanding.

[45] A pasha or pacha (the latter is more familiar in French) is, strictly speaking, a high-ranking Turkish officer. The title was, however, sometimes bestowed in literary parlance on potentates of a greater magnitude, as in Captain Marryat's breezily cynical *Arabian Nights* pastiche *The Pacha of Many Tales* (1836), with which Ponson might have been familiar. Simiane is, of course, accusing the Baron of having the mentality of a harem-keeper.

[46] The reader will recall that the Baron was in Heidelberg exactly two months after the tailor's daughter's clothes were apparently stolen from her corpse, and then–according to what he told Simiane at the beginning of Part Two–spent a further three months scouring Europe for some trace of his Gretchen; that would imply that it is now late April or early May in 1725. Simiane's remark in Chapter XXIV that he has now been a widower for "nearly 18 months" confirmed that timetable, although the observation at the beginning of chapter XXV that he had first seen the towers of the Baronne's château "14

months before" suggests a shorter interval. This reference and subsequent ones, however, imply that the events narrated in Part Two take place in late summer. A more specific reference at the beginning of Part Three will confirm that the Baron's account of his movements appears to have mislaid three months. The time-scheme of the story would, however, be far more coherent if he had not, so that the events related in Part Two did take place in late April and those in Part Three in December.

[47] Emmanuel-Armand, Duc d'Aiguillon (1720-1782) was Louis XV's chief administrator in Brittany at a much later date, but he would only have been four years old at this point in the story.

[48] The park at Chaillot, in Paris, was the site subsequently chosen for the erection of the Palais du Trocadéro in 1878, whose name then displaced the older one. The second park named, more usually known as the Buttes-Chaumont, was still under construction when *La baronne trépassée* was serialized, on an elevated site that had played a key role in the defense of Paris in 1814.

[49] The phrase Ponson uses is *écorné du cerveau*, whose literal translation would be more like "a lesion in the brain." This might, indeed, be the modern diagnosis of the particular problem that the Baron appears to have, but Simiane is obviously using metaphorical argot, so I have substituted the slang phrase.

[50] I have transcribed the text's reference to *un courant d'électricité* directly into English, although the modern reader will understand–even if Ponson did not and the Baron de Nossac certainly could not–that what he actually means is that the horse and its riders might provide a point of conductivity capable of channeling the electrical force of a lightning-strike. Benjamin Franklin's famous experiment with the kite and the key was, of course, still far in the future in 1724, as was the scientific and literary fashionability of the notion of "atmospheric electricity."

[51] The Marabout text, from which I am working, has no prior reference to a weapon in this chapter. Whether some text is missing from that version, or whether Ponson had simply forgotten to mention that the Baron had taken a pistol from the saddlebag of the young woman's horse, I cannot tell, but I suspect the latter.

Part Three

[52] This paragraph confirms the adjustment made to the story's time-scheme in Part Two (see Note 46) and creates an awkward problem in terms of its continuity. The text makes it perfectly clear that the Baronne died in December 1723, some time between December 11 and 18–the uncertainty arises because the time given for the Baron's convalescence after the duel is initially given as *huit jours* [a week] and subsequently as *quinze jours* [a fortnight], both terms being conventionally approximate. This means that the ultimatum regarding the Baron's remarriage contained in the Baronne's will must have been due to elapse in mid-December 1725, when the Baron's fortune ought to have reverted to Hélène Borelli's family. Although it is now March 1726, however, the Baron is still possession of his fortune. It will soon transpire that he is, in accordance with the terms of the Baronne's will, living in the house in the Île Saint-Louis in which the unlucky couple spent the first part of their ill-fated wedding night. The exact date is subsequently reported to be March 12, and the text also states that the deadline is two days away. The three months that were arbitrarily added into the story's chronology in Part Two have, therefore, thrown the whole plot out of kilter.

[53] At the time Ponson wrote *La baronne trépassée*, Longchamp was in the process of being redeveloped as a pleasure-ground; the famous racecourse was opened there a few years afterwards. In 1726, however, it was still the site of an nunnery, which remained there until it was abolished in the wake of the Revolution, in 1790. The area lying between Paris and Longchamp, however–the Bois de Boulogne–would have be-

gun its gradual development into a complex of parks where Parisian society delighted in putting itself on display.

[54] It is not clear which festival is being celebrated; of the five candidates who might be considered the patron saint of laundresses, none has a feast day in March. The festival of the one saint whose only protégées are washerwomen, St Hunna, is celebrated on April 15. In literal terms, a *rosière* was a girl awarded a rose as a prize for being the most virtuous in her village; the term was, however, more commonly applied in a cruelly metaphorical sense to spinsters left, as the English phrase puts it, on the shelf.

[55] Once again Ponson's history is out of joint; Louis XV would have recently passed his 16th birthday at this point in the novel's rickety time-scheme.

[56] The Villeroi who had served as Governor of France was Nicolas de Villeroi (1598-1685), who had done so under Louis XIV; this Villeroi can only be his son François (1644-1730), who was a famous General and Maréchal de France.

[57] Armand, Duc de Richelieu (1696-1788) was the great-nephew of the notorious Cardinal.

[58] Alcibiades was an Athenian General and statesman, who began his career as a pupil and friend of Socrates but subsequently became legendary for combining–and perhaps spoiling–his natural gifts of good looks and immense ability with unbounded willfulness, insolence and capriciousness. A famous anecdote relates that the gesture he made in cutting off the tail of a dog owned by his mistress Aspasia had a tremendous impact on public opinion–a tale that was retold by Ponson's *bête noire* Villiers de l'Isle Adam, among others.

[59] Philippe Quinault (1635-1688) was a prolific dramatic poet who was scathingly satirized by Nicolas Boileau but built a more solid reputation with his librettos for Classically-based operas whose music was provided by Jean-Baptiste Lully. He did not, however, write a *Didon*. By far the most famous operatic adaptation of that story in the relevant period is Henry Purcell's *Dido and Aeneas* (c.1688), which had a libretto by

Nahum Tate; it is not entirely inconceivable that Quinault might have provided a French translation of it, but it is more likely that Ponson is improvising.

[60] Cochin-China was a French colony lying between Cambodia and Annam, around the Mekong Delta; its capital was Saigon. It was eventually incorporated into South Vietnam.

[61] I have left many of the culinary terms in this menu in French, as befits haut cuisine, but thought it best to use the familiar English equivalent of *marmelades d'anguilles* [jellied eels]; *Xérès* is the French version of Jerez, and refers to sherry.

[62] The phrase *hors de cause*, here translated as "don't count," can also imply "above suspicion"–a double entendre that is obviously intended.

[63] *Les aventures de Télémaque*, composed in 1695 or thereabouts by the Abbé Fénelon (1651-1715) and first published (in a pirated edition) in 1699, was the most widely-circulated French text of the 18th century, partly because it includes an allegorical utopia highly critical of Louis XIV. Seen as a whole, it is a pedagogical romance couched as a companion-piece to *The Odyssey*. In the story, Télémaque, accompanied by Mentor, undertakes a series of educational adventures after falling in love, rather unfortunately, with the nymph Eucharis; they include a descent into Hades. Although its invocation as a Gobelins carpet design is entirely plausible as an item of period detail, Ponson might well intend the reader to imagine a parallel between its hero and the Baron.

www.ingramcontent.com/pod-product-compliance
Lightning Source LLC
Chambersburg PA
CBHW060347030726
47497CB00003B/625